The Problem Professor

A Doro Banyon Cozy Historical Mystery-Book 4

D.S. Lang

Book Cover by Karen Phillips

Editing by Alyssa Colton

ISBN ebook: 978-1-962039-10-9

ISBN paperback: 978-1-962039-11-6

Author's Notes

I love doing research, and it was great fun to delve into details about train travel in the 1920s. Each line was somewhat different in terms of service, train length, stops, and so on. Overall, going by rail could be a wonderful, luxurious experience for those who could afford top-notch accommodations. The decoupling that occurs in the book was a rare event, but it suited the plot.

Colorado College is a real school with a solid history as a progressive institution. Thanks to my friend Ellen. an alum, for fact-checking the details! Pikeley College is a fabrication. No such university existed, nor do I imagine that any real person resembles Professor Mathers. Having held the title of Visting Assistant Professor for several years (it was a job where the title and salary were worlds apart), I never knew anyone like him. Like all my characters, he is fully fictional.

It is great fun to make up characters, places, and all for novels because, like Doro, I have a vivid imagination.

D.S. LANG

I hope you enjoy the book! Happy sleuthing!

Chapter One

Mid-August 1929

After Dorothea Banyon locked her suitcases, she surveyed her bedroom. Not exactly hers, since she did not live in Colorado with her parents, but they reserved the space for her annual visits. Three months out of the year, for the past few years, Doro had laid claim to the lovely room, which was reminiscent of the one from her childhood. Rose and pink and ivory created a welcoming respite.

Unlike previous days, when toiletries had covered the vanity and clothes had hung from the corner hall tree, all was now in order. She and her best friend, Agatha—Aggie—Darwine, had cleaned and straightened the room earlier. They had also put dust covers over the furniture because Doro would not be back for nine long months.

Ambivalent feelings hit her. Although eager to return to Michaw, Ohio—her hometown—she hated to bid goodbye to her parents. Maybe someday, her mother's health would improve enough to leave Colorado, which was only one reason for Doro not to move west. Two others were as potent. If Doro moved, Gramma Rose would be without family in the Michaw area. Then, there were friends at home. One in particular rose in her mind's eye. But was he still a friend? A tap on the door drew Doro's attention back to the present. "Come in." She would have time enough later to consider what, or who, waited back home.

Her maternal grandmother, Rose McLaren, stepped inside. "Breakfast is ready, dear."

"I'll be right down," Doro replied, her heart in her throat as she fought back a rising tide of emotion. "I just want to take one last look around the room."

A sympathetic smile touched Gramma Rose's lips. "As much as I look forward to going home, I feel torn about saying goodbye to your parents. It's one of the reasons I've only come twice before now. Leaving is hard." Her voice grew rough with emotion.

"Those times were when Mother was in the sanatorium," Doro commented. "You stayed for six months that first visit."

The septuagenarian nodded. "Your father had his job at Michaw College, and you were still in high school. Even though your uncle was here, he and your mother needed help. Of course, I wanted to be with Julia as much as possible. She was still mighty sick back then."

Julia McLaren Banyon, Doro's mother, had fallen ill when Doro was in high school. The diagnosis of consumption had hit the family hard, especially when the disease lingered and worsened. Finally, doctors had suggested she go to Claremount Sanatorium in Colorado Springs, close to where Doro's Uncle Peter, her mother's big brother, had lived. For a time, Doro and her father had hoped the change would be short-lived. When it became clear the dry climate was preferable, Professor Banyon took a job at Colorado College and joined his wife. Doro, guardedly optimistic that her parents would eventually move back and wanting to be near her grandmother, had remained behind. "I know you did, and Mother was grateful. So were Dad and I."

"I'm grateful to you, too, Doro." Gramma crossed the room to put an arm around her granddaughter. The top of the older woman's head barely came to Doro's chin, but they had the same sea-blue eyes and similar hairstyles, although Rose's bob was silver, while Doro's locks were medium-brown. When she looked at her grandmother and mother, Doro could easily imagine herself in future decades. "Your uncle stayed here longer than I imagined he would, mostly because of your mother."

Doro smiled. "Uncle Peter doesn't let any grass grow beneath his feet." After his brother-in-law moved to the Springs, Peter McLaren had left for California. Since then, he had gone on to New Mexico. Luckily, he always found work as an accountant.

"So true. You could've moved out here with your parents, but you've stayed in Michaw to be close to me. I appreciate it more than I can say, my dear."

After returning the hug, Doro stepped back. "I love Michaw as much as you love Sylvania. We're people who like to stay where we've been planted."

A lilt of laughter left Gramma Rose. "We are." After a brief pause, her grandmother continued. "Now, you have more than one reason to remain in Michaw."

Uneasiness crept through Doro. Aggie had spent the latter half of May, June, and part of July in Sylvania with Gramma Rose. Then, the pair had traveled from Ohio to Colorado together. Since their arrival a month ago, Aggie had mentioned Everett Mallow several times. Ev, the Michaw College campus security officer and deputy town constable, shared ownership of Tee, a stray puppy found the previous fall, with Doro. Most of Aggie's remarks about Ev had centered on the dog, but there was always an undercurrent, along with speculative glances from Doro's parents and grandmother, whenever his name arose. At least Aggie had not revealed Ev suggesting he and Doro step out—or her turning him down. Refusing had been hard, but Doro's longtime goal, becoming the head librarian at Michaw College, meant forgoing marriage. The school, like so many others, did not employ wives. Her family knew about her dream, so she repeated her stance. "I love my job."

Her grandmother's silver eyebrows rose a fraction. "You could be a librarian at another school."

Since there was no suitable answer, Doro made a general observation. "I love Michaw." Doro scrambled for something else to say, something that would head off any mention of Ev, because Aggie had surely discussed the handsome lawman with Gramma Rose. When her mother tapped on the door and entered the room, Doro was saved from further discussion.

"Breakfast is ready. Come and eat while the food is hot." Although Julia Banyon's voice held warmth, her eyes—so much like her mother's and daughter's—glistened with repressed tears.

Doro felt her throat constrict, but she smiled. "I'm ready." And she was. As ready as she ever would be. Not for the first time, Doro wished her mother could return to Michaw—and be healthy there.

With that, the three generations of women went to the dining room, where Aggie and Ebediah Banyon, Doro's father, were helping themselves to the array of food on the buffet.

After morning greetings were exchanged, the group took their places at the massive mahogany table. For a few moments, while the others enjoyed the dishes in silence, Doro covertly studied her parents. Despite her sadness over the impending separation, Doro's mother looked healthy and happy. Her hair, the same shade as Doro's, was cut in a stylish bob, much like those of her mother and daughter. Not a trace of gray was visible and only a few lines scored Julia Banyon's pretty face. In her early fifties, she still had the lithe figure of a girl. Doro's father, with his hazel eyes and dark brown hair, was equally youthful in appearance and manner. They were an attractive couple in looks and temperaments.

"This is a wonderful repast, Julia," Rose said. "Meals on trains are good, but there's nothing like a hearty, home-cooked breakfast."

Doro's mother grinned. "Luckily, it wasn't cooked by me, since my repertoire is limited to cookies, soups, and stews."

Grandmother's lips twitched. "You got your kitchen skills from me, I'm afraid."

"And they've come down to me," Doro added with amusement.

"Your sugar cookies and shortbread were popular at our recent town events," Aggie pointed out. "And delicious."

"All the McLaren women make luscious sweet treats," Ebediah Banyon observed with a wink at his daughter.

"Without Mrs. Churchill, we wouldn't have much variety in meals," Julia Banyon said. "She's a jewel of a housekeeper."

"I'd be happy with whatever you cooked," her husband said, "but these scones are wonderful."

"They certainly are," Gramma Rose agreed.

Doro nodded because her mouth was full of the delicious baked good. Aggie, with the same issue, also bobbed her head up and down.

"Mrs. Churchill is packing a basket with two flasks of cold tea, some sandwiches, and fruit. I'll ask her to put scones in it, too," Julia said.

The travelers expressed their gratitude before Aggie spoke. "I'd love to have her recipe. Doro and I plan to do more baking this fall. It's fun to putter in the kitchen and to see people enjoy the results."

Doro shot her friend a look of surprise, but Aggie kept focused on Julia Banyon. Although her shortbread had been a big hit during the Michaw May Days festival, Doro knew nothing about plans to bake more often. Twice a year—Christmas and May Day—was enough for her. At least, it always had been.

"How wonderful." Doro's mother smiled as she turned to her daughter. "You're busy with school, but it's good to practice cooking skills. You never know when they might come in handy."

Such comments disturbed Doro, who looked around the table for other reactions. Her father was focused on his meal, while her mother maintained an expectant expression. Prior to now, Julia Banyon had only asked about Ev in the context of him caring for Tee all summer. But what had Aggie said to Grandmother that might have been passed on? What speculation had occurred behind Doro's back? Why were leading remarks arising now? To ward off further uncomfortable conversation, she offered her usual reminder. "The kitchenette in my faculty apartment doesn't lend itself to extensive culinary concoctions, and I'm busy with my job at the library and teaching my course on the mystery novel. Those efforts are important to getting tenure." She smiled at her father. "You know how hard that can be."

"Indeed," he replied, "but your life doesn't have to be only the college."

"Of course not." Although Doro agreed with the sentiment, she had been focusing on work to the exclusion of everything except writing and sleuthing. The train trip home would provide time to consider her future, and Everett Mallow's potential role in it. But giving up her lifelong goal would be hard, if not impossible.

When everyone finished eating, Doro's father went to bring the automobile around, while Julia Banyon walked into the foyer with Aggie, Doro, and Gramma Rose. "All of you look like seasoned travelers, and fashionable ones at that."

"Thank you for having this outfit made for me, Mrs. Banyon," Aggie said as she touched the deep green coat frock with its coordinating neck scarf and hat ribbon.

"It was my pleasure," Doro's mother said. "The dressmaker was right about using a modified beltline, because this style suits your figure nicely."

"It's something we'll keep in mind when we shop in Sylvania. The drop-waists don't flatter all of us," Gramma Rose was dressed in her own version of the same style. The major difference was the more somber gray color and the longer skirt.

Doro studied her grandmother and her best friend. "You're both wearing new togs. I'm in what I wore to come out."

Her mother smiled. "You've taken a little more interest in your clothes, so that ensemble was new to me."

Gramma Rose nodded. "We shopped last spring with train travel in mind. The drop-waist dress suits Doro, since she's slender like you, Julia, and the navy color is serviceable and pretty."

Julia Banyon's lips twitched as her attention went to Doro's head. "And you bought a matching cloche."

"That's the only kind of hat she'll wear." Gramma Rose tapped the brim of her burgundy bucket hat with its gray silk band. "Aggie and I like something different."

"So, I see," Julia said, "but I'm not sure I'd recognize Doro in any other style of headwear."

"Hilarious, Mother," Doro replied. She was about to say Ev admired the way a cloche framed her face, but wisely refrained. After a hug and kiss with her parent, she stepped toward the door. "I'm afraid we need to be on our way." When moisture pooled in Julia's eyes, Doro had to blink hard herself. In a reflexive action, her hand went to the locket dangling from the gold chain around her neck.

"I love seeing my locket on you," her mother said in a choked voice.

Doro's father, who had returned to the foyer, clasped his wife's fingers. "I do, too."

Doro bit hard on her lower lip to keep it from trembling. When she gained a modicum of control, she responded. "I've worn it every day, since you gave it to me, Mother. I treasure it."

"I'm glad," Julia Banyon murmured.

"So, am I," Doro's father added. "We're all together in the photos inside, just like we are in spirit."

Doro's mother offered a soft smile. "And we always will be."

"We will," Doro agreed, but she could say no more, and silence fell over the group.

Gramma Rose and Aggie picked up the slack, and the next moments passed in a blur of more hugs and farewells before the travelers went out to where the Packard was parked. After Doro's father stowed the bags in the trunk, he joined the women in the vehicle. All of them waved farewell to Julia, who stood on the front porch with her hand in the air.

When the house was out of sight, Doro leaned back in the seat. Beside her, Aggie reached out and patted her hand.

All too soon, her father pulled up in front of the busy train station. After helping his mother-in-law out, Dr. Banyon opened the trunk. A cheerful porter arrived immediately with a luggage cart. Within a short time, the bags were on their way inside where the man would see they got in the right compartment.

Aggie and Gramma Rose went into the train station, which was busy on this Tuesday morning, while Doro stopped outside with her father. Once again, bittersweet regret formed a lump in her throat. "Thank you for another lovely summer," she murmured. How she missed the old days when they were all together in Michaw.

His gaze scanned her face. "Your mother and I enjoy having you here. Baxter did, too." A grin tugged at the corner of his mouth.

"He's still doing well." Even as she spoke, Doro wondered how long that would continue. Bax was an elderly dog. He had not even come downstairs this morning, and she had not wanted to wake him up to say goodbye. He slept often now.

"He is," her father agreed. "Maybe you can bring your little Tee next summer. I hear some trains allow dogs on board."

"She would adore that," Doro murmured, but what would Ev think? He loved the little dog as much as she did. Would he part with Tee for three months? She shook off the errant thought.

"I hope you can convince your grandmother to come again. Seeing her was good for Julia. Aggie was kind to accompany Rose. Perhaps, she'd do that next year."

The comment evoked other possibilities. "Aggie said little about Wade Lammers, but the two of them have been stepping out. Wade wants to court and marry, but she'd have to quit her job, as things stand now."

Ebediah Banyon's expression grew solemn. "Your grandmother shared that with your mother in a letter. When the board of trustees meets next week, the policy of not employing married women is likely to be rescinded. Between you and me, it's what I've heard from reliable sources. I correspond with a few of my old colleagues, you know."

"I do. You're missed on campus," Doro told him.

Emotion flared in his gaze. "I miss the school, but I need to be with your mother."

Doro nodded. "I understand."

"I won't suggest again that you move out here, because you have good reasons to stay in Michaw," her father said. "As I told you, the college's policy toward having wives as employees is apt to change."

"Wives maybe, but not mothers, so it won't help Aggie because Wade has three children."

"That change will come. Soon, I hope, which won't benefit Aggie now, but it could help you."

Warmth surged into Doro's cheeks. "I don't know what Aggie has said or Gram has written, but Ev and I are only friends." If that. Their parting in May had been less than congenial.

Her father put up one hand. "Neither revealed anything that your mother and I didn't discern from your letters."

The comment reminded Doro of what her mother's best friend, who was a Michaw College secretary, had said in May. The woman often wrote to Julia Banyon, who wrote back. Exchanges about Doro's social life had been a favorite topic, much to her dismay. Evidently, Doro had given away more than she figured in her correspondence. "I wrote very little about Ev."

He shrugged. "You wrote enough to let us know you respect him, enjoy his company, and spend time with him. When two young folks are your ages, that often leads to courtship. I know you've always planned to focus on your career, but times are changing and women may be able to work and have families soon. I hope so. Your mother taught before we married, and she filled in for a while afterward."

"But I came along, and she had to quit," Doro observed.

"We were both thrilled to welcome you," her father said with a broad smile.

"I know." She could not have asked for better parents, but Doro was sorry her mother hadn't had more options. "I was a lucky little girl. I'm still lucky."

Her father squeezed Doro's hand. "We're fortunate to have such a wonderful daughter." He paused before going on. "As I said, I firmly believe the board will allow married women to work at the college. It's less likely they'll allow mothers, but you never know. Besides, you're a few steps from having children."

"Quite a few," she murmured. "Aggie is much closer, but working and having a family seems fraught with its own challenges. Wade's mother and sister have helped him since his wife died. I suppose they still would."

"Knowing his folks, I'm sure Aggie and Wade can rely on them to pitch in, when needed."

But how much help would be necessary? Wade's mother ran a boardinghouse, which kept her busy. As Doro considered Aggie's situation, she thought about her life. Who would help if she married, had children, and kept working? Her grandmother was past seventy and several miles from Michaw. What if a child fell ill while both Doro and Ev were at work? Which of them would rush to school to pick up a son or daughter? And one parent would have to stay home with an infant. Which one?

Doro inwardly chastised herself. As her father had stated, she was a long way from having a family and, considering her abrupt departure in May, Ev might no longer be interested in stepping out, let alone marrying.

Her father's voice cut through Doro's thoughts. "In any case, you'll be home when word comes down. That will give you a better idea of future possibilities."

The statement hinted at a query. Since Doro did not want to discuss Ev, she branched into a related area. "That's the main reason we're leaving a week earlier than originally planned. Aggie wants to hear the news and see Wade." As for Doro, her feelings were mixed. Learning the board's decision was important, but facing Ev might be tricky.

He nodded. "So, you said."

Doro shifted from one foot to the other. "Gram doesn't like to be away for long, either."

"It's kind of you to change your schedule, and I'm sure you and Aggie will be welcomed back with open arms."

"Dad..." Doro's voice trailed off.

Her father interrupted before Doro could say more. "Times are changing, maybe not as quickly as you'd like, but married mothers will hold jobs sooner or later. Neither your mother nor I will tell you what to do, but I'll admit we both worry about you being all alone in the future. You've wanted to be the head librarian at Michaw College since you were a little girl. We've always supported that dream, but we hoped attitudes toward wives and mothers working would've changed by now." He ran one hand over his face. "Progress can be slow."

"You're right," Doro murmured.

He laid his hands on her shoulders. "Your mystery novel is excellent, and writing is a career open to married mothers. Just like being a poet is. Working from home might be easier than juggling a regular job with a family. I know some of my female colleagues struggle at times."

"But the male ones don't," she said. A note of angst threaded through her voice. When had she first realized her options were fewer than the boys in her class? Doro did not remember, although she recalled her disappointment at hearing all the things girls should not or could not do.

"Not as much, and it isn't fair," her father said. "I know Wade Lammers, and he's a good man. He'd do more than many husbands and fathers, but he has a job that calls him away at odd hours occasionally. That's something they'll have to consider, if they marry. Like I said, writing could be easier for Aggie and for you, if you ever consider marriage."

The last phrase offered options, so Doro did not comment. Instead, she considered the meat of her father's observation. Over the summer, she had finished her book and shared it with her parents, her grandmother, and her best friend. All of them loved the whodunit, but she sidestepped that topic. "You seemed positive when Aggie mentioned focusing on her poetry in the future."

"She's talented," he said. "One of my colleagues read some of her work, and he'd be happy to send it to a publisher he knows. I didn't tell Aggie, but she's going to polish her book of poetry and let me see it again."

Pleasure spiraled through Doro. "You've supported the dreams of many of your former students, but I won't tell her."

"Good, because I can't guarantee publication, but I feel optimistic," he replied. "Now, we better get into the station, because you don't want to miss your train."

"No, I don't," she agreed, but the conversation left Doro with plenty to consider.

She and her father had not gotten far when a rumbling voice rang out. "John, how nice to see you!"

The form of address did not surprise Doro, since no one close to her dad ever called him by his first name. Instead, they used his middle moniker, which he preferred, and she understood why. Ebediah was old-fashioned, and her father was not.

A stout man, a valise at his feet, stuck out one hand to her dad.

Doro's father reciprocated. "Are you heading out or returning home?"

"On my way to Chicago for a presentation. Going through Kansas City," the other man replied before his gaze shifted to Doro. "Is this your daughter? You mentioned her spending the summer with you and your wife. I believe she may have met my own missus."

"This is my daughter Doro." He turned to her. "This is Professor Staunton Mathers, who is a science professor at Pikeley College," Doro's father said by way of introduction.

After she exchanged greetings with Mathers, Doro continued. "You must be on our trains, sir. We're going through Kansas City and to Chicago on our way home."

He doffed his bowler to reveal thin, graying hair swept to one side and held in place by an ample coating of Brilliantine. On either side of the swath, his shiny pate gleamed in the light. "I am on both, so we'll see each other along the way. Now, if you'll excuse me, I want to grab a donut and coffee. My wife didn't let our housekeeper know I was leaving this morning, so breakfast wasn't on the table in a timely manner."

The comment perplexed Doro. Couldn't Mr. Mathers have informed their help? Or fixed a light repast himself? Her gaze traveled over the man, whose black suit—while well-cut and expensive—was not in the latest style. Nor were his spats. The white protective covers stood out in stark contrast to his highly polished black shoes. Doro had seen no one wear the accessory for several years. His entire ensemble would have been fashionable a decade or two ago. Not so now.

"We don't want to hold you up," her father said.

Mathers kept his focus on Doro. "When you marry, Miss Banyon, be sure to put your husband's needs first. It's the duty of every decent wife." Then, the man donned his hat, grabbed his bag, and went on.

Doro stood in stunned silence as she watched Mathers waddle away. After a moment, a memory came to her. "Mrs. Mathers came to luncheon a few times, and she invited us to her home for tea and lunch, too. Is she his wife?" Disbelief echoed in her voice. Luann Mathers was a willowy blonde in her early twenties.

"She is," her father replied.

As Doro turned toward him, she saw the frown on his face. "She has to be thirty years younger." Not only that, the young woman was soft-spoken and pleasant—hardly a match for blustering, bossy Mathers. How had they gotten together?

"You're right. He's thirty-three years older." A rough sigh left Doro's father. "Mrs. Mathers' father, Daniel Truman, and Staunton were colleagues. Daniel's wife died almost a decade ago during one of the Spanish flu outbreaks, and he dealt with heart problems for nearly as long. Luann was only nineteen when he passed three years ago. With no other family and little means, she turned to Staunton for help. Some people thought he might take her as his ward, but few figured they'd marry. I surely didn't."

"It's hard to picture the two of them together." Doro watched as Mathers heaved himself on to a stool at the station café. "When Luann came for luncheon, she was always in a hurry to leave before her husband got home. I pictured a handsome young fellow, not..." She withheld an unflattering observation about the portly professor. Looks were not everything, and his manner was more off-putting. Much more. Doro searched her mind for recollections of visits to the Mathers' home. Once, she had caught sight of a young man leaving from the back garden. He had been clad in a natty suit with a fedora pulled low over his hair, and Doro had figured he was Luann's spouse. Now, she knew that was not the case. Was he another relative? "Does Luann have a brother?"

"No, she was an only child," her father replied. "Why do you ask?"

"No particular reason." Doro did not want to cast aspersions on young Mrs. Mathers. Perhaps, the man had been a student of the professor, not someone interested in a private talk with Luann. "So, it's just Luann and her husband. No other relatives?"

"It is. Your mother and I have been to their home for dinner occasionally. I didn't know Luann well before her marriage, but she seems more reserved now." He offered a taut smile. "Unfortunately, we don't have much more time to chat, so we should find Aggie and your grandmother."

Although a host of questions about the Mathers' union flickered through Doro's head, her father was right. The train would leave soon, and she needed to be on it.

Within moments, Doro saw her grandmother and Aggie. She hurried toward where they were standing among the crowd on the platform. "I thought the train would be here by now."

"It's in the yard," Gramma Rose replied. "A porter told us that three cars are being added at the end of the train. One is where we'll be housed."

"They have to do some jockeying around, since a crew sleeper car and the caboose need to be reattached after the new cars are added." Aggie chewed on her lower lip. "The porter assured us they'd hurry, but another passenger mentioned the need to take time. He said something about the right couplers and how they should be inspected to pull sufficient weight."

"I'm sure that will happen," Doro's father said.

Before the conversation went further, a strident voice rang out—the voice of Staunton Mathers, who had left the café, two donuts in one of his enormous hands. He was nearing the platform. Doro was not the only one who swiveled to see what caused his outburst. The entire crowd gaped at the man. With one glance, Doro saw Mathers was furious. But why?

"I hope you're leaving town for good, you blackguard," Mathers, his round face flushed, shouted at a tall, lean man thirty-odd years his junior. When the object of Mathers' wrath stepped away, the older man grabbed his arm. "Can't look me in the face, Grayson?"

The younger man's nostrils flared with a sharp intake of breath. "Let me go, Professor." His fluid baritone was firm but calm, and his handsome features were carefully schooled.

"Let you go? I'll help you go far away from here and from my wife," Mathers ground the words out, but there was no mistaking his rage. Or his accusation.

Doro stared at the younger man, who was close to Luann Mathers' age. With his dark good looks and her fair beauty, the two of them would make an attractive couple, but Doro could not envision the shy girl stepping out behind her husband's back. But what about the figure who had slipped away from the Mathers' house? Could it have been this young fellow?

Grayson shook off the older man's grip and stepped away. "I'm not going away for good, Professor. I'll return in a couple of weeks." The words held a note of challenge.

"If you're half as smart as you think you are, you'll clear out-of-town forever," Mathers muttered. "Because, if I see you anywhere near my wife, you're a dead man."

A snicker left Grayson, but his voice held no trace of amusement. "You're the one who ought to stay away from her."

The professor's pastries fell to the floor as he grabbed the lapels of the younger man's suit jacket. "How dare you? She is my legally wedded wife, and you better remember that."

The words were barely out of the professor's mouth when Doro's father rushed to intercede. "Staunton, release him now. You're making a fool of yourself."

"That's nothing new," Grayson added. "The professor is a problem. A big problem that needs to be solved, and I have an idea about how to do it."

Mathers' eyes nearly bulged out of his massive head. "You're an impudent pup that ought to be put down."

"Staunton," Dr. Banyon spoke in a quieter tone. "Go on your way."

Several moments passed before Mathers took Dr. Banyon's advice. Then, he turned on his heel and stalked away without another word. He crushed both donuts in the process.

"Thanks, Dr. Banyon," Grayson said as he straightened his suit coat. "Mathers is an old fool."

"You haven't helped matters, Grayson," Doro's father replied, a stern expression on his face.

"I'm not leaving Colorado Springs on a permanent basis. I shouldn't have to."

A period of silence preceded Dr. Banyon's response. "Do yourself and Luann a favor by staying away from her. Mathers won't back down, and you'll only create trouble for her and yourself."

Anger flashed in the young man's dark gaze. "She needs some fun in her life, not a pompous old goat who treats her like an expensive doll." Grayson touched his hat. "I appreciate that you mean well, sir, but you aren't in my shoes, or in Luann's."

Another young man, the same height and build as Grayson but with light auburn hair and green eyes, hurried up. "I heard your confrontation with Mathers from halfway across the station. Please say the old coot isn't on our train."

Grayson grimaced. "I'm afraid I can't do that, Phin."

"Do you know where he's headed?" Phin asked.

Doro's father spoke up. "Professor Mathers is going to Chicago. What about the two of you?" He looked from one to the other. "Classes begin in two weeks, so I'm surprised you're not getting settled for the term."

"We would be, but my father died the day before yesterday," Grayson replied. "Phin is going with me."

Dr. Banyon offered his condolences before issuing more advice. "Steer clear of Mathers, if you can. He's got a bad temper, and you've run afoul of him. Both of you."

Doro sensed an unspoken undercurrent. How had both young men gotten on the bad side of Mathers? And how bad was it? Again, she wondered about the man she'd seen leaving the Mathers' property. Too bad the stranger's hat had hidden his hair color because both Phin and Grayson were of similar height and build.

"We'll keep away from the professor, sir," Phin said, in a reassuring tone. "He likes to make trouble, but we'll ignore him."

"Good. Be sure you do," Doro's father said.

"Sorry, miss." The one called Phin turned toward Doro and touched the brim of his bowler hat.

Dr. Banyon introduced her to Grayson Bailey, the brown-haired fellow, and Phineas Spieth, the redhead. "Gentlemen, this is my daughter, Professor Dorothea Banyon."

"We've heard about you and your exploits as an amateur sleuth," Grayson said, his eyes sparkling with good humor.

"We sure have," Phin agreed with a grin.

When she glanced at her father, Doro saw pride in his expression. She was beyond lucky to have parents who were pleased with her accomplishments. So many young women were encouraged to marry as soon as they left high school. "I've been part of a team in every investigation."

"Someone has to lead a team, though," Grayson pointed out.

Because she had always played a major role, often *the* major role, Doro shrugged. "I enjoy solving whodunits."

"And you're always successful?" Phineas asked.

"So far, yes," she replied with a chuckle.

"Crooks better be darn smart around you, I guess," Grayson observed.

Doro smiled. "It would be better if no more crimes happened. I teach a course on the mystery novel, so reading whodunits is a more pleasant way to play sleuth." Although not nearly as exciting.

"Luckily, no crimes occurred while you were visiting," her father said. "Let's hope none occur on the train."

"You're from Ohio, right?" Phineas asked.

She nodded. "I am."

"We're probably on the same train, at least as far as Kansas City," Grayson put in.

"My grandmother, my best friend, and I are on that train. After the first leg, we'll transfer and continue on to Chicago before changing there for the last leg home," Doro said. "Are you from Kansas City?"

"Phin is, but my family lives in Joplin, Missouri," Grayson replied. "Now, we should go. It was nice to meet you, Miss Banyon."

Phin offered similar sentiments before the two friends went on their way.

Dr. Banyon pulled out his pocket watch. "The train is already ten minutes late in leaving, but let's get all of you closer to the edge of the platform."

"That was quite a scene," Gramma Rose observed as the group moved along.

Doro's father released a pent-up breath. "Sorry. I was afraid they'd come to blows." He explained who the older man was. "Both Gray Bailey and Phin Spieth are at odds with the professor. Although young Bailey has always studied at Colorado College, he took a class with Staunton as an undergraduate, which isn't unusual. A number of students do. Bailey also studied with Luann's father. That's how the two became acquainted. Antagonizing Staunton Mathers isn't a good idea." Dr. Banyon's gaze scanned the three women. "Phineas is Gray's friend. He's also a graduate student, but he left Pikeley College, where Mathers teaches, between his sophomore and junior years. I've heard rumors about why he left, but who knows if they have validity? In any case, his animosity isn't as personal as Gray's. At least, not to my knowledge. If you see, Phin, Gray, and Mathers together, go the other way."

"It's not like you to exaggerate, John, which makes your warning troubling," Gramma Rose said, as she studied her son-in-law. "Is there a chance they'll engage in fisticuffs? If so, I'd say the younger man has the advantage."

Dr. Banyon's lips twitched. "As always, you get right to the point, Mother Rose." His good humor ebbed. "They've almost gotten into physical altercations a few times, since faculty and students from both colleges attend various programs together. I hoped their confrontations would be eliminated, but that obviously hasn't happened. As for Phin, he's made some nasty comments about Staunton. Although he isn't the only one,"

Her father's concern gave Doro pause. "Professor Mathers insinuated that Mr. Bailey might be smitten with Mrs. Mathers. Is that the source of their problem?"

Her father nodded. "Again, the details have eluded me, although I believe the two stepped out before Dr. Truman died."

"Luann Mathers' father?" Doro asked for clarification.

"Yes," Dr. Danyon replied. "He and Staunton were colleagues for years."

"I missed the first part of the confrontation, but that older man is Luann's husband?" Aggie asked in a stunned tone.

"He is," Doro told her friend.

"Something of a misalliance," Gramma Rose observed.

Her son-in-law nodded. "In any case, give the trio a wide berth, if they're together. With luck, they'll behave on the train, although Mathers can be cantankerous about poor service, which he identifies as anyone not catering to him."

Doro thought back to the professor's remarks on how to be a good wife and wondered if Luann was at his beck-and-call. Then, there were Bailey's remarks. But it was none of her business and, even if she asked, her father did not engage in gossip. Perhaps, she would learn more on the train. While Mathers was not apt to provide information, Bailey and Spieth might. Learning about their issues with Mathers was not like solving a genuine mystery, but the puzzle piqued her interest. Most puzzles did.

Chapter Two

A fter another ten minutes, the train stopped at the platform. Following a flurry of activity, Doro, Aggie, and
Gramma Rose said their last farewells to Doro's father before
getting on-board. A porter helped them find their drawing
room compartment, where their bags were already in place. The
lodging was larger and finer than Doro's usual rail accommodations, but her parents had insisted on paying for a space large
enough for all three women.

"Our sleeping compartment on the way out was lovely," Aggie said as she swiveled to take in the entire area, "but this space
is luxurious."

"It certainly is," Gramma Rose agreed. "Although I didn't
want Julia and John to fuss, all three of us can be together."

"I understand why this type of compartment is called a drawing room," Doro observed. "It's furnished like one, and the
sofa and lounge chairs look comfortable. At night, we'll have
four full beds, and we can hang up some of our clothes, if we

want." She gestured to the closet. "I always have a lavatory in my compartment but no closet, just a clothes rod. Since I only need one bed, the spaces have been cramped. This is roomy." She flung out her arms and spun around. The other two chuckled.

"And wonderful. We could spend the entire day in here and not feel confined," Aggie added.

"We sure could," Doro agreed.

"True, but we'll want to go to the dining car for meals," her grandmother said. "Except for lunch today, when we can enjoy the basket your mother sent."

Doro nodded, since she had no intention of limiting herself to staying in the compartment. Despite her father's admonition about Bailey, Spieth, and Mathers, she was curious. Bumping into the younger men might answer some of her questions. She wondered about Luann Truman Mathers and Grayson Bailey, and about how Phineas Spieth had also gotten on the professor's bad side. Had one of them called on Luann when her husband was away from home? It should not matter, but curiosity was calling, as it did often.

After stowing their belongings and having lunch, the three women settled by the wide window and watched the scenery pass. Gramma Rose dozed off an hour after they left Colorado Springs, so Doro and Aggie became engrossed in their own books as the train sped along.

***

As the train continued southeast out of Colorado Springs, the topography slowly altered. With the mountains behind them, the ground grew flatter and, when they connected with the Acheson line and headed due east, the elevation change became marked. Shortly after they got on the Topeka line, Gramma Rose woke up.

"I see we're into Kansas," she said.

"We are," Doro agreed. "No matter how many times I make this trip, I'm always amazed at the miles and miles of empty spaces. In Ohio, there's farmland, but you don't go far without seeing a building, a vehicle, or people. Here, it's completely different."

"It sure is," Aggie agreed. "I was stunned when we came out. Nothing to see for hours on end. Or so it seemed."

"There are isolated ranches and small towns in places, but you girls are right. This part of the country is different from northwest Ohio," Gramma Rose observed.

A slight shiver went through Aggie. "Maybe it's being raised in the city that makes me feel uneasy about not seeing any living beings for a time."

"Probably so," Rose said. "We've hit a couple of whistle-stop stations, and there'll be a few more before we get to Dodge City."

"Which is the next big town. Not that it's so large," Doro said.

"Since there's not much to see, I'm going back to my book," Aggie said.

"Me, too," Doro added, and Gramma Rose agreed.

As they went farther into Kansas later that afternoon, the sky darkened. Doro flipped on one of the sconce lamps before peering out at the storm clouds gathering on the horizon. "It looks like we're headed into bad weather."

Seated on the sofa across from Doro, her grandmother stirred and followed her gaze. "You're right. We could be in for a rough ride on this next section of the railway. That happened the first time I went out to see your mother. It was right about in this area, too." Gramma Rose clucked her tongue. "We get powerful storms in Ohio, but nothing like I saw that day."

Aggie, sitting next to her friend, leaned over for a better view. "I've heard about tornadoes in this part of the country. Huge ones. Maybe the train will stop at the next station, so we can get off for a while."

Rose leaned across to pat Aggie's hand. "We were late getting out of the Springs, so they'll want to get back on schedule, if possible. But don't worry. A tornado is unlikely. Just some thunderstorms ahead."

The concern knitting her friend's brow made Doro offer additional reassurance. "I've been back-and-forth to Colorado every summer for years. Before Dad moved, we went together. Since then, I've traveled on my own. There have been a few storms while coming or going, but nothing terrible. We'll be fine."

"If you say so." Aggie sounded less than comforted.

A chuckle left Doro. "You didn't have problems on the way west, did you?"

"No, but there were clear skies for the entire trip." Aggie waved her hand toward the outside. "Those are ominous clouds. And what about the couplers for the extra cars? Remember the man on the platform? He was worried."

Although she knew next to nothing about trains, Doro rushed to placate Aggie. "He wasn't with the railroad, so he's no expert."

"That's true. I'm sure the cars are secured," Gramma Rose said. "Although I experienced a tremendous storm once, the train continued on with no trouble."

Since Doro knew Aggie fretted, she aimed for distraction. "In a few days, we'll be back home. You must look forward to seeing Wade."

The dismay ebbed from Aggie's expression. "I am, and I'm eager to hear what the board of trustees decides about employing married women, even mothers."

For a moment, Doro considered revealing her father's perspective but, not wanting to get her friend's hopes up, she resisted. "It won't be long before we find out." As she studied her friend's expression, Doro noted the tension there. "Times are changing, and other colleges employ married mothers."

"I know," Aggie murmured. "I met a woman professor with a family when we visited your dad's campus. Remember when I went to the lavatory, and you wondered why I took so long?"

After searching her memory, Doro nodded. "You said you got turned around."

"I did, and a gracious lady helped me find my way. While she was escorting me to the history department, we talked about being professors, and I mentioned the Michaw College Board of Trustees meeting soon. I also said I hope they allow women with families to teach," Aggie said.

"What did she say about that?" Gramma Rose inquired.

"She's a wife and mother. Three children, like Wade." Aggie cleared her throat. "Professor Sumner, that's her name, is glad she can keep teaching, but it isn't easy to juggle everything. Her husband is a doctor, so he gets called out at odd hours. Like Wade. They have a part-time housekeeper, which helps. But a doctor earns more than a constable, so they can afford to hire someone."

Since Aggie's uneasiness was apparent, Doro pointed out his support. "Wade's family helps now, and they would if you two marry. I could pitch in, too."

"Of course, they would, and so would I," Gramma Rose added. "It doesn't take long to drive out to Michaw from Sylvania. My old Model T is reliable."

A soft smile touched Aggie's lips. "Thanks to both of you, but Professor Sumner made me stop and think. Her mother lives with them, and she helped until she had a heart attack. Now, she's limited in her activities. Wade's mother has already had one attack, not to mention her boarders requiring her attention. During the school year, she has to tend to their needs."

Aggie's dismay worried Doro, mostly because she had made valid points, ones that Doro needed to consider, too. "I don't know Professor Sumner, but perhaps she was feeling worn out when you ran into her."

"It's summer vacation," Aggie pointed out. "If she's tired now, how will she be during the term?"

The question made an excellent point, and Doro was not sure how to address it. Luckily, her grandmother stepped in.

"Sometimes, anticipating difficulties is more unnerving than facing them," Gramma Rose observed. "I'm not saying it's easy for women to work and maintain a home, but widows often do it because they have no choice. Most of them don't have professional positions like the two of you and Professor Sumner. I doubt if one type of job is simpler to balance with a family. I didn't do it myself, but times are changing. Perhaps, someday, most women will work."

"Perhaps so," Doro said, but such a thing was hard to imagine. To offer additional reassurance, she mentioned her father's observations, although she did not cite him as the source. "Wade is a good man, and he's already used to caring for his kids. Doesn't he cook and clean?"

"He cooks most of the meals," Aggie admitted. "His sister comes to clean once a week, but Wade keeps the house in order on a daily basis. Mostly, he does a good job. And the children help."

Abruptly, Doro wondered if Ev cooked. His studio apartment had a tiny kitchenette, so he ate most of his meals in the men's faculty residence, but what had he done as a policeman and a federal agent, the jobs he had held before coming to Michaw? As far as cleaning, Doro had only seen his campus accommodation once, when she'd dropped off Tee in May. The place had been spotless, so he was not a slob.

"You look pensive, Doro," her grandmother said.

Warmth rushed into Doro's face. Her errant thoughts would not be shared. Nor would she give them more time. "Just thinking about our arrival home." Which was partly true. She addressed Aggie. "Wade is meeting the train, isn't he?"

Aggie, a smile replacing her frown, nodded. "Since we arrive in Sylvania on Friday evening, he'll be there."

"I like Wade," Gramma Rose said. "He's a fine young man."

"He is," Doro agreed. Although the lawman was fifteen years older than her friend, to a septuagenarian, Wade must seem youthful.

Their conversation was interrupted by a knock on their door. Doro opened it to find the conductor, Walter Sayers, in the corridor. The man, of medium height and build, with nearly coal black hair and equally dark eyes, had introduced himself when they boarded the train. As he had then, Sayers ran one finger inside his heavily starched shirt collar.

"Looks like we'll be running into some big storms ahead," he said. "Dinner will be served early in the dining car, so go soon. It'll fill up as folks get the word. We started at this end of the train, so you're finding out first. The big dining car has already prepared meals, but a few folks riding up front may filter back. We never know."

"Thank you," Doro replied before the man moved on.

"That doesn't sound good," Aggie said after the door closed behind Sayers.

"They're being cautious," Gramma Rose said. "Let's freshen up and have dinner. A hot meal will be lovely."

"It will. We can eat something and come back here," Doro suggested. "Even though sunset is a couple of hours off, the storm clouds will make it get dark early, so we won't see much scenery for the rest of the afternoon."

"We can play whist," her grandmother suggested.

Doro and Aggie chuckled because Rose McLaren suggested her favorite card game at every opportunity.

***

When the three women arrived in the dining car ten minutes later, only a handful of tables were occupied, so they easily found one and sat down. Despite the dinner hour being moved up, the usual formal place settings were ready. Sparkling sterling silverware, crystal wine and water goblets, a starched linen cloth with matching napkins, and a small vase of flowers provided an elegant touch on every table.

"Let's sit farther back," Doro said, moving on and taking a deep breath. "The aroma of bread is heavenly."

"It is," Aggie agreed, "and there must be ham baked with cloves."

"You're both right. I also smell coffee. A fresh-brewed cup sounds marvelous," Gramma Rose said. When they decided on a table, she continued. "Train travel has come a long way since I was a girl. We couldn't have gone all the way from Sylvania to Colorado Springs when I was born. Of course, my father had to hook up the horses to go even the shortest distance. Motoring is much easier."

"Some folks were still using horses when I was little," Doro said. "A couple of the farmers outside Michaw haven't made the change yet."

A sigh left her grandmother. "Not everyone wants to move with the times, but they will eventually."

Doro and Aggie exchanged a long look, since both young women knew the sentiment all too well. *Eventually* was a word they had heard often, especially in regard to women's roles.

The arrival of a young waiter, tall and thin, interrupted. "Good afternoon, ladies, I'm Joshua," he said with a smile. "I'm sorry we don't have our usual menu, but the kitchen staff is rushing to serve dinner before we encounter the storm, which could be within the next couple of hours. The head chef is back here, since he's already prepared food for the main dining car."

Doro glanced around. "This is a combination car, isn't it? One that was added in the Springs?"

"Yes, miss," the young waiter said. "With two extra cars, another dining one was necessary. Otherwise, folks back here would have a long walk to the one that was already in place. It's a bit unusual for the chef to move around, and this kitchen is smaller, but the food will be good. In any case, he has a compartment at the end of the train, so it works out."

"I sure it will," Gramma Rose agreed, "and we're grateful an earlier meal is being served. We'll be tucked into our compartment playing cards before we run into the rain."

"Very good, ma'am," the young man said as he pulled a slip of paper out of his pocket. "We have a tomato and cucumber salad, trout, baked ham, sweet potatoes, and green beans. There's also fresh baked rolls and a custard for dessert. We'll have more choices tomorrow."

"That's a nice offering on short notice," Gramma Rose assured him before giving her order.

Doro and Aggie followed with their preferences, but a strident voice intruded. "Waiter, waiter. Get over here. I've been waiting for far too long."

Doro shifted to see Professor Mathers, his broad face flushed with anger, waving one huge hand in the air. Recalling the train station debacle, and her father's observation about the man being demanding, she felt a surge of dismay. Was it too late to find a table far away from him?

"We saw him in the station," her grandmother murmured. "He was unpleasant there, too."

"Mr. Mathers often travels this route. Too often," the young man replied with a frown. "I work it a lot myself, so I've met him."

The professor shouted again. "Can you hear, young man?"

"Sorry, ladies, I'd best see to him," the waiter said before darting to the other table. His voice did not carry, but Mather's did.

"I want a steak, a baked potato with sour cream and butter, plenty of rolls, coffee, and pie à la mode for dessert." Although Joshua stood next to his table, Mathers bellowed at him.

A middle-aged couple, just entering the car, halted in place. When the woman gestured to the nearest table, her husband nodded. After helping his wife into a chair, the man sat across from her, facing the debacle. Doro decided they were both wise: the lady for wanting a table far from the noise and the man for monitoring the situation.

Meanwhile, the waiter took one step back. "Professor, we aren't able to accommodate special orders this evening. We're likely to run into a line of heavy thunderstorms within the next hour or two, which is why we're starting dinner service early."

"Nonsense," Mathers insisted. "The cook must've baked potatoes and pies already. Grilling a steak won't take long."

Doro saw the waiter's shoulders rise and fall as if he had taken a deep breath. The poor kid, and he was no more than nineteen, did not deserve to be treated so abominably. No one did.

"I apologize for the inconvenience, but we have a limited menu," the young man replied, his voice louder and edgier than before. "The chef will be pleased to fix any meal you want tomorrow."

"Do not speak to me in such a tone," Mathers replied. "Get that cook out here. I want to talk to him."

Doro witnessed the scene with dismay. Joshua's tone had been controlled and respectful. Was the professor always so demanding and obnoxious? Her father's comments had indicated that might be the case.

As the exchange went on, more diners entered: a man of around forty and a boy who appeared to be in his early teens. Unlike the couple, this pair took their places next to Doro's table. The gentleman nodded to the women, while the boy gaped at the professor before they both got seated.

Another waiter, close to forty and wiry in build, approached the Mathers' table. "You're disturbing other guests and picking on someone younger than yourself, which ain't surprising. Joshua already explained about this special situation, didn't he?"

A harrumph rumbled out of Mathers. "As often as I travel this route, I expect better service. Clyde, remember that one of my friends is with the railroad. I'm sure he won't be pleased when he finds out how I've been treated." The man's voice was loud enough to echo through the entire car, while his gaze fixed on the older waiter.

Anger flared in Clyde's gaze. "Throwing your weight around, as usual, but you don't scare me. You can't take nothing else from me. Not after what you did."

The color in Mathers' round face deepened. "You miscreant. How dare you? I don't know why you haven't lost your job, but that will change as soon as I get to my destination."

When Clyde moved toward Mathers, Joshua grabbed his arm. "Don't."

The older man glanced over his shoulder at his junior colleague. "He ain't ought to talk to you, or nobody else, like he does. He's got away with too much for too long. That's gotta end." Clyde's voice rose with every word.

Doro looked around the dining car, but no one moved to intercede, although all eyes were on Mathers. Perhaps, it was best if passengers did not get involved. Where was the conductor? Should she look for him?

Before anything else was said, Grayson Bailey and Phineas Spieth, just entering the dining car, intervened. Bailey stopped at the table, while Spieth stood a couple of paces behind him. "Mathers, you need to lower your voice and let these men do their jobs. All of us are being inconvenienced, but you're the only one acting like a spoiled brat. But you always want your way, don't you?"

Evidently, the two young graduate students had heard most of the debacle. Bailey's features were carefully schooled, and

Spieth's jaw was set hard, but the former's tone had cut like a knife. Doro's continuing survey, an effort to find someone who might quell the growing tension, was interrupted by the professor's strident voice.

"How dare you?" Mathers surged to his feet, knocking over the small table and his chair in the process.

Both waiters jumped back to avoid shattering glass. Water and flowers, from a crystal vase, scattered across the floor, while the linen tablecloth and napkin hung askew. Gasps resonated through the car as other passengers reacted.

Mr. Bailey, who stood his ground, put one big hand against Mathers' barrel chest to hold him in place, but the older man plowed forward. As he did, shards of glass crumbled under his feet. When the professor lunged at him, Bailey pushed hard to keep him at bay, which caused Mathers to fall over the up-ended the table and into one across the aisle. Luckily, no one was sitting there, but the lovely settings scattered everywhere. Mathers labored to his feet and again sprang at Bailey, who stood his ground. Spieth released a humorless guffaw before shoving Mathers into his chair. "Sit down and stay there."

"You insolent whelp. You haven't changed a bit. Always obnoxious," Mathers bellowed. His narrowed gaze went from one young man to the other. "I've had a theft on my property recently. Probably about the same time you two got back in town this month and back in June."

Gray looked incredulous. "Now, you're really reaching."

"You are," Phin agreed. "You'd be smarter to look at your current students, or at least the ones you've cheated recently."

Once again, the professor's face became beet red. "How dare you?"

Phin chuckled. "You said that already."

"Let's find a table," Gray said.

"As long as it's far from old man Mathers," his friend replied. "That way, we can ignore the coot. He's making a fool of himself again. Maybe we should go to the other dining car. There's a bigger one up ahead. Or the club car should offer light fare."

"Most of the passenger cars are nearer those places, which will mean they're filled. Let's stay here. Despite the old coot," Bailey said.

Mathers' face turned purple as he stood to confront Spieth. "You're as bad as he is, and you're even more foolish. I have influence with your professors, who already know about your previous academic problems. They may find your thesis to be inadequate, you young pup, and I can tell you right now that's a strong possibility, if I have any say. Consider going home for good."

Spieth, an angry flush nearly blotting out his freckles, grabbed the old professor by his lapels. "You won't get away with that. I'll see to it." When he let Mathers go, the professor stumbled backward and again tumbled to the floor.

"How dare you touch me?" Mathers roared. "You'll pay for this, Spieth. Mark my words."

Spieth's response was to turn away. "Come on, Gray, let's find a table at the other end of the car. Being near this old buffoon will spoil our appetites."

"Good idea," Bailey, his face fixed in a frown, replied before both young men retraced their steps and found a place to sit.

Joshua helped Mathers to his feet. "Are you all right, sir?"

The professor jerked free. "No, I'm not. I want to speak with the conductor. First, however, get this table cleaned up and bring the cook out here."

"Yes, sir," Joshua said before picking up the debris littering the floor.

Mathers, still fuming, turned on Clyde. "Aren't you going to help him, you good-for-nothing ignoramus?"

The older waiter fisted his hands. "Get out of our way."

Before the professor could respond, Gramma Rose called out to him. "Take a seat with us for a few moments. That will make it easier for the waiters to get your table back in order."

Doro and Aggie exchanged a stunned glance, but said nothing as Mathers levered himself into the empty chair at their table.

"Thank you," he said, but his voice did not hold even the slightest note of gratitude. "The behavior of servants and young folks is appalling."

What Doro found appalling was the professor's arrogance. Not that Bailey and Spieth had acted with decorum. And what had goaded the older waiter? Mathers must have an inkling. "Clyde seemed upset." The man's comments evoked curiosity. How well did the waiter know the professor? Did they have some connection outside the railroad?

A harrumph left Mathers. "Clyde Oscar is ignorant and ill-mannered. The railroad should not tolerate such behavior, and I shall see that his superiors know."

"You wouldn't want to get him fired." Gramma Rose spoke in a cajoling tone. "A fine, respected scholar like yourself is above such antics."

Mathers' expression softened as he turned to the septuagenarian. "You came to my home with Mrs. Banyon and these young ladies, I believe."

"Your wife was kind enough to invite us on several occasions," Gramma replied, "but I only saw you once in passing. I'm Rosalyn McLaren, Julia Banyon's mother. I believe you formally met my granddaughter Dorothea at the train station, and this is her best friend, Agatha Darwine. There wasn't a chance for us to be introduced."

Doro grimaced. The debacle between the professor and the two young men had taken front stage, and Mathers seemed intent on a continued spectacle.

A slight smile formed on the professor's thick lips. "It's good to see young ladies traveling with a chaperone. Old-fashioned virtues make girls more appealing to decent men." He chuckled. "You two aren't really girls, but you're still of marriageable age."

His archaic attitude and subtle criticism had Doro fuming. With her twenty-sixth birthday in three weeks, she did not consider herself a spinster, although others might. Besides, the term was old-fashioned and insulting, words that described the professor. "Sir..." Before she could say more, her grandmother interceded.

"Since the Great War, times have changed. Many young women, like Doro and Aggie, wait to wed, and they have careers." Gramma Rose spoke in a calm tone, but steel glinted in her gaze.

"Foolishness, if you ask me. We have only a few female professors at Pikeley, thank goodness," Mathers said.

"Colorado College has some. A few are married with children. As my grandmother said, times have changed." Doro could not keep an edge from her voice.

"Which is not necessarily a good thing," Mathers retorted with a scowl. "Your Michaw College is small, isn't it?"

Doro could not disagree with the assessment, but small schools were often trailblazers. "It is, but Michaw has been known as a progressive school. Soon, we expect the trustees to allow married women, even mothers, to work there."

A harrumph left Mathers. "Your father once mentioned the college was all-male before the Great War. Foolish to change the policy. Women ought to be home with a husband and children."

Again, Doro inwardly grimaced. Sadly, he was not alone is his sentiments. The previous fall, some male professors at Michaw had tried to turn back the hands of time, but they had failed. The school remained a co-educational institution. "Not everyone agrees with that sentiment," Doro said.

"Trustees at your little college may be weak, but bigger schools seldom promote women. Nor do many hire them," the professor said. "Wise practices that smaller entities ought to mimic."

Doro bit her lip to keep from chastising the man for his backward ideas. She knew well that a number of major universities rarely hired and elevated women, mostly because of men like Mathers. In some places, procedures were changing, partly due to more girls getting degrees, which she pointed out to the professor. "Many young women attend college now, and some expect to use their degrees."

"Foolishness," Mathers muttered. "Same with allowing the lower classes to get a college education. They get above themselves and resent being put in their places. Jealous of their betters, too, and that only leads to larceny and worse."

His rambling evoked a one-word question from Doro. "Larceny?"

"Yes, larceny. We've been plagued by my papers coming up missing, right in our home. It's why I'm strict with Luann about our guests. She'll welcome anyone through the door," the professor said.

"I hope you aren't referring to us." Doro could not keep a note of sarcasm from her voice.

"Not at all, my dear," Mathers replied. "When our butler's been busy, Luann has invited students and former students inside. Several times, the papers on my desk were in disarray afterward."

"That doesn't mean the students handled them," Gramma Rose pointed out. "Perhaps, a servant inadvertently disturbed them."

"Or maybe Luann did," Aggie added.

A snort left Mathers. "The help knows better, and so does my wife."

Doro considered his revelations. The furtive figure had come from the library side of the house. She had not noticed any papers in the man's possession, but they could have been tucked into his jacket. But why take items from Mathers' desk?

At that point, Joshua hurried over and addressed Mathers. "Your table is restored, and I'll get your meal right away, sir."

"See that you do," Mathers said with a sneer. "I should've gone to the other dining car. However, it's a long way up there. If the help is better, some of them ought to come back here."

After the young waiter rushed off, Gramma Rose gave the professor a polite dismissal. "Enjoy your dinner in privacy."

For a moment, he did not move or speak. Then, he rose, nodded, and returned to his table.

"What a boor," Aggie murmured, her eyes wide.

"There is no excuse for such atrocious behavior," Gramma Rose said. "None at all. The other two young men were right to intercede, but their rude comments didn't help. John told us to steer clear of them, and he was right."

While Doro agreed, she remained silent. The confrontation in the Colorado Springs train station rose in her memory. The threesome evidently had a history, a checkered one, according to her father. What about Mathers' accusations of theft? Had the man she'd seen been one of them? But who was the man? Gray? Phin? Or someone else? And what about Mathers' threat? Could he influence professors at another school? Doro did not think so, but the man had obviously wanted to scare Mr. Spieth. And what had Mathers meant about Spieth's history? What was there to know? Her glance went to where he and Grayson Bailey were sitting. Both young men looked calmer, but how long would it last? And what about Clyde? What was the waiter's connection to the professor? Last, but far from least, Mathers' attitude toward women appalled Doro. Avoiding him, even when he was alone, was now her strategy.

The young waiter returned with the professor's meal, but the man did not thank him. Instead, Mathers fumed about the chef. "Where is Andre? I know he's working this run, since I asked the conductor when I got on. Get him out here now or I'll be reporting the two of you to my friend, along with Clyde."

"Sir, he's very busy," the young waiter said in a placating tone.

Mathers banged his beefy fist on the table. Luckily, the glassware had not yet been replaced, but the silverware clattered to the floor. "I'll go to the kitchen, if I must."

Joshua, who looked at wit's end, nodded. "I'll get Chef Andre, sir."

After the young man dashed off, Doro turned to her dining companions. "Mr. Mathers is worse than Dad told me. He's beyond demanding."

"He's an oaf," her grandmother said. "The chef has his hands full, especially with two kitchens to supervise. All the dining car workers do, too. It's appalling that Mr. Mathers is so focused on himself. I only invited him to sit with us briefly so he'd stop harassing the waiters." She glared at the man, but he was busy chastising the older waiter.

"I need clean cutlery," the professor said. "And there are still shards of glass on the floor."

The waiter, his thin face set in severe lines, looked to be near the breaking point. "We got almost all of it, and we have others to serve." His tone was harsh and hard.

Mathers clucked his tongue. "Such incompetence."

At that moment, the chef, flushed and flustered, approached Mathers. "Sir, I can't prepare special meals tonight. We are rushing to feed everyone before we encounter the storm. This run, I have a large kitchen and a small one to supervise. I'm stretched thin, and so is my staff. Tomorrow night, I will be happy to take your order, but not now." Nothing in the man's tone indicated any pleasure at agreeing to the professor's wishes. Quite the contrary.

"Ridiculous," Mathers roared. "It takes no time for a decent cook to grill a steak."

Andre's face went crimson and his dark gaze grew stormy. "I am a chef, sir. Not a mere cook."

A harrumph left Mathers. "Cook or chef. Do your job and fix me a steak."

The chef's cheeks puffed out as he sucked in a long breath. "Sir, my job is to serve all passengers, not to cater to a demanding few."

When Andre turned away, Mathers grabbed the sleeve of his chef's jacket. "I have a friend who is high in this railroad. Rest assured, I'll report your uselessness to him."

Andre yanked his arm loose and spun to face the professor. "Useless? Useless? I've worked at the finest hotels and restaurants. Thankfully, only a few diners were as gauche as you. Few passengers are, either."

"You jackanapes," the professor shouted. "You better have something decent for me to snack on tonight. It's too long between dinner and breakfast on the regular schedule. Now, you've moved the evening meal up, so I'll need something substantial. See that it's where I can easily find it."

Because Mathers still failed to modulate his voice, passengers turned to stare. Doro noticed Phineas Spieth leaning sideways and shaking his head. She hoped he and Grayson Bailey stayed at their table.

"Do not wake me or my staff," the chef shot back. "The key will be where you can locate it. So will food. As for the time of the meal, the other kitchen is serving now, as well, and that is at the conductor's request."

"You'll be sorry you were so rude," Mathers blurted out. "Very sorry."

The chef glanced at the professor over his shoulder. "Someone needs to make you sorry for being such a clod." Andre stomped off, leaving a sputtering Mathers in his wake.

While Mathers fell silent, whispers went through the other diners, all of whom had observed the latest squabble. As the professor glanced around, his gaze fixed on Doro and her table. "I'm sorry you ladies had to experience the awful rudeness of the help. Some folks don't know their place."

Doro wanted to say Mathers was the dolt, but she did not want to stir him up again. Or have him return to their table. The other diners deserved peace.

"I hope we have a quiet interlude during dinner," Gramma Rose put in. Her somber tone and fixed expression undergirded her assertion.

"Me, too, madam," the professor said. "It's appalling for workers to make such a stink."

Doro rolled her eyes. The man clearly did not discern her grandmother's displeasure with him. Luckily, the exchange was halted by Joshua bringing their meals. Doro, nervous about Mathers hollering again, held her breath, but Clyde brought the rest of his food at the same time. Despite complaining more,

Mathers dug into his dinner as if he had not eaten for a week. The women went about consuming their cuisine in a more genteel manner.

Joshua returned to check on them periodically. He also stopped at Professor Mathers's table. Since the older man continued to air complaints, Doro, Aggie, and Gramma Rose expressed their appreciation and gratitude. All of them relaxed when Mathers made his way out of the car.

He pushed Joshua, who had just come to check on the three ladies, off to the side as he went. "You need to let people by."

The waiter nodded, but his expression was grim. When Mathers was out of sight, Joshua's shoulders slumped, as if in relief.

"I'm so sorry the professor was so rude," Doro said.

"Do you know him?" Joshua asked.

"We met at the train station in Colorado Springs. He's acquainted with my father, who is also a professor, although not at the same college," Doro replied. "He was quite rude to the chef. Is that typical?"

"They've had several run-ins over how food is cooked. The professor likes his steaks well done, which can make them tough. Chef Andre explained that to him many times, but to no avail." Joshua shook his head. "The chef can be temperamental, which doesn't help the situation."

"I'm sure it doesn't," Aggie said.

"We've heard there's another dining car up ahead," Doro commented. "Why doesn't Professor Mathers eat there?"

"It's a dozen cars ahead of us. There's more space, since the kitchen is in a separate carriage with a few tables. This car was added when the extra passenger carriages were," Joshua said. "Chef Andre oversees everything, and the head cook wouldn't kowtow to the professor's demands, either, so that wouldn't help the situation."

Doro absorbed the information. The words between Andre and Mathers had been heated, but no worse than the contretemps with Bailey, Spieth, or Clyde. Knowing it was not the only time the pair had crossed swords weighed heavily on Doro. She had met the professor only a few hours earlier, and he had been at odds with four men during that time. "Please tell Chef Andre how much we enjoyed the meal," Doro said, hoping compliments might mollify the man.

Aggie nodded. "It was delicious."

"It most certainly was," Grandmother added with a smile. "The chef is a magician."

A slight smile touched the young waiter's lips. "I'll tell him, ma'am. He'll appreciate that." Before going about his other tasks, Joshua assisted Gramma Rose with her chair. Then, he bid the women a good evening and went on about his job.

"Since we're finished with dinner, why don't we go back to our drawing room and play cards?" Gramma Rose asked.

"I'd love to kick off my shoes and get comfortable," Aggie said.

"That sounds good to me, too," Doro agreed, but her mind whirled with the drama from dinner and from the train station.

Chapter Three

An hour later, thunder rumbled in the distance, and the three women turned away from their card game to look out the windows.

"We're almost in the storm," Aggie said. "Look at those clouds. They're nearly coal black."

Although sunset was an hour away, Aggie was right. Darkness loomed on the eastern horizon. Undoubtedly, so did thunder, lightning, and rain. The tremor in her friend's voice, and knowing storms made Aggie uneasy, had Doro offering reassurance. "We'll be fine."

"Of course, we will," Gramma Rose added with a smile. "Trains are made to endure all kinds of weather."

Although Doro was not sure that was true, she agreed for Aggie's sake. "Certainly, they are."

Aggie, her eyes wide, looked at the other women. "I hope so. I remember our Palm Sunday tornado in 1920, and it was terrible."

Doro recalled it, too. The whirlwind had wreaked havoc around Michaw: cattle killed, roofs torn off, barns leveled. "I remember, too. We were spending time in the garden. When clouds rolled in and the wind whipped around, we all went to the storm cellar."

"Very wise," her grandmother said. "I left your house shortly before the bad weather set in. I'd just gotten to my place when we heard thunder rumbling in the distance. My neighbor hurried over to ask if she could join me in my basement. Of course, I agreed. We got inside ahead of heavy rain." Gramma Rose laid her hand over Aggie's. "The tornado didn't affect Sylvania, but I saw the aftermath in Michaw. Devastating. That was the first one to hit our area in my entire life, and I've lived a long time." Her smile intensified. "I doubt if another bad one will come close to me."

Aggie released a long sigh. "I'm sure you're right."

Since her friend sounded far from certain, Doro made a suggestion. "Let's finish our card game, have a snack, and go to bed. When we wake up in the morning, the storm will be behind us."

"A fine idea," her grandmother said.

Aggie's response was to nod.

By the time the women got into bed, rain pelted the windows, and winds howled around the car. Although they had turned off the lamps, lightning flashed so frequently that darkness stayed at bay for almost two hours. When the rolling thunder subsided, Doro heard her grandmother's light snores and grinned. Rose McLaren never had trouble sleeping. The woman could drop off in the middle of a conversation and wake minutes later, fully alert. According to Doro's mother, Rose had always had the gift of catnapping. For Doro, who sometimes tossed and turned, it was a true blessing, and one she envied.

***

Sometime later, a noise woke Doro. Almost immediately, she felt the train jerk before coming to a stop. Questions tumbled through her sleep-addled brain. Had the train derailed? Had there been a collision?

"What was that?" Aggie asked as she sat bolt upright.

"I'm not sure," Doro replied before peeking out the window. A flash of distant lightning provided only the slightest clue. "We stopped. Maybe we ran into something."

"I heard the noise, but what would we hit?" Aggie asked.

Doro swung her feet to the floor and pulled on her robe. "A tree?" She could not think of anything else, and violent storms often created that sort of damage.

"What if the train derailed?" Aggie asked. She got up from her bunk, which was across from the windows and crossed to perch on the edge of Doro's bed. "I can't see a thing. It's pitch black, so we must be miles from a town."

"Probably so. Last night, the conductor said we'd reach the next station before dawn. It can't be much past midnight," Doro observed.

The light next to Gramma Rose's bunk came on before she spoke. "It's two o'clock."

"What do you think happened?" Aggie asked.

"I'm not sure," the older woman replied. "Doro could be right about a tree being on the tracks."

"But the train stopped. Surely, the tree can be removed, so we aren't stuck." Aggie's voice quavered.

"We won't be stopped for long." Gramma Rose also got out of bed and donned her wrapper. "Someone will be along to explain the situation, and I want to be decent."

"Good idea," Aggie agreed before putting her robe on and returning to sit by Doro.

The three women continued to speculate until, ten minutes later, a knock sounded at their door. Doro hurried to answer. Joshua, looking barely awake, stood in the corridor. "Sorry to bother you, miss, but we've had an accident. The conductor says not to worry. He's checking with the engineer as best he can."

"What do you mean? Can't he walk through the cars to the locomotive and discuss it?" Doro asked, perplexed by the boy's response.

"No, miss. We hit something or such and the combination dining-kitchen car and all the cars after it got decoupled from the rest of the train," Joshua replied. "The engineer will figure it out soon, I'm sure. With several cars and the caboose detached, he'll notice a change in drag and stop. Then, the conductor and him can talk somehow or another."

Since workers on trains usually communicated through lamp signals, getting information passed along would be challenging, especially during steady rain. Perhaps, the men would meet outside. She hoped so, because being stuck on the rail line was cause for concern. "It seems like we've finally gone through the worst of the storm," Doro observed.

"Yep," the young waiter said. "It's still a soaker out there, but a couple of the crewmen are looking at the tracks. There's only the brakeman, the flagman, the conductor, and us dining help left back here. The rest of the men are in the cars that were farther up."

The news was not reassuring to Doro, but help would certainly be sent when the engineer realized what had happened. Could he back up the train and return? She had never seen that done, so Doro did not know if it was possible.

"Do you know what caused the decoupling?" Aggie asked.

One of his thin shoulders rose and fell. "Not sure, miss, but I gotta alert other passengers." Joshua nodded before moving on.

After closing the door behind him, Aggie spoke again. "That passenger at the station had a valid concern when he mentioned the couplers needing attention."

"Maybe so," Doro had to admit. "We'll get details later, I'm sure."

"I hope so," Aggie said.

Doro sighed. "There's not much sense in trying to go back to sleep until we get word about the problem and a solution." She went to the window and strained to see out.

"I agree," her grandmother replied.

Doro gazed outside. "I can make out flashlight beams and lantern lights, but not much else."

"Like you said, something could be on the tracks ahead of us," her grandmother pointed out. "We'll have to wait until someone comes to let us know. Until then, why don't we have a snack? There were several scones left."

"Sounds good," Doro agreed.

"It does," Aggie chimed in.

Within minutes, the three were enjoying a late-night repast. They had barely finished when another knock interrupted. Once again, Doro jumped up to answer.

Joshua, his expression grim, nodded to the women. "There's nothing on the tracks, so no one knows what caused the decoupling."

No matter what the cause, repairs were needed. "Will they be able to fix it right away?" Doro asked.

"No, miss. It got bent bad somehow, so we'll have to wait for a replacement part," the young man replied before turning away.

"Wait," Aggie echoed. "How long will that be?"

His gaze went to her. "Sorry, miss, but we aren't sure. The main part of the train stopped down a way when they realized what had happened. The brakeman ran down and talked to the crew. They're going on. When they reach the next station, word will go out that we're stuck. That stop is a two-man operation, so help will have to come from farther up the line or from behind us."

"They're going ahead without us?" Aggie asked, her tone incredulous.

Joshua nodded. "Since the coupler can't be fixed here, there's not much choice."

"How many cars were left behind?" Doro asked. He had mentioned the cars earlier, but she had been half-asleep.

"The dining car, this one, the next one with more passenger compartments, a sleeper car for us crew, and the caboose, of course." Joshua shifted from one foot to the other. "I'm real sorry, but we have food at least."

"How long will we be stuck on the tracks?" Aggie asked.

"I'm not sure, miss, but don't fret. Word'll go out that the trains behind need to hold at the nearest station or pull off into a siding," the young man said. "As for getting help to come, a crew will either head out of Colorado Springs or come back from Wichita. Now, I need to alert other passengers. When we know more, I'll be back."

Doro considered his response. "A siding is the rail line that loops off the tracks and back, right?"

"Yes, miss," Joshua replied. "I really need to tell the others."

"Thank you," Gramma Rose said before the young man went on.

After closing the door, Doro sighed. "I wonder how the coupler got damaged."

"So do I," Aggie added. "Is that common?"

Gramma Rose shrugged. "It's never happened during my travels, but I've heard of such incidents. In any case, help will be on the way soon, so let's get more sleep."

"I suppose we should," Aggie replied, but she looked uneasy.

Although Doro also felt off-kilter, she fought for an even keel. "By morning, the coupler may be fixed, and we'll be on our way again." Doro smiled, but she also wondered how the damage had been done—and how hard a repair would be.

***

When Doro woke early on Wednesday morning, pale light filtered into the compartment. The car was still stationary, so repairs had not yet taken place. Although not surprising, she wished help would arrive soon. As always, Doro felt ambivalence about leaving one place to go to another but, once she was en route, she preferred for the trip to speed along. That had been true when she'd left Michaw in May, and it was the same now. Although leaving her parents pulled on her heartstrings, Michaw was home. No matter where she went or lived, it always would be. How Doro wished her mother's health would improve enough for the family to reunite in Ohio. Maybe someday. For now, she wondered how late they would get into Sylvania.

Not wanting to wake Aggie and Gramma Rose, Doro crept out of her bunk and tiptoed into the dressing room, gathered clean clothes, and availed herself of the lavatory before stepping into the outside corridor. No sights or sounds indicated others were up. This particular car had only four drawing room compartments, while the next one housed six smaller accommodations. Although Doro had seen a few people in the dining car, she'd only met Bailey, Spieth, and Mathers. Since she was not sure where they were housed, Doro wondered if they were in the other part of the train. If so, there'd be no more listening to them argue, which would be lovely.

Briefly, Doro wondered whether to wait for her grandmother and her best friend or continue on. Breakfast would be served soon, which meant the kitchen staff was up. The other workmen must be, as well. That thought led her to the end of the car. Perhaps, she could see something from the gangway vestibule.

When she reached the closed space between the carriages, Doro peered outside but saw nothing except an expanse of land—the same panorama that had been outside their windows the previous afternoon. As they had sped by, the landscape had seemed more and more barren. Eastern Colorado and western Kansas were in the Great Plains, which was obvious to a train traveler. Long expanses of land stretched in all directions, with no sign of habitation nearby. Although some rolling terrain was in the distance, most of the land was flat. Hurtling along, the area seemed benign. Being stuck, it took on a more ominous feeling.

Doro chastised herself for the errant thought. Train robberies were a thing of the past, so they were perfectly safe. Weren't they? A niggling finger of trepidation traced her spine, but she shook it off. Perhaps, she should read some of Aggie's poetry instead of the rest of her whodunit. Less fuel for her vivid imagination might be advisable at present.

Since the dining car was next, she went on in case the kitchen staff had news. And maybe coffee brewing. Restless, interrupted sleep had taken a toll. Although the tables were bare and no one was around, she heard voices from the kitchen, which was situated to one side. Although the words were indistinct, the tone was obvious. Something was wrong. Wanting to find out what, Doro rushed forward.

The kitchen door was ajar, so she could see some of those inside—the conductor, two waiters, and a crewman—all of whom were standing in a small circle and looking at the floor. Curious, Doro took several more steps. Every head turned toward her.

"Miss, please stay out," Joshua said as he approached her. With one hand, he gestured toward the door. "You shouldn't see this."

Doro shifted to look past him. All she saw was a pair of highly polished shoes with spats and an upended cracker barrel. Broken saltines were strewn across the floor. Suspicion bloomed inside her. "What happened?"

"It's Mr. Mathers," the young waiter replied.

The answer was not surprising, since the professor's footwear had stood out to her in the train station, but the confirmation evoked more questions. "Why was he in the kitchen? What happened to him? A heart attack? A nasty fall?"

"Probably came for a snack. Always does," Joshua said, "but he got stabbed."

The response held her momentarily mute before evoking troubling thoughts. Surely, the man hadn't fallen on a knife, which meant his death was not an accident. Instead of voicing her ideas, Doro sought more information. "Who found Mr. Mathers?"

The young man's pallor increased. "I did, miss. I was coming to help prepare breakfast, and he was on the floor."

"Had he been here long?" she asked. "Do you know?"

His thin shoulders went up and down. "Not sure, because I didn't want to touch no dead body, so I went for the conductor right off."

Doro offered a smile. "Understandable, but how did you realize he was dead?"

The young waiter swallowed convulsively. "I called out to him. When he didn't say nothing, I went over and sort of poked at him. Didn't make a move. That's when I noticed he wasn't breathing."

"I see," Doro murmured.

Mr. Sayers came to stand by Joshua. "Miss Banyon, this isn't a place for a young lady."

With effort, Doro maintained her composure. Most men would say the same thing, so chastising him for his bias would do no good. "I've found two murder victims myself, sir. I investigated them and two other cases successfully."

The man's dark brows shot up. "I thought you were a college librarian."

Doro confirmed his supposition. "I am, but I also teach a course on mysteries." She did not add that it was a study of novels, not real-life cases. Why undermine her status as a detective? "After a murder last fall, one of the ones I investigated, our campus security officer said I make a fine amateur sleuth. Chances are, I have more experience than anyone currently on the scene." She sounded defensive, but it was all true. "Is there a lawman who can handle the crime?" Many trains had a railway police officer, so she assumed this one did. But was he nearby or on one of the cars that had continued on?

The conductor shook his head. "There was a guy on the train, but he's not stranded with us. Not sure what we can do until help comes. We're sorta stuck as far as finding out the details." His gaze slid to Mathers and back.

"You don't need to be," Doro offered. "I'm happy to help. My friend Aggie Darwine worked with me on several cases, and I know she'll pitch in." When Sayers opened his mouth to speak, Doro rushed on. "It's important to preserve clues and the crime scene. We can guide you in doing that and also look for witnesses."

Sayers gnawed on his lower lip. "I wish I could contact someone up the line."

For the first time, Doro was glad communication had not evolved to that level. Being unable to summon immediate help might mean she and Aggie could investigate. "It's a shame, but we can ensure you have the proper details to share when help arrives."

"I dunno." The conductor took off his cap and scratched his head. "You're not duly appointed lawmen."

Had he put a slight emphasis on men? Uncertain, Doro pressed her point. "Aggie and I have worked with our campus security officer, who's also a deputy constable, and with the town constable. Both of them would say we're fine detectives." Which was true. But they would discourage the young women from getting involved in a murder, especially when a killer was loose somewhere in the abandoned section of the train. The idea gave Doro pause, but it did not put a stop to her offer. "We know proper procedures."

"You found two killers? Wasn't it dangerous?" the man asked.

Although the memory of being tied up by one murderer surfaced, Doro pushed it back. "Not really. We're cautious. Besides, a thorough investigation takes time. Help will be here long before we finish." While that scenario was most likely, solving the mystery could happen quickly. It had in the past.

"Then, I suppose it's all right for you to look at the body, but as far as investigating, I don't like the idea," the conductor said.

Annoyance filled Doro. If she was a man with the same qualifications, would he object? Probably not. Doro resisted further comments. Instead, she braced herself to study the scene, but it was not gruesome.

Mathers laid face down on the floor. He might have fallen asleep there, except for the wet splotch around a slash on the back of his suit jacket. Since she had read plenty of whodunits, Doro recognized a stab wound, even though this was the first one she'd seen. No knife was in view, but a smart killer would take the murder weapon. As she moved for a better view, Doro noted a gold watch and chain next to the body. Robbery must not have been the motive. She turned to face the men. "If there's a physician in one of the cars stuck here, fetching him is proper protocol."

Sayers looked skeptical. "Dr. Myles Cartwright and his wife have a compartment in the next car, right next to your drawing room."

When the conductor did not continue, Doro reined in her impatience. "Will you send someone to get him, or should I go?"

Sayers turned to Joshua. "Tell Dr. Cartwright what's happened and ask him to come here."

"Yes, sir," the young waiter replied before taking off at a trot.

Doro focused on the other two men, Clyde and the other man. "We haven't met," she said to him.

"I'm Albert Rogers. I'm a brakeman," he replied.

Doro introduced herself before going on. "Joshua found Mr. Mathers, but did either of you see someone near here before or immediately after?"

The brakeman glanced at the conductor. "Our security man isn't on this part of the train, but he'd look into this, if he was."

A harsh breath left Doro. Was the man afraid to answer? Maybe, because his response did not match her question. She looked at Clyde. He didn't seem like the sort to wait for permission. When his gaze met hers, Doro offered a light smile.

"I come along just as Joshua were running out to get help. He was shaken up, so I told him to fetch Mr. Sayers, and I come in to check the body." Clyde jerked a thumb at the brakeman. "He wanted some coffee before going out to take another look at the coupler, so he was here a few minutes later."

"I see," Doro said before turning to the other man. "So, you haven't checked it again?"

The man again looked at the conductor, whose jaw tightened. "Miss Banyon..."

Doro interrupted. "It's Professor Banyon."

Sayers pursed his lips. "You can ask a few questions. Very few."

"Thank you," Doro replied, although she felt little gratitude. "You haven't been outside today, Mr. Rogers?"

"I was earlier, when the cars come apart," he replied.

"We heard the cars somehow got decoupled. Is that common?" Doro asked.

"Not in my experience. The couplers gotta be real strong with good connections in order for cars to stay together on steep slopes and when the train speeds up," Rogers told her.

Doro filed those details away for future reference. "I've heard cars are coupled at a train station."

"In the rail yards. It can be a dangerous job, although not so much since coupling ain't manual no more. Still, you gotta be careful." Rogers' gaze flickered to Clyde, who had gone ashen.

For a long moment, Doro studied the older waiter. Had that statement upset him? It certainly appeared so, but she supposed all rail workers were aware of hazards. "Are the couplers checked often to ensure they're in good shape?"

Rogers nodded. "I've worked the rail yards and there can be pressure to move fast, especially if a train was late getting into the station and cars needed to be switched out."

Which is what had happened in the Springs. "Switched out for what reason?" Doro asked. "Because cars were added?"

Sayers replied. "Yep. We needed two extra carriages with compartments for this leg. They had to be added in the rail yard. Another dining car was necessary, too. That's why we were short of time getting folks off-and-on in the Springs. Luckily, few left there. But many boarded and most, like you and your party wanted larger compartments." Accusation underscored the words.

"Would the extra weight weaken the coupler?" Doro inquired.

The conductor shrugged. "Maybe. Maybe not. I'll let someone higher than me decide."

Doro figured he'd also like someone higher up to handle the investigation, but how long would it take to get help? That was not her most burning question, so she pressed on. "Both of you immediately agreed with Joshua about the professor being dead?" She looked from Rogers to Clyde."

The brakeman nodded. "I fought in the Great War. I knows a dead man when I sees one."

"I'm sorry you had to witness another death," Doro said. Anyone who had served in the trenches of France had seen far too much devastation.

"At least them dead men were fighting for their country. This one didn't do nothing for nobody." Clyde jerked his thumb at the body. "Not surprised someone stabbed him. He had his fair share of enemies, and for good reason."

The utter lack of sympathy stunned Doro, while the observation about Mathers having many detractors made her consider who might have killed the man. Someone who clashed with him recently seemed most likely. Grayson Bailey and Phineas Spieth came to mind. So did the chef and Clyde. But the professor had also berated young Joshua, who had found the body. Uneasiness crept through Doro. Having found two murder victims herself, Doro realized the first person on the scene was not always the perpetrator...but sometimes, he or she was.

"I came as fast as I could," a man said as he entered the kitchen.

Doro turned to see a tall, sparse fellow with a neatly trimmed beard and close-clipped black hair approach the body. Although she had seen the man and his wife in the dining car, Doro had not realized he was a physician. "You must be Dr. Cartwright."

He turned to Doro. "And you are?"

"Doro Banyon. Professor Banyon." She added the last, since the man looked like he might order her out. And she was not going.

He blinked several times. "I see. Are you related to Professor Mathers?"

"No, but he was a colleague of my father," she replied, although the pair did not teach at the same school. Doro continued by offering the same explanation she had given to the conductor.

After a moment's hesitation, Cartwright nodded. "For now, stay back. I want to do a cursory examination."

"You won't disturb the body," Doro suggested.

The doctor turned a stern gaze on her. "Of course not. I've been to a couple of crime scenes in my practice, and I know what to do, and what not to do." He strode to the body and bent down.

For several minutes, silence hung heavily in the room. Doro noted that neither the older waiter nor the brakeman watched, while the conductor's gaze flitted to and from the body every few seconds. As for Joshua, he was nowhere to be seen. As soon as Dr. Cartwright rose, Doro asked about the waiter. "Where is the young man who fetched you?"

"He's getting the chef, who will have to figure out how to feed folks. With a dead body in here, he'll have trouble fixing breakfast," the doctor replied.

The conductor clasped and unclasped his hands. "It's bad enough we're stuck. Not feeding passengers isn't acceptable."

A shrug moved the doctor's shoulders. "Perhaps, the chef can put together a cold collation. As Professor Banyon said, we shouldn't disturb the body until a lawman sees the scene."

Mr. Sayers looked even more flustered. "Help to repair the coupler is coming. There won't be no policeman, because no one but us knows about the murder. We're between stations. The next big one up the way is another two-and-a-half hours. Colorado Springs is the closest behind, which is farther. The whistlestop towns often don't have a lawman, or only one with little experience. They can alert folks about us being stuck, but we can't get word out about the dead body until we're moving again." He shifted from one foot to the other.

"Is there any chance help will come by the roadway, if there's one close to the rail line?" Cartwright asked.

The conductor released a long sigh. "Not much chance. A highway lays a few miles ahead along this part of the track, but it's not heavily traveled. The nearest town is about ten miles north, maybe a little less. A handful of ranches are in the general area. Not close to us, though." Sayers fingered his cap brim. "If the chef doesn't get here, I'll go for him. We've got to have a plan to feed folks."

Before the last sentence was out, Chef Andre came rushing in. "What happened?" His gaze traveled around the group before fixing on the floor. "Who is that?"

The question seemed odd, since Professor Mathers often traveled the route, and the chef knew he was on board since they had locked horns the previous night. Besides, Mathers and Andre had exchanged comments about a snack and, even face down, the professor was easy to identify.

"Professor Mathers has been stabbed," the conductor replied. "Can you see if any knives are missing?"

The chef stared at him. "We don't have an inventory, and knives come up missing from time-to-time. There's no way to check on any but my own set, and they're locked in that cabinet." He gestured to a tall white cupboard off to one side.

Doro noted the padlock on the doors and felt the possibility of finding the murder weapon and getting fingerprints slip away. "What about the type of knife, Doctor? Can you make a guess?"

Briefly, the physician hesitated. Then, he replied, "A four-to-six-inch serrated blade is my hypothesis."

"Plenty of kitchen knives fit that description," Andre put in without a trace of emotion.

"Do you see anything out of order, other than the deceased and the cracker barrel?" Doro asked.

For a moment, the chef scanned the room. "That towel looks damp, and it doesn't belong hanging out of a knife drawer."

That comment and a perusal removed Doro's last hope about fingerprints. The white cloth was wet with water and blood, so both blade and hilt must have been cleaned. Looking through the knives would not help, if that was the case.

"The body needs to be hauled away, so we can prepare for breakfast." Again, Chef Andre spoke without a shred of concern.

Doro's surprise escalated. She had not liked Mathers, but she felt sympathy for him. Others, it seemed, did not.

"He can't be moved yet," Dr. Cartwright put in.

"No, he can't," Doro added. "We need a lawman to check the scene."

The chef stared at Doro. "And how will I prepare meals? It'll be hours before help reaches us, and they won't bring a sheriff or marshal along."

"Unfortunately, that's true," the conductor said. "Dr. Cartwright, are you sure we can't move the body?"

Fresh annoyance prickled along Doro's nerve ends. She surely had more investigative experience than the physician, but the conductor virtually ignored her.

"It's best to have a lawman look the scene over," Cartwright said, "but this is a special circumstance."

"It certainly is," the conductor agreed before addressing the chef. "Do you have any space in the cooler?"

Not only did the suggestion appall Doro, the men ignoring her was galling. "I still think you should leave Professor Mathers where he is, inconvenient or not."

Sayers, Cartwright, and Andre all scowled at her. The conductor was the first to respond. "Your local lawmen may kowtow to you, Miss Banyon, but we won't."

Although she was not usually fussy about being called by her proper title, Doro felt the need to insist on it now. "It's Professor Banyon, Mr. Sayers, as I pointed out to you already."

Red climbed into the conductor's cheeks. "Sorry," he mumbled in a voice that held no hint of regret.

"Nevertheless, what Sayers said is right," Andre, his tone as cutting as one of his kitchen knives, said. "I cannot function with a dead man underfoot. We have space at the back of the cooler. I suggest wrapping him and putting him there. Any lawman worth his salt can investigate without the corpse being laid out here."

Although his implication, that she was not a good detective, hit Doro hard, she did not react outwardly. Arguing with him and the others would be futile, so she resolved to conduct a clandestine inquiry and solve the case before any lawman came along. "It's your kitchen," she said to Andre, "but I can stay here while you and your team prepare breakfast." His dismissive attitude and terse tone could be a sign of guilt, which meant watching him was wise.

The chef glared at her. "And why would you be here, miss? As you say, it's my kitchen, and a small one at that. Go back to your compartment. Breakfast will not be served for an hour."

Doro braced her hands on her hips. "Sir, you speak out of turn. You can't order me back to my compartment." Dealing with imperious men was not new to her, but Doro was usually more diplomatic. The chef's arrogance was too much to bear, especially since the conductor and the doctor weren't supporting her. The local lawmen—Wade and Ev—didn't kowtow to her and Aggie, as the conductor had suggested. They respected the two young women and treated them as equals. She glared at Sayers. "Isn't the conductor in charge of all train workers?"

Sayers flushed. "Of course."

Before he could say more, the chef spoke again. "This is Sayers' first run as conductor, so listening to those of us with experience is wise."

The color in the conductor's face deepened to scarlet. "I've got plenty of years working on the railroad. Many more than you, Andre." Sayers turned to Cartwright. "What do you think about the body? Leave it here or move it?"

Fresh annoyance had Doro biting her tongue to keep from lashing out. Would they act the same way if she was a male amateur sleuth? She doubted it.

The physician hesitated a moment. "I agree with Professor Banyon about leaving the body where it is. The railroad security man riding up front might come with the repair crew, since he could want to see why the cars got decoupled. He can take over at that point."

Sayers shifted from one foot to the other. "That's likely. Decoupling isn't common, and studying the break would help determine if there was foul play, which I doubt." He turned to the chef. "We won't be moving the professor."

The chef's glare turned into a glower. After muttering something under his breath, he stalked toward the preparation area.

As he turned away, Doro addressed him. "Although we can't be certain one of the knives in the drawer was used, or that it wasn't wiped clean, please use only your own knives until prints can be taken." Despite her doubts that any would be found, even if the murder weapon was in the drawer, she felt the need to follow proper procedures.

"That's a good idea," Cartwright put in.

Although the chef sent a stare over his shoulder, he said nothing. Doro went on. "Someone should stay to make sure the body isn't disturbed. Maybe one of the crewmen?"

Uncertainty flickered in the conductor's gaze. "I can't spare none of my men. I got very few here."

"Then, allow the professor to stay," Cartwright suggested.

The man went up a notch in Doro's regard.

Several long moments passed before Sayers responded. "All right."

Sayers' agreement seemed reluctant, but Doro did not care. If she observed the kitchen staff, she might uncover a clue.

With a glance over his shoulder at Doro, Andre said, "Stay out of the way."

A harsh retort was on the tip of Doro's tongue, but she bit it back. "I'm here to observe. Nothing more." Observe and gather evidence, but she did not reveal the latter.

Andre's attention swept around the room. "I only need my staff. The rest of you must go."

The brakeman hurried off, with only a few whispered words to the conductor on his way out. Dr. Cartwright, his countenance grim, faced the chef. "Make sure you don't disturb the body. I'll be back later." He nodded at Doro and Sayers before slipping away.

"Professor Banyon, I need to ensure the passengers are comfortable and let them know a meal of sorts will be served," the conductor said with a slight emphasis on her title. "Please stay out of the chef's way. He and his people need to prepare breakfast."

Although the chef did not look back, he interceded. "Send my other waiter back here."

While Sayers still looked uneasy, he nodded. "I will."

"Would you be so good as to tell my grandmother and my friend where I am?" Doro asked. "They were both sleeping when I left our drawing room."

"Of course," Sayers said before he disappeared.

Doro perched on a high stool near the doorway. Since watching the meal preparation held little interest for her, she focused on Mathers' body. He must have come to the kitchen for a snack, something more than one person might predict due to last evening's conversation. "Were you aware he came to the kitchen this morning?"

Andre spun on his heel and glared at her. "Everyone in my crew figured he would. So, would every person in the dining car last night. Now, be quiet so we can work."

With that, he returned to his tasks, and Doro fell silent. She wanted details, but the chef was not apt to answer more questions now, so Doro sat quietly and considered the array of facts surrounding the professor. And who might have done him in. The list was not short.

Chapter Four

Ten minutes later, a flushed and breathless Aggie appeared in the kitchen's doorway. Andre immediately issued another warning.

"Stay out," the chef bellowed.

Aggie looked from the chef to Doro. "We heard what happened from the conductor." Her attention went to Mathers' body, and her face grew white.

"Let's step into the dining room," Doro murmured, "and I'll explain everything."

The two young women went into the adjacent area before Aggie whispered a question. "What's going on? I know Professor Mathers was stabbed, but the conductor didn't share details."

"I'm afraid we don't have many." Doro continued by revealing what she knew.

Aggie shook her head. "Another murder with no leads."

"I wouldn't say that," Doro commented.

Her friend's eyebrows rose a fraction. "Since you stayed in the kitchen, you must've convinced the conductor to let you investigate."

"Sayers didn't go that far. He wasn't eager to let me stay, but a doctor is on board, and he supported me, although not with gusto. Anyhow, we can look into the case, but we need to be circumspect."

Aggie rolled her eyes. "That doesn't sound like we have official permission."

"But the conductor didn't forbid us, either." Doro revealed the exchange between Sayers and Andre. "The conductor is new at being in charge, so he may not challenge us. He'd be more likely to ignore what we do, unless we uncover important clues before a lawman arrives on the scene."

"But when will that be? The murder occurred after the rest of the train went on."

"True, but a railroad security officer may come with the repair crew. At least, that's what was discussed in the kitchen. Decoupling isn't a common occurrence."

Dismay shadowed Aggie's hazel eyes. "Do they think someone tampered with it? Or maybe the rush at Colorado Springs kept the coupler from being connected properly, like we discussed."

Doro shrugged. "No one knows. The added cars might account for the problem or rushing could be the cause. According to the brakeman, a coupler has to be strong, especially on steep inclines and rough rails."

"I'd rather think the coupler was weak or damaged than believe someone tampered with it," Aggie said. "Besides, we already talked about it being tricky to mess with the cars in the rail yard. But I keep thinking of what the man on the platform said. Maybe hurrying kept the couplers from being thoroughly examined."

"That's probably what happened, but we aren't likely to know for sure until repairmen study the broken coupler. Even then, I'm not sure if the conductor will share the news with us."

Aggie narrowed her gaze. "He really doesn't want us investigating?"

Doro lifted one shoulder in a half-shrug. "He won't kowtow to us."

"Kowtow?" Aggie echoed. "Why did he say that?"

"The context was he isn't kowtowing to me like our local lawmen."

Aggie's jaw dropped. Then, she laughed. "Mr. Sayers doesn't know Wade or Ev."

"Or us."

"So very true," Aggie agreed, her voice laced with amusement.

"But he'll know us better by the time we get to Kansas City." She reined in her own humor. "Mr. Sayers was wavering, so he may be more supportive after word spreads about the murder. Passengers will be upset when they find out. That could put pressure on him. Since I already told him about the two of us being amateur sleuths, he might welcome our help sooner rather than later."

"What exactly did you say?" Suspicion undergirded the question.

Laughter rumbled out of Doro. "I didn't exaggerate. We've solved two murders and a poisoning. You can't deny that."

"I didn't do much on the first murder case," Aggie pointed out. "You and Ev teamed up then."

At the mention of the handsome campus security officer, Doro's pulse sped up. Since she did not want to discuss him at the moment, she brought up another successful investigation. "You and I also discovered who stole an examination."

A grin lit Aggie's face. "We most certainly did."

Memories flooded Doro's mind. The young women had met a decade earlier when Aggie, a student worker, was under suspicion for stealing or losing a test. Doro, her father, and another student had worked to find the real culprits. During the process, Doro and Aggie had formed a friendship that had only grown closer over the following years. "I didn't mention that."

"Just as well. It hardly ranks with murder or poisoning." Aggie's expression grew solemn. "Since you didn't agree that there are no leads, I assume you have some."

"Professor Mathers wasn't well liked, from what we observed," Doro began, "which means he had multiple detractors. Maybe even enemies."

"Probably," Aggie responded. "So, Grayson Bailey and Phineas Spieth are among your suspects." It was a statement, not a question.

"They're at the top of my list."

Aggie chuckled. "You always get a list started quickly."

"It's only in my mind so far. I'll jot down notes after the kitchen is cleared." Doro chewed on her lower lip. "I don't trust Chef Andre not to tamper with the crime scene."

Aggie's humor evaporated. "You think he killed Mathers?"

Doro waved one hand in the air. "Maybe, but Joshua is also a possibility."

"Joshua? The waiter? He's so polite and unassuming," Aggie said. "I can't believe he'd commit murder."

"I don't want to believe it, but Professor Mathers humiliated him in front of the entire dining car. Joshua was visibly upset."

"Who wouldn't be?"

Doro pressed both hands to her forehead. "You're right. Another interesting detail is a key to the kitchen being put out for the professor. I'm not sure where."

"So, the professor typically went to the kitchen and fixed his own food. From last night's discussion, I wasn't sure."

"Sometimes he did, but no one is crystal clear about his habits."

For a moment, Aggie seemed to weigh what Doro had shared. "What if Mathers demanded someone fix food for him?"

"He'd probably wake a crewman up."

Aggie folded her arms across her middle. "That's a possibility, but would a waiter prepare food?"

"I doubt if the professor would want his treat prepared by someone who wasn't skilled," Doro admitted. "Mathers might've woken Andre, although the chef clarified that shouldn't happen."

"Would the chef kill him for that reason?"

"Sometimes, the motive is weak," Doro replied before summarizing the chef's comments and ending with, "I found the professor to be obnoxious, too, but I'm sorry he was murdered. Chef Andre didn't show a shred of concern, which is disturbing."

"I agree. The lack of sympathy is appalling." Aggie's attention went to the kitchen door. "What about Clyde? Was he in there?"

"He was, and he was as callous as Andre," Doro replied before quoting the waiter.

Aggie shook her head as if in disbelief. "It's difficult to understand being so hard-hearted. I didn't like Mathers myself, but that's not a motive for murder. I'd like to know what's between Clyde and the professor. The antipathy was palpable at last night's dinner."

With one hand, Doro brushed a lock of hair off her face. "Joshua didn't want to say much about Clyde's grievance with Mathers. The older waiter's comment about the professor taking something from him was cryptic."

A soft sigh left her friend. "I wish Wade and Ev were here to help us."

The yearning in Aggie's voice echoed inside Doro, although she did not pine for anyone herself. Especially not Everett Mallow. But the idea did not go away, even as she protested. "They'd take over. At least Ev would try."

"He didn't take over the last time," Aggie said.

"Ev and Wade were flat on their backs during most of the investigation," Doro pointed out. Three months earlier, after judging a baking contest during Michaw's May Days festival, the two lawmen had fallen ill, leaving Doro and Aggie to figure out the source of the problem and pursue several suspects before the perpetrator had been found and apprehended.

"The two of them arrested the culprit." Aggie's lips twitched. "With our help."

"It was more a case of them helping us," Doro said with a lilt in her voice. Both men had issued concerns, but neither had told the two friends to stop investigating. Neither had suggested bringing in outside help, either. Ev and Wade appreciated their detective skills, which was more than could be said for Sayers and Andre.

"They both said as much." Some of Aggie's amusement fled. "Do you believe we can solve this murder before the law arrives? That seems like a Herculean task."

Doro shifted from one foot to the other. "The engineer will have a repair crew sent. They may bring a railroad security man, who isn't likely to have more experience than we do."

"Wade worked railroad security before coming home after his wife fell ill," Aggie pointed out.

"Some people didn't think that gave him the right experience to be the town constable," Doro recalled. "They figured the council offered him the job out of sympathy after he and the children were left alone. Criticism continued for a while, although it's died down in the last couple of years."

Aggie nodded. "He's mentioned expecting the constable's job to be as straightforward as railroad work. But there have been more big cases. On the trains, even when he investigated a robbery, the police took over eventually."

"That's what will happen now, I'm sure. With no way to reach any lawmen, we'll have to wait until we get to a station, I suppose." Doro did not consider that to be a bad thing. "In the meantime, we can poke around." After the statement was out, she bit back a chuckle. When Ev used *poke around* to describe Doro's penchant to dig into mysteries, she bristled. Now, it seemed like an apt phrase. Or maybe he was always in the back of her mind, whether she was ready to admit it or not. "We should go into the kitchen to observe."

"Can they fix breakfast with a dead body in there?"

"They're walking around him." Doro released a pent-up breath. "How is my grandmother doing?"

Aggie beamed. "You know Gramma Rose. Nothing gets her down. She wants to hear all the details."

Laughter rumbled out of Doro. "I'm not surprised. She chatted about our adventures, as she calls them, with Mother. The two of them love mysteries as much as we do." Memories momentarily drove the current case from her mind. "It was fun to discuss our latest investigations with them." And wonderful to be with family.

"But not every detail," Aggie added with asperity.

Doro shrugged. "They don't need to know about us being held captive by a killer last December."

Several seconds elapsed before Aggie responded. "Luckily, your grandmother doesn't come to Michaw often. Even so, she may hear the story at some point."

Doro mulled over the possibility. Anyone in Michaw might let the information slip, but would it matter? "She won't share the encounter with my mother, who would press harder to have me move to Colorado. Gramma Rose, too." Rose McLaren had spent her entire life in Sylvania, and she had no plans to leave. Although the older woman would have supported Doro in whatever she did, Rose kept her granddaughter's secrets, if only to avoid upsetting her daughter. Luckily, Gramma Rose did not know all of what Doro did in pursuing justice.

Aggie's hazel eyes took on a teasing glimmer. "Plenty of reasons to stay in Michaw."

Because she knew Aggie would bring up Ev again, Doro put up one hand. "I need to get into the kitchen. Breakfast will be served in under an hour, so bring Gramma Rose back with you. With luck, we can chat with Grayson and Phineas."

"Are you planning to question Joshua?" Aggie asked.

"He found the body, so I'll start by asking about that. Depending on what he says and how he acts, I may have more queries."

Another grin lit Aggie's face. "I'm sure you will."

After her friend left, Doro went back into the kitchen. The men continued their frantic pace, while Chef Andre shouted commands. Several more minutes passed before Joshua, his face flushed and sweaty, returned.

"Sorry, I wasn't back sooner. The conductor needed help," the young waiter said.

Andre spun to face him. "You're dining car staff. Get an apron on and get busy."

Joshua gritted his teeth, as if to restrain an angry retort, but his eyes flashed with fury. A chill went through Dodo because he looked nothing like the amiable young man who had served them the previous night. He was in a subordinate position, which had to be frustrating. But was his frustration bad enough to make him violent?

As she perched on the stool again, Doro considered the other suspects. Talking to Joshua would be natural, but how would she approach Grayson and Phineas? Much more carefully. And what about Clyde? Getting information out of Chef Andre was apt to be the most onerous task. Perhaps chatting with others about him would be her best first step. During the process, she might glean details about the older waiter's grudge against the professor and determine if it merited further inquiry. Surely, someone on board knew details about what Mathers had taken from Clyde. And that had to be the source of the animosity between the two.

***

Fifteen minutes later, the sound of passengers arriving in the dining car reached Doro, who slid off the stool. Andre and his staff had trays piled high with sweet rolls, bowls of fresh fruit, and flasks of coffee. The chef barked orders at the waiters as they went about the final preparations.

"Tell people we have an even more limited menu than last night," the chef ordered in a terse tone. "Go around and let them help themselves to sweets and fruit. The water for tea will be hot soon. Until then, they can have coffee or wait."

The two waiters responded by heading into the dining area. While they went back-and-forth serving passengers, Doro maintained a place by the door. During that time, the conductor returned with an old sheet.

"We should cover Professor Mathers," he said when Doro gave him a questioning glance.

"Good idea." As Doro helped Sayers drape the material over the body, she shuddered. Although the professor was not the first murder victim she had seen, any death troubled her. Even so, the image popping into Doro's mind was of Ev collapsing at the May Days festival.

Remembered fear gripped Doro. Not knowing what was wrong when he fell to the ground had been one of the scariest moments of her life. Ev's usually bronze complexion had looked pale and waxen. Within a short time, Wade had been nearly as ill, and both men had been confined to bed for days. But they had not died. And they had been perfectly fine when Doro left home in May. Still, she wondered if she would ever forget the sight of Ev, ashen and weak, crumpling into a heap. For a long moment, she had feared he was dead. And she had never admitted those feelings to him, because they revealed so much.

Abruptly, the chef's voice cut off the roll of memories. "Get out of our way. Serving breakfast is an onerous task with a corpse in the middle of my kitchen. Having you two here only adds to the problem." Andre waved a hand in the air as he stared at Doro and Sayers.

The man's total lack of sympathy again struck Doro as odd. Did Andre realize he was a suspect? He surely would after she asked him some questions. But the others came first because the chef, despite his attitude, lacked a powerful motive.

"You'd best leave the kitchen," Sayers said.

Why the conductor agreed to the chef's demands, Doro did not know. Since arguing was futile, she nodded. "Of course," she murmured before stepping through the door ahead of Sayers.

"Doro, join us," Aggie called out.

A glance around the area located her friend and her grandmother at a nearby table, so Doro waved before turning to the conductor. "Since a railroad security man is coming, I understand your reluctance to let Professor Darwine and me investigate." She didn't really, but a concession might mollify the man.

He shifted from one foot to the other. "It's not personal, Miss Banyon. That is, Professor Banyon. Now, if you'll excuse me, I have other duties to perform."

After Sayers turned on his heel and exited the car, Doro joined Aggie and Gramma Rose. Frustration had her releasing a long pent-up breath.

"That sigh must mean Mr. Sayers is still against you girls investigating," her grandmother said.

"He's against amateur help, although he didn't exactly restate his objection just now, so maybe there's hope," Doro replied in a glum tone.

The older woman frowned. "I'm worried about a killer on the loose. Digging into details could be dangerous, especially in our current circumstance." She glanced out the window. "We're far from a town, which means the murderer can't escape easily. He's here on the train. It could be anyone. Someone who might watch you two."

"True," Aggie murmured. "Maybe we should back off this time."

Consternation filled Doro, but she had no chance to respond.

The sound of a voice being cleared interrupted before a man sitting at the table behind Aggie turned to face the trio. "Sorry to intrude, but I couldn't help but overhear some of your conversation. My name is Stefan Boggun." He gestured over his shoulder. "That's my son, Stefan, Junior."

Doro recognized the pair from the previous evening.

After the women introduced themselves, Boggun nodded. "We heard about someone dying, although we didn't realize it was a case of murder."

"No, we sure didn't," his son said. "What happened?"

"We don't have much information," Doro replied. Although somewhat hesitant to respond in full, allowing false gossip to spread was not wise, so she shared the pertinent facts.

Mr. Boggun's gray eyebrows shot up. "How awful. I feel sorry for young Joshua. Finding a body when he reported to work had to be a terrible shock."

"I don't know. It sounds exciting," his son put in. The boy's brown eyes gleamed with interest. "The dead man was the one putting up a stink last night, right? After seeing that, I'd say there's a bunch of suspects."

The boy's eager interest, along with his assessment of Mathers, had Doro fighting not to laugh. "A few," she said.

"I heard you say something about being an amateur," the boy said. "Like an amateur sleuth?"

"Son, don't pepper the ladies with questions," his father put in before looking back at Doro. "I'm sorry. He loves to read mysteries, especially Sherlock Holmes."

"That's all right," Doro assured the older man. "All three of us are whodunit aficionados."

"Really?" young Stefan asked. "Who's your favorite author?"

"I love Agatha Christie's books," Doro replied.

"So do I," Aggie added.

"I enjoy her work, as well," Gramma Rose chimed in.

Stefan nodded enthusiastically. "She's a real good author." He looked from one woman to another before glancing back at Doro. "But what about being an amateur sleuth? Are you?"

"The girls have successfully investigated several cases," Gramma Rose said with pride.

"Really. How neat." The boy whistled.

"Son, that's not appropriate inside," Mr. Boggun said. "Whistling is for outdoors only."

"Sorry, Pa." Stefan quickly turned his attention back to the women. "So, are you going to crack this case?"

When Doro met Aggie's gaze, she saw her friend's amusement and Gramma Rose looked to be fighting a smile, as well. "The conductor doesn't want us being too involved."

"We heard you say that, but a killer is on board. Seems like someone oughta investigate," young Stefan insisted.

Since Doro held the same perspective, she found supporting Sayers' orders to be difficult. But what should she say? Even though she planned to dig a bit, admitting as much might not be wise. After all, her grandmother was right about not evoking attention from the killer. She glanced at her grandmother, who gave a slight nod in response.

"I've shared my anxiety with the girls. We don't want to make the murderer uneasy," the older woman said.

A solemn expression replaced the younger Boggun's eager look. "No. Of course not." Disappointment underscored the words.

Doro focused on the elder Boggun. "You mentioned hearing about the death. Who told you?"

"Conductor Sayers came around to the compartments," he responded. "He didn't want to say how it happened, but my boy already overheard Joshua when he and the chef were walking down the corridor around seven o'clock. They must've been on the way to the kitchen after the murder."

"That's about the time Joshua fetched the chef. Have you heard other passengers discuss the death?" Doro inquired.

"Few are left in this part of the train," Boggun observed. "A doctor and his wife and another couple with a mother-in-law are in the drawing-room car. Two college boys, a retired army officer, an elderly widow, and a newlywed couple are in the car with regular compartments. The chef is housed there, too. Of course, the professor's accommodation was also in that car."

"You know a lot about the passengers," Aggie commented.

A smile curved Boggun's lips. "I'm a newspaper publisher, so I like to keep track of details around me. I never know when a story might cross my path. It's second nature to me, since I started working on my grandfather's paper when I was a boy. First, running errands and then, writing copy."

Little wonder the man was interested in the murder, Doro thought. "How fascinating," she murmured.

"It is," young Stefan agreed. "I want to be a reporter, too. Or a mystery writer. Or both."

"Then, you need to spend more time on your compositions for school," his father advised. "You're going to high school this coming year, so you need to work harder."

Stefan grimaced. "That's so boring. When I'm a reporter or an author, an editor can fix my mistakes."

Aggie stepped back into the conversation. "It's important to write well yourself, if you want to be respected."

The boy stared at her with wide eyes. "Do you write?"

"I write poetry, and I teach English at a small college in Ohio," she replied.

A chuckle rumbled out of Mr. Boggun. "Listen to the experts, my boy."

Color crept into Stefan's cheeks. "Sure, Pa."

Doro saw the waiters making progress toward their tables, so she hurried to offer a warning. "If Mr. Sayers didn't share the cause of the professor's death, it might be best not to tell other passengers. Creating panic won't help anyone."

"Then, we'll keep quiet," Boggun assured her. "Won't we, son?"

Although Stefan looked disconsolate, he nodded. "All right, Pa."

"It's important for people to feel safe," Gramma Rose said. "Especially an elderly widow."

The comment surprised Doro since Rose McLaren never referred to herself as old. Maybe it was a ploy to keep the boy quiet.

"Yes, ma'am," young Stefan said. "I won't say anything."

"Good," Gramma Rose replied.

As soon as the single word was out, Joshua appeared at the Bogguns' table. Father and son turned to him, while the women went back to talking among themselves until the young waiter served them.

"This looks good," Gramma Rose told the young man.

"We'll be able to serve a better lunch," he replied without looking at any of them.

His furtive manner telegraphed anxiety. What its source might be was in question, so Doro proceeded with care. "I have a couple of questions for you."

His eyes went wide. "I don't have no time to talk."

"This won't take long," Doro assured him.

He glanced up-and-down the car, which was empty except for the Bogguns and Doro's party. "Mr. Sayers don't want us talking about what happened to the professor."

"Mr. Boggun and his son already know the truth," Doro said. "Young Stefan overheard you and the chef talking."

The color fled from Joshua's face. "We ain't supposed to upset the passengers, and I sure didn't mean for no one to hear."

"Of course, you didn't," Gramma Rose put in. "Mr. Boggun and his boy won't say anything, so you need not fret. And there's no one else to overhear."

Joshua nodded as he turned back to Doro. "What's your questions?"

Wanting to waste no time, she went ahead. With the utmost discretion, Doro pulled out a notepad and pencil before jotting down a note. "Chef Andre mentioned Professor Mathers knowing where the kitchen key would be. Did you know?"

"Nope. I don't have no key," Joshua answered in a soft whisper.

"How did you plan to get into the kitchen when you arrived early this morning?" Doro asked.

A flush rose in his face. "I—uh—I thought the professor unlocked the door to get food. He don't usually lock up after himself."

For a long moment, Doro studied his face. Although she was not sure Joshua was being forthright, Doro did not call him on it.

"Did the professor ever wake a waiter or a chef?" Aggie posed the question, also in a subdued tone.

"He woke whoever he wanted, whenever he wanted," the young waiter replied. "Sometimes, a chef. Sometimes, a waiter. Sometimes, the conductor, or so I've heard." His taut expression telegraphed apprehension.

"Did the professor ever expect the food to be brought to him?" Doro asked. From the previous evening's exchanges, she figured he retrieved a key. But was that always the case?

"No, he liked to go to the kitchen and be served there if he wanted a hot dish," Joshua said. "Complaints about the man have circulated from station to station for a good, long time."

Gramma Rose gasped. "He expected someone to cook for him in the middle of the night?"

The waiter clutched the tray. "That wasn't unusual, from what I know." He looked around the table. When he spoke again, his voice was a barely audible whisper. "Like you heard last night, Mathers had a friend who's a big shot with the railroad. If the professor wasn't happy with the service, he reported to his buddy right away. Or so I've heard from other men on the line."

"Surely, it isn't typical for passengers to expect food service at any hour of the day or night," Gramma Rose said.

"No, ma'am, it isn't," the waiter agreed. "Mathers was one of the few who did. Actually, the only one I know about."

Doro tapped her pencil against the notepad. Questioning a potential suspect required extra caution, but if Joshua was only a witness, he could share valuable details. Would the young man tell the truth? She would have to gauge his responses. Having Aggie join in would provide another set of ears and eyes. "The cracker barrel was open, but nothing else seemed out of place. Did you note anything?"

Joshua shook his head. "Nope."

The reply added nothing, so Doro pressed on. "Would cheese and crackers have sufficed as a snack for the professor?"

"Along with some sardines, perhaps. The man fancied those, according to other waiters," Joshua said. "And a sweet to finish."

"He usually had more of a small meal than a snack, from what you're saying," Gramma Rose observed.

"He did," Joshua agreed.

"And he was well-known among all the railroad waiters?" Doro suggested.

A grimace shadowed the young man's face. "Someone like him, who carps a lot and has big wigs as friends, gets talked about. Mostly warnings not to run afoul of him."

"I see." Since other passengers were entering the dining car, Doro spoke the two words in a low voice. How many others on the train might have had a motive to kill the man? And how would she find out?

Aggie leaned one elbow on the table. "If he didn't want a cooked repast, did he bother the chef?"

"I only been on the train when he was a few times," Joshua said. "But I heard he didn't usually get a chef up. More often, he woke one of the waiters or the cook, but he'd gone to the lounge car before the decoupling, so he isn't with us now. Besides, the cooks only assist the chef. They don't generally cook themselves, unless it's a pressing matter."

The title of cook seemed odd for someone who did not actually perform the task, but Doro let it go. If the cook was in the other part of the train, he was not involved in the crime.

The waiter looked around again. "I gotta serve other tables." He extended the platter of sweets. "Please help yourselves. Clyde will be along with coffee and fruit." Joshua rushed to the next table without a backward glance.

Before any of the ladies could comment, the older waiter arrived. While he was serving, Doro presented an observation. "Joshua said he'd heard about Professor Mathers from others."

Clyde shot an angry glare at the young waiter. "He knows better than to gossip. Take whatever he said with a grain of salt."

His reaction seemed disproportionate to the boy repeating tittle-tattle. "He only shared what's been discussed among employees at various stops."

When Clyde met Doro's gaze, the tension drained from his face. "Oh, I see."

Since the man did not continue, Doro offered details. "Joshua heard the professor was a problem on many trips."

"Every trip would be more accurate," Clyde snarled. "Mathers was a nasty piece of work, who liked to bully those he considered beneath him. Especially youngsters." Something akin to sorrow replaced the anger in his expression. "He weren't fit to teach young folks." The vehemence in Clyde's tone was stunning.

"How do you mean?" Aggie asked.

During the silence following the question, Doro recalled a conversation with Luann Mathers. The young woman had hinted at her husband's waning interest in teaching. But how would a railroad waiter know that? Asking the volatile Clyde was likely to evoke another outburst, so Doro offered a general observation. "I suppose you heard people discussing him, especially when they traveled to or from Colorado Springs."

For a moment, the waiter looked blank. Then, he nodded. "That's right. Plenty of folks knew about him. He were never quiet on board. Always a braggart. Not that he had much to brag about, but lies were his stock in trade."

"Did he brag about his job, his wealth, or something else?" Gramma Rose asked.

"All of that," Clyde replied. "He had some fooled, but not me. I knew what he were really like."

"Joshua does, too," Doro observed.

"Yep," was the waiter's single word answer.

Again, there was a lull in the conversation. Aggie filled it with a statement. "It had to be unnerving for him to find Professor Mathers."

A slight nod came from Clyde. "True enough. The poor boy ain't had it easy."

"In what way?" Doro asked.

Clyde glanced down the aisle before responding. "His folks died when he were twelve. For a time, he lived with a spinster aunt. She run a boardinghouse along the rail line, and some workers without no family stayed there. He helped her with heavy work and upkeep. When she passed last year, Joshua couldn't run the place alone. Since he don't have no other relatives, he got a job on the railroad. He wants to move up to a position with higher pay in the future." He pursed his lips. "Mathers knew that and got the boy to do his bidding with the threat of getting Joshua fired always in the background."

"Joshua told you that?" Doro asked.

Clyde nodded. "We get plenty of chance to chew the fat when we work the same run, which is pretty often."

"How awful for him," Gramma Rose said. "The professor was not a nice man."

Coming from Doro's grandmother, that was a harsh judgment. To Doro, Mathers seemed much worse than *not nice*. "No, not at all," she added before returning to the case. "So, it's fairly likely that Professor Mathers rousted Joshua out of bed."

"Possibly," the waiter said. "But I doubt it, cuz I woulda heard him. My bunk is next to the kid's."

"And you didn't hear anything?" Doro wondered if Mathers had roused Clyde. Would the waiter admit it?

"Nope. Nothing at all," he replied.

"How long have you worked for the railroad?" Gramma Rose asked in a conversational tone.

"More than fifteen years," Clyde said.

"So, you must like the work," she continued.

"Mostly, I'm happy," he replied.

The man had been far from happy during the previous evening's meal service, and Clyde had exhibited no cheer earlier.

"I suppose few passengers are as demanding as Professor Mathers," Doro observed.

"True," Clyde said. "Now, I gotta finish serving." After nodding to the women, the conductor went on.

Since more passengers were entering the dining car, the three women ate without further discussion of the murder. But the case filled Doro's mind.

Chapter Five

A petite, white-haired woman was one of those arriving. When she paused inside the door, she leaned heavily on an ornate walking stick. Since there were no empty tables between them and the lady, Doro made a suggestion. "Perhaps, we should ask her to join us. She must be the widow traveling alone."

"What a thoughtful suggestion," her grandmother said with a smile. "Introduce yourself, Doro, and ask her to sit here."

Within moments, Doro returned with the woman and made introductions. Aggie and Gramma Rose welcomed her.

"Thank you. I'm Mrs. Mavis O'Brien, and I'm pleased to meet you all." After sitting down, the woman continued. "Thank you for letting me join you. Traveling by myself is lonely, and I'm not used to it yet. It was always Mr. O'Brien and me."

"Did you lose your husband recently?" Gramma Rose asked.

"Less than a year ago," Mrs. O'Brien replied. "We were married for over fifty years. No children, but we had several nephews and nieces. I'm going to Kansas City to visit with one of the girls and her family."

"How lovely," Gramma Rose said before sharing the travel details for her party.

"It's so nice you can all be together," the elderly widow observed. Although she appeared to be near eighty, she had a liveliness that belied her years.

"We didn't see you at dinner last night," Aggie put in.

"I stayed in my compartment. Getting ready for the trip wore me out, so the young waiter was kind enough to bring me a tray. I hated to ask, what with the storm coming." She tsked-tsked. "Now, someone has died, from what the boy told me when he came around to say breakfast would be informal. A storm, a decoupling, and a death. It's not been a calm excursion."

Doro exchanged glances with Gramma Rose and Aggie before responding. "No, it hasn't, but help is on the way."

"Good. I hate to be stuck out here for long." A low laugh escaped Mrs. O'Brien. "When I was a girl, my parents and I took the train back east a few times. Once, a big payroll was on board, and a gang stopped the train and took the money. No one was killed, but the security guard was shot. Scared the willies out of me. I was only ten."

"It sounds scary," Aggie murmured.

Mrs. O'Brien smiled at her. "When we were first married, my husband had a hard time convincing me that train travel was safe."

"Did you take frequent trips back then?" Aggie asked.

"Not so often," Mrs. O'Brien replied, "but he was a conductor, and I fretted something awful about him."

That information made Doro wonder if the widow was acquainted with Mr. Sayers or other workers on board? "You must know a lot of men who work for the railroad."

"Not so many anymore. My husband retired a decade ago," she replied.

"Both Mr. Sayers and Clyde are long-time employees. Have you met them in the past?" Doro asked.

A grin lifted her fine features. "Oh, yes. My husband would be happy to see Mr. Sayers working as a conductor, since he's wanted the job for years." Mrs. O'Brien beamed. "Of course, Mr. O'Brien knew him much better than I did, and much longer. Mr. Sayers and I only became acquainted when he was posted as a stationmaster a few years back."

"We heard he's a new conductor," Doro observed.

"That's right. This is his first run being over the whole train," the widow said. "It's not easy to take charge, and now he's got a lot of problems to handle, along with supervising the entire crew."

"Most of them are in the other part of the train," Gramma Rose pointed out.

"They'll get a conductor at the next big station," Mrs. O'Brien said. "But that's a way up the line."

Clyde returned with coffee, which he poured for Mrs. O'Brien. "Joshua will bring you some sweet rolls, and I'll be back with fresh fruit for everyone."

"Thank you so much," she said. "We haven't chatted, but how is your wife doing?"

The waiter briefly bowed his head. "It's a struggle."

"I can only imagine. Such a terrible loss for both of you," Mrs. O'Brien said, her voice soft with sympathy.

"Thank you. It was." He cleared this throat. "I'll be right back."

Although Doro wanted to ask why Clyde and his wife had suffered a loss, she did not wish to appear callous. She shot a questioning glance at her grandmother, who gave a slight nod.

"You know Clyde and his wife well?" Rose McLaren asked.

"I've known him for many years but only met his wife at their son's funeral. Many railroaders were there." She sighed. "It was a horrible situation."

"In what way?" Aggie voiced the query in a sympathetic tone.

After a sip of coffee, Mrs. O'Brien laid down her cup and stared into it. "Custis, their son, was killed in a rail yard accident." She looked around the group. "Although safety improvements have been made over the years, the yards can still be dangerous, especially for inexperienced workers. Custis had only been on the job for six months when he was pinned between two cars."

All three of the other women gasped. "That's dreadful," Gramma Rose murmured.

"It certainly is," Aggie agreed. "I wonder why the boy didn't become a waiter like his father."

"A rail yard job was open, so Custis took it. He wanted to earn money quickly, so he could go back to school," Mrs. O'Brien explained. "Waiting for a position on a train crew would've meant a delay in obtaining funds. He was so eager to finish his education."

The widow's knowledge could be key, but Doro preceded with caution. She did not want to sound snoopy, as Ev sometimes said she was. "Go back to school? Why did he leave?" Doro echoed. "Poor grades?"

"Heavens, no. Custis was a bright student. He graduated at the top of his high school class and got a scholarship to Pikeley College."

Mention of the school intensified Doro's interest. "What was he studying?"

Mrs. O'Brien put one forefinger to her temple. "Science, I believe. When he was in school, Custis came to our home quite a few times for supper. A lovely young man. So polite and pleasant."

Anxiety churned in Doro's stomach. Professor Mathers taught science. "Why did he leave school?" she asked again.

A frown darkened the widow's face. "He lost his scholarship, although I don't know why. My husband fell ill about the same time. Custis stopped to see him before leaving the Springs, but he didn't tell us exactly what happened." She paused for a moment. "I hope you don't think I'm gossiping, because I hate folks who carry tales. But you asked about Clyde, and that always makes me think of his boy." She dabbed at her eyes. "Sorry. My husband and I got close to Custis. It was almost like having our own grandchild."

Gramma Rose patted the other woman's hand. "I understand, and we're sharing information, not gossiping."

Mrs. O'Brien offered a watery smile. "Thank you."

Doro barely registered the exchange between the two older women because she was focused on the comments about Custis leaving Pikeley. Could his departure be related to Mathers? If so, that might give Clyde a motive to kill the professor. Doro tucked the idea away. She, Aggie, and Gramma Rose could discuss it later. Since Clyde came back in short order, the group did not pursue more questions.

"Here you go, Mrs. O'Brien," he said with a smile. After putting a plate of sweets in front of her, he placed a big bowl of fruit in the middle of the table before focusing on the widow. "If you need anything at all, send word to me. I want to make sure you're comfortable and not worried."

"No reason to fret," she assured him.

A puzzled expression shadowed Clyde's lean face. "I thought you might be concerned about the murder."

"Murder?" she echoed. "What murder?"

Before Clyde responded, Doro jumped in. "The conductor didn't want passengers to know about the professor's cause of death yet."

A harrumph left Clyde. "Mrs. O'Brien ain't just any passenger. She's part of the railroad family, so I figured he'd tell her."

Had the waiter actually thought that? Or was he purposefully disobeying orders? Doro was not sure. Nor could she be certain Clyde wasn't the killer.

"No, he didn't." The widow spoke in a breathy murmur. "What happened and where?"

Clyde opened his mouth, but Chef Andre—who had stepped into the dining car—called out. "We've got hot water for tea, and I need it taken to the tables."

"Gotta go." The waiter hurried off.

In his wake, Mrs. O'Brien looked at Doro. "You know about the murder?"

Doro explained how she had found out, and her grandmother shared that the two girls were amateur sleuths. "We've worked several cases," Doro added.

"So, you're investigating this one?" the widow asked.

"Not really. Mr. Sayers wants to wait for a railroad security officer. One should come with the repair crew, just to ensure the decoupling was actually an accident," Doro said. If the widow was friendly with Sayers, she might reveal their plans. No sense in further annoying the man.

"I'm no expert, but it's likely a weak coupler. At the station, I heard about them adding more cars. My husband always insisted on checking the couplers himself, because they can be damaged or weakened. I doubt if Mr. Sayers had time, because the train was late pulling into the Springs. I figured we'd be way late leaving, but we were only a bit behind schedule. Railroad officials don't like delays, so sometimes crews are pushed hard to hurry." Mrs. O'Brien helped herself to fruit and took a spoonful of the mixed melon, berries, and cherries.

"So, it's possible that a weak coupler was missed," Aggie stated.

The widow nodded. "It doesn't happen often, but it can. At least no one was hurt."

Doro's suspicion about someone purposefully vandalizing the coupler subsided, but she did not dismiss the idea. "That was fortunate." She paused before continuing. "How long have you lived in Colorado Springs?"

"Almost all my life," the widow replied. "Born and raised there."

"Were you acquainted with Professor Mathers?" Gramma Rose posed the query.

"Oh, my, no. He and his folks moved in much higher society than my family. I'd heard the Mathers' name, and I've seen the mansion. But I never saw the professor, and I know little about the college, other than what Custis told us."

"What did he say?" Doro asked.

A pensive expression fell over her face. "He loved the school at first. For the first three years, we heard nothing but good about it. He met other students with similar interests, and he spoke highly of his instructors. Then, he seemed upset and uneasy. He never said why but, like I told you, my husband fell ill, and Custis probably didn't want to bother us with details. Later, I thought his grades might've gone down. But I don't know. It's hard to believe when he was such a fine student. Why would he suddenly fail?"

The previous evening, Mathers had ranted about female students and lower classes being in college. Had he given the boy poor marks due to his status? If so, were the grades low enough to cancel his scholarship? Doro needed to find out.

When Joshua returned with coffee, Mrs. O'Brien beamed at him. "It's wonderful to see you again."

"Good to see you, too," the young waiter replied.

The widow replied in a whisper. "Professor Banyon says you found a dead body this morning. I'm so very sorry."

His face went white. "It was a shock," he admitted, "but I'm not supposed to talk about it until the security man comes. Mr. Sayers made that clear."

"I would never advise going against him," Mrs. O'Brien stated. "But these two young women have solved several cases. They might be able to gather details to help the security man when he gets here. Identifying the killer will be important to the higher-ups."

Joshua chewed on his lower lip. "I'm sure that's right."

"Do you know where Mr. Sayers is now?" Gramma Rose asked.

"He just went to meet with the flagman and the brakeman in the caboose. They're eating there, and he'll be back in an hour," Joshua replied.

"Maybe you'd talk with Aggie and me after the diners are gone," Doro suggested. Many had already left the car.

He shifted from one foot to the other. "I dunno."

"It won't hurt," Mrs. O'Brien assured him. "Besides, don't you like reading whodunits? Clyde said you did a while back."

"We both enjoy reading whodunits, too," Aggie told him. "Putting pieces of a puzzle together is challenging and gratifying."

Joshua nodded. "My aunt liked those books, and I read a few of hers."

"Now, you're part of a genuine mystery," Aggie added. "You may have a key clue and not realize it."

A thoughtful expression crossed the young waiter's face. "Maybe."

"Why don't you finish your work and come back?" Mrs. O'Brien suggested. "I'll retire to my compartment, but I'll see you later, I'm sure."

"All right." With that, the young waiter continued to the only other occupied table.

After finishing her food and beverage, Mrs. O'Brien laid her napkin aside and glanced around the table. "I'm nervous about a killer being on the train."

"My nerves are on edge, too," Gramma Rose replied. "The girls are used to this sort of thing, so they aren't as bothered, although I've urged them to be cautious. No sense in antagonizing the killer."

Mrs. O'Brien's hand flew to her mouth. "Perhaps I shouldn't have encouraged Joshua to talk with you. What if the killer overhears? I got carried away thinking about the whodunit part."

"It's unlikely the murderer will see two young women as serious detectives," Doro pointed out to ease the older ladies' minds.

"We've run into opposition in the past," Aggie added.

"Women are doing a lot more than they did when I was young," Mrs. O'Brien commented. "I think it's a good thing."

"So do I," Gramma Rose agreed. "As long as the girls are careful, I don't object to them sleuthing, and they're safer together."

The widow nodded. "I wish I wasn't traveling all alone."

Only a moment passed before Rose McLaren proposed a suggestion. "You could come to our compartment. We have a drawing room, so there's an extra bed."

"I wouldn't want to intrude," Mrs. O'Brien said, although with no enthusiasm.

After a quick study of the woman, Doro seconded her grandmother's suggestion. "We have plenty of space, and you wouldn't be intruding."

"Not at all," Aggie agreed.

"If you're sure," the widow said.

Doro and Aggie restated their support of the idea.

"It'll be lovely to have someone closer to my age with us," Gramma Rose said. "Now, if you finished, let's go. The girls can come along when they're ready."

After the two older women departed, Doro focused on Aggie. "I didn't realize my grandmother was so concerned. It sounded like having another person in our compartment eases her mind."

"Doesn't a killer roaming the train bother you at all? This isn't like our previous cases. Then, we could take refuge in our residences. Remember when we were digging into the lost exam? I stayed at your house for a couple of nights. During the last three investigations, we've both lived in Wheaton Hall, which is secure."

What her friend said was correct. Both her family home and the women's faculty residence had offered safety. "You're right, and I'm not discounting that there's a murderer on-board, and no lawmen. Even though Wade and Ev were out of action in May, you and I took precautions when we were out-and-about. We will now, too."

Aggie nodded. "Let's say we have no leads. That should keep the killer from targeting us."

"Good idea," Doro observed as she glanced around. "Even though Joshua isn't the best suspect, we can start by telling him we're at square one. Since the car has cleared out, this is a good time to chat with him."

After a look at the other tables, Aggie agreed. "He's the only one in here, so let's get going."

Doro called for the young waiter to join them, which he did, but not in a hurry. "We need to clean up," he said.

"It won't take long for us to ask you a few questions," Doro assured. "Please take a seat."

"I can't do that when I'm working. I'd get in trouble," Joshua insisted.

"It's rather awkward to look up at you," Doro added.

Aggie smiled and gestured at an empty chair. "Sitting down for a few moments won't hurt anything."

After a moment, Joshua took the seat, but his expression remained uneasy.

With the situation on a more even keel, Doro went on. "You already said you found the body when you reported for work."

"Yes, miss. He was on the floor, just the same as when you came," Joshua said.

"From what you've already said, he's well-known among crewmen," Aggie observed.

The young waiter nodded. "Folks talk."

With luck, they had also discussed why Clyde and Mathers had been at odds, but Doro resisted the urge to ask outright. First, she wanted to allay Joshua's anxiety. "And none said anything good about the professor," Doro suggested.

"I never heard nothing nice," Joshua confirmed.

Since that was the prevailing sentiment, Doro went back to the events of the morning. "We heard Professor Mathers and Chef Andre quarrel," Doro said. "That was typical?" Getting additional confirmation could be useful.

The young man nodded. "Chef Andre can be high-handed. So was Mathers. They clashed because the professor demanded special treatment, like he was royalty. Andre didn't like that. I been on a few runs where the two of them had rough words."

"I imagine others resented Mathers' behavior, too, from what you've told us," Aggie said, her tone soft and cajoling.

Joshua grimaced. "Yes, miss. The professor made it hard for all of us, especially the dining car staff. He had lots of likes and dislikes. Although we had no way of knowing if he'd be on a certain train, Mathers thought his favorites should be stocked. If they weren't, he hollered at whoever told him."

"Like last night when he scolded you," Doro observed.

A flush climbed into the young man's lean cheeks. "He does it with everyone."

"But he threatened to have you fired for your attitude," Doro said. "Does that happen to everyone?"

He bowed his head and rubbed the back of his neck. "Mathers knew I want to be promoted. Whenever we crossed paths, he reminded me about his friend."

"The one who's a boss with the railroad," Aggie added.

"That's right. Then, he'd demand I wait on him like he was royalty," Joshua said in a hushed voice. "I didn't like it, but I did whatever he asked."

After a brief interlude of quiet, Doro made an observation. "I'm surprised he didn't wake you up to make him some food."

Joshua's head shot up. "I wasn't in the kitchen until I reported for work." His tone was defensive, and his eyes flashed in alarm.

"I didn't say you were," Doro told him.

The color in his face deepened. "I don't know why he didn't get me. But he didn't."

"And you don't know who might've been in the kitchen with Mathers?" Aggie asked. "Another passenger, perhaps."

"I don't think so, miss," Joshua replied. "The kitchen is locked up overnight."

"Last night, Chef Andre told the professor about the key being in its usual place. Would it be easy for someone else to find?"

The young waiter's gaze went to the table. "I dunno, but putting a key out goes against the rules."

An interesting tidbit. "But it's not unusual for a key to be available for the professor?" Doro asked.

"Not at all," Joshua admitted.

"You know where it's left," Aggie suggested.

Joshua's expression gave the truth away, and when he spoke, he made the admission. "Chef Andre usually leaves it in a pouch hanging from his compartment door when Mathers is on board. I heard others say that way, the chef isn't disturbed as much."

"Was the key being left out common knowledge?" Aggie asked.

"Only the kitchen workers know," Joshua replied. "Like I said, it's against the rules to give out keys to passengers."

"Is Conductor Sayers aware of the practice?" Doro made the inquiry.

"I doubt it. He might've seen the pouch on the chef's door, but he wouldn't know what it was for, I s'pose," he replied.

Since Sayers was new to the job, Doro was not surprised by the response. She was about to ask more about the key, when Chef Andre stuck his head out of the kitchen and stared at Joshua.

"I want to finish the breakfast clean-up before I have to start lunch, so get moving." The chef barked out the order.

Joshua nodded at the chef before turning back to the two young women. "Anything else?"

"The conductor said he doesn't know Clyde well," Doro observed. "Do you?"

The young waiter's gaze moved to a point past Doro's shoulder. "Some, but I only been with the railroad for a year."

Joshua's failure to look her in the eye as he spoke bothered Doro. "Clyde was angry with Mathers last night. Did that happen often?"

The young waiter briefly looked her way. "Clyde can be quick to fly off the handle."

"Does he get angry with you?" Aggie asked, dismay roughening her voice.

Joshua shook his head. "No, miss. Never. He gets emotional sometimes."

"Since his son died?" Doro asked.

The young man's eyes went wide. "I dunno. Maybe."

His reaction increased Doro's tension. "Mrs. O'Brien mentioned Clyde's loss."

Joshua's shoulders bobbed up and down in an odd shrug. "She'd know cuz of her husband working for the railroad. I only been with the company a year," he repeated. He glanced at the kitchen before standing up. "If I don't get back to work, Chef Andre will get after me."

"We understand," Aggie said in a soothing tone. "You go on along."

Although Doro wanted to ask more questions, letting the boy leave was a wise strategy—for the moment. "Thank you for your help. Since we have no leads, every morsel is important. Just don't mention us asking you to the conductor."

"Cuz he don't want you snooping," the young man said.

Since Joshua had heard Sayers' admonitions, Doro did not disagree. "He thinks a railroad security man can investigate."

"I like Mr. Sayers, but he's real scared to do something wrong and get demoted." After a nod, Joshua went into the kitchen.

When the waiter was out of earshot, Aggie sighed. "He's probably right."

"He is, and I suppose he heard as much from one of the older crewmen. As for his responses, they weren't all that helpful, and his reaction to questions about Clyde was odd."

"The boy might be nervous, but I agree. He didn't want to provide much information. Either Joshua was covering up for Clyde, or he's involved—as the killer or as a witness."

Doro jotted more notes down. "Both are possible. Joshua knows more than he's told us. I wonder if he realizes why Custis left school." She chewed on her lower lip. "Phineas went to Pikeley for a couple of years, but he must've transferred several years ago from what my dad said."

"Maybe before Custis was a student?"

Doro reviewed what they knew. "Custis died about a year ago, shortly after leaving school. Phineas and Grayson graduated from Colorado College then, because they started graduate school last fall. That means Phineas transferred three years ago. He spent his freshman and sophomore years at Pikeley."

"When Custis must've been enrolled there at the same time."

"Yep. From what we know he was," Doro agreed.

"It's a small school, isn't it?" Aggie asked. "I didn't see the campus when we were in the Springs, but I got that impression from your father."

"The enrollment is about eight-hundred," Doro replied. "From what my father has told me, students from Pikeley and Colorado College socialize with one another, so Phineas and Grayson should've known Custis, in any case. Those two are also among my suspects, but they might answer questions about him, if we're careful asking."

"Those are good observations," her friend said. "Are you putting them ahead of Joshua?"

"So far, I'm not ranking the suspects, except for putting Joshua down the list. What do you think?"

"Not ranking them is fine for now. Since Joshua found the body, he might've seen the killer. Or heard someone come or go from a compartment as he was heading to work. I'd label him as a potential witness, more than a suspect."

Doro nodded. "While the killer might not have seen him. Or, if Clyde is the murderer, Joshua could be covering up for him."

"I agree on both counts." Aggie's attention moved to the kitchen door. "When do you plan to interview Chef Andre?"

"Whenever I can," Doro muttered.

A chuckle left Aggie. "He isn't likely to cooperate, from what I've seen."

"If Andre refuses, we have no standing to make him."

A rueful expression crossed Aggie's face. "I wish Ev and Wade were here. We could use their authority as lawmen."

Doro could not deny the facts. The men could insist on interviews and such, when she and Aggie could not. That did not deter her, though. "They weren't around when we solved the mystery of the lost exam."

"True, but that didn't involve physical harm to anyone."

"We didn't know that when we started digging into the case. The thieves could've reacted badly and tried to get even with us," Doro said. "But that's beside the point. We're a good team without help from any lawmen."

Aggie pursed her lips. "Maybe, but a murder is serious business. And, as your grandmother and Mrs. O'Brien noted, this killer is stuck here—just like we are. I'm not saying we shouldn't look into the case. I'm just saying we should be careful."

"You sound like Ev." The words were out before Doro considered the wisdom of such an admission.

A grin lit her friend's face. "Because he worries about you, which isn't such a bad thing."

Everything considered, Doro had to agree—but silently, not aloud. "We'll be cautious and, if we get a strong sense of who's guilty, we won't tell anyone other than Gramma Rose and Mrs. O'Brien." She drummed her fingers on the table. "Let's not share too much with them. I don't want to cause more concern."

Aggie's expression relaxed. "Good thinking. Now, what's next?"

"It seems like the clean-up is almost over, so I'll ask Clyde to answer a few questions. Then, I'll approach Chef Andre." Doro paused for a moment. "Are you going to stay for both interviews?"

Aggie smiled. "Absolutely."

When the older waiter, who had come out of the kitchen, got closer, Doro spoke to him. "Sir, would you mind answering some questions?"

His gaze flitted away and then, back to Doro. "I suppose so, but I don't know nothing."

"You never know what you might recall." She gestured to the empty chair beside her. "Please sit down."

After he dropped into the seat, Clyde nodded. "Don't mind if I do. I were up half the night telling folks about the problem. Then, in the kitchen before dawn and plenty to do ever since."

"We won't keep you, because you'll have the same situation at lunchtime," Aggie said.

"Thanks. I'm hoping to go back to my berth and get my feet up. Not as young as I once was, and this job ain't getting easier," he replied.

Doro noted his lack of concern at sitting on the job. Perhaps, Clyde felt more secure in his position than Joshua did. "You've been with the railroad a long time, right?" Starting with a benign question, one that was already answered, seemed wise.

"Over fifteen years, with a break in the middle when I went to war. Started as a waiter and still in the job," he said. "The wife wishes I were home more. That won't happen for years yet."

"How often do you get home?" Doro asked.

"Every couple of weeks or so. It depends on what trips I'm on. Kitchen help stays on-board for an entire run. The others ride certain sections. If I'm lucky, a run ends close to my hometown. Otherwise, I gotta hitch a ride, which can shorten my break by a day or more," Clyde said.

"Are you usually with Chef Andre's kitchen crew?" Doro asked.

A scowl darkened his narrow face. "Unfortunately, that happens too often. As you've seen and heard, he's tough. With his help and with passengers who annoy him. This trip is making him worse, cuz he got the big kitchen car and the partial kitchen here. Course, he don't have to fret over the other one now."

Doro studied the waiter's face. Although his observations were negative, he did not seem angry or upset. Nor had he mentioned his own altercation with Mathers. "Are other chefs easier to work with?"

"Most is high-strung, but not so vocal as Andre. Peace and quiet make work easier, but I can handle whatever he dishes out."

"I'm sure you can," Aggie observed. "But what about passengers? Does he have spats with many?"

Clyde shook his head. "Only a handful ever got to him. Professor Mathers were one. Last night's argument were far from the first."

Again, the man did not mention his attitude toward the murder victim. If Clyde continued to avoid the topic, Doro had to bring it up. For now, she bided her time.

"Did they usually argue over food quality or selection?" Aggie inquired.

"That and the way Chef Andre treated the professor—not with the proper deference. Them's Mathers' words."

Again, Doro made a few notes. "We've heard the chef left his key hanging on his compartment door at night. Were many people aware of his habit?"

"All the dining crew were, and any passengers who ever wanted an after-hours snack probably knows," Clyde replied.

"Do many people want to eat when the kitchen is closed?" Aggie asked. "I'd never consider asking, not that I'm a veteran train traveler."

Clyde's thin lips flattened. "Because you is all nice folks. Not bossy or demanding, like some."

"Like Professor Mathers, you mean." Doro offered the observation in a controlled voice.

The waiter's jaw tightened. "He was a nasty piece of work."

A repeated, but valid, observation. When he did not say more, Doro got to the core of the matter. "Last night, you said Mathers couldn't take anything else from you. What did you mean?"

The man glowered at her. "Ain't none of your business."

His harsh response reminded Doro of the previous evening. Clyde could be pleasant, but something—something related to the professor—was stuck in his craw. Did it relate to his son? Since she feared questions about Custis would drive the man off, she avoided the topic. For now. "Your conversation with Mathers was as hostile as the one with Chef Andre." Her words were both observation and accusation. Clyde took them as the latter.

"I ain't listening to this." He jumped to his feet. "You got no call to accuse me. You oughta be looking at them two college boys and finding out what Mathers did to them. They both got plenty of reason to hate him."

Aggie spoke before the man stalked off. "Sir, my friend wasn't accusing you of anything. She just wants to help find the killer. I'm sure you do, too. None of us wants to be stranded in the middle of nowhere with a murderer amongst us."

Silently, Doro offered gratitude for the perfect comment. An innocent man would want the villain identified, even if he hated the victim.

Clyde shoved his hands into his jacket pockets and rocked back on his heels. "The professor got what he deserved."

"But we don't know if the killer has others in his sights," Aggie put in. "Doro is known as an amateur sleuth, and I've assisted her. What if the guilty party wants to keep us from investigating? We could be in danger. You wouldn't want that."

The waiter shook his head. "Of course not, miss."

"Then, you'll answer a few more questions?" Doro asked.

His reply was to sit down again. "I didn't kill the man, so you don't need to know about our history. That's private business."

Seeing he would not be budged, Doro resigned herself to getting the details elsewhere. "Can you think of any other passengers on this train who might've wanted a late snack?"

His forehead furrowed, and several moments passed before he responded. "One of them two students asked about food when we was alerting folks to the emergency. Like I said, you oughta talk to them."

"Which one?" Aggie asked.

"Spieth. The other was asleep," Clyde replied.

"He didn't wake when you knocked?" Doro asked.

"Nope," was Clyde's reply. "The two of them was in the club car a good part of the evening. Probably played cards and had refreshments."

"Meaning, liquor," Doro said.

One of Clyde's narrow shoulders bobbed up and down. "I don't snoop into what passengers bring with them."

The comment provided little enlightenment, so Doro made a noncommittal reply before posing a pointed question. "What time did you and Joshua finish going through the cars last night?"

He rubbed his forehead. "Around three. Afterward, we all met in the kitchen for a bit. Then, I went straight to my berth. Joshua wanted to check the coupler, so he went outside with the conductor and brakeman. Curious, like any kid. His bunk is by mine, but I never heard him come back. Went into a deep sleep right off." A sigh left him. "If you don't have no more questions, I could use some shut-eye."

"We don't want to keep you," Doro said, "but thanks for your help." Such as it was.

"Sure thing," he said before shuffling off.

Aggie braced one elbow on the edge of the table. "We could hear the crew rapping on doors two or three compartments away from us, so it's hard to believe the knocking didn't wake Grayson Bailey up."

"That bothers me, although he could've been intoxicated." Dismay flickered through Doro. "We know Grayson and Phineas are in the same car as the professor was, so they could've overheard an exchange between him and the crew member who woke him."

Aggie chewed on her lower lip. "And followed him to the kitchen later?"

"It's possible. Both seemed irate at Mathers."

"Chef Andre did, too," Aggie said. "And Clyde was plenty mad. Not to mention he didn't want to tell us the source of his anger."

Doro drummed her fingers on the table. "Mr. Bailey might've imbibed to drown his sorrows. Seeing Mathers had to upset him."

Sorrow etched Aggie's features. "I feel terrible for him and Luann. If Grayson Bailey didn't kill Mathers, they still have a chance at happiness. If he did..." Her voice trailed off.

"Let's hope he was drinking to forget. If he was too drunk to hear a knock, Mr. Bailey couldn't have rallied in time to kill the professor."

"You're right, but what if he was faking sleep to cover up his plans?"

Doro rolled her pens between her hand. "That would be devious, but possible. What did you think about Clyde saying the grudge between him and Mathers was personal, so we don't need to know?"

"It seemed like an evasion, because he was plenty willing to answer other questions."

"And point the finger at Grayson Bailey and Phineas Spieth," Doro murmured.

"Not without reason," Aggie said. "Mr. Bailey has a clear-cut motive, but we don't know as much about Mr. Spieth."

With a sigh, Doro leaned back in her chair. "It was obvious Grayson is in love with Luann Mathers, and being spurned can be a powerful motivator."

Aggie drummed her fingers on the table. "He wasn't really spurned. Luann was virtually forced to marry the professor, according to what Grayson said."

After putting her pencil and notepad down, Doro folded her hands in her lap. "My dad was surprised by their marriage, which doesn't mean she was forced into it. Grayson Bailey made it seem that way, but how do we really know?"

Aggie's eyes widened, as if in disbelief. "Surely, you don't think a nineteen-year-old girl who had been stepping out with a handsome young college student, would suddenly switch her affections to a grumpy, overbearing man more than twice her age?"

Doro offered a rueful smile. "No, I don't, which gives Grayson more motive for killing Mathers. Now, Luann is free. Or she will be when her mourning period is over." She thought back to her father's comments. "In the train station, my dad said plenty of people were stunned by the marriage. He was, because he figured Mathers would become her guardian, not her husband. I wish I'd asked him more about it."

Sadness darkened Aggie's gaze. "That poor girl. I hope Grayson Bailey didn't murder her husband, because she'll need someone to lean on. The help didn't seem fond of her when we visited."

"I agree. They acted more like spies than servants. But I'm sure my parents will visit her as soon as they get word about the murder. They'll help Luann, in whatever way possible."

Aggie nodded. "I'm sure they will, but it won't be easy for her if Grayson did it."

"You're right. We have other suspects, though. Several of them." Doro studied her notes. "Chef Andre, Clyde, and Joshua, in addition to Grayson and Phineas. We may turn up others as we ask more questions."

A frown fell over Aggie's fine features. "I hope there aren't too many more, because that will make solving the case in a short time nearly impossible."

Doro could not repress a grin. "You believe we can solve it before help arrives?"

Optimism replaced frustration in Aggie's expression. "The crew coming to repair the coupler will get here in a few hours. If a security man is with them, he might figure out who killed Mathers, but I'm skeptical."

"Due to what we know about Wade's security job on the railroad," Doro suggested.

Aggie nodded. "Wade has said himself security officers aren't policemen. Although a handful have that experience, most don't. We'll see about the one who shows up here."

"Chances are he'll put the murder in the hands of the law in the next big town," Doro commented. "We'll gather as many details as possible and defer to the security man. I hope he won't be someone who thinks women belong at home caring for a husband and children."

Aggie grimaced. "That's why you're keen to solve the mystery. Because the conductor poo-pooed us being involved."

"Partly," Doro admitted, "and partly because I'm tired of hearing what women couldn't and shouldn't do."

"Times are changing." Aggie rolled her eyes and grinned.

"So, we keep hearing," Doro murmured before returning to the case. "Let's talk with Chef Andre before he goes back to his compartment."

"That won't be pleasant."

"You're good at winning people over, so I'll rely on you to soften him up," Doro said with a smile.

"I can try," Aggie replied.

The two friends headed to the kitchen where clean-up was underway. Andre, a scowl on his face, turned toward them. "Passengers are not permitted in here. Sayers let you in earlier, but that won't continue. This is my bailiwick."

"We won't get in your way, Chef," Doro said. "We just have a few questions."

Andre narrowed his gaze until his eyes were dark slits. "I don't have to talk with you. Get out."

Doro did not mince words in responding. "Since you and Mathers had a run-in last night, and it wasn't the first time from what we know, you're a suspect, Chef Andre."

A harrumph left the chef. "I do not wish to be interrogated in front of my underlings."

His tone, expression, and wording telegraphed the extent of his haughtiness. No wonder he and Mathers had clashed. Both were arrogant and obnoxious. Doro bit her tongue to keep from saying as much. "Perhaps we could sit at a table in the dining car."

"All right," he muttered.

The group took seats away from the kitchen door, but Andre's countenance remained stony.

After releasing a pent-up breath, Doro laid her notepad on the nearest countertop and got her pencil out. "We've heard about Professor Mathers often wanting a late-night snack. Isn't that right?" Starting with an established fact often eased the way into more difficult topics.

The wiry chef faced Doro. "Often is not quite right. He wanted something every night. More than once, I suggested he take food to his compartment after dinner. But, no, he never knew what he'd be craving at two or three or four in the morning." Disdain underscored every word. "If he wanted hot food, my cook or I had to get up and fix it. More than once, his repast needed to be a steak with a baked potato. Can you imagine?"

"I can't," Aggie put in. "It was wrong to get you or others up to cater to him."

The chef's scowl intensified. "He didn't care about right or wrong. The man was a clod."

Andre's continuing lack of sympathy bothered Doro, but she pressed on. "Did he wake you last night or take your key?"

Something akin to surprise flashed in the chef's beady eyes. "I wouldn't give a key to him."

Doro shrugged. "That's not what you said during yesterday's dinner service."

When Andre looked at the women, color surged into his thin face. "It's against company policy to give keys to passengers, but I need rest. Not to be woken up at ungodly hours. We're here until ten at night and back at six in the morning. I have to sleep sometime."

"That's understandable," Aggie murmured.

He ran one hand over his face. "I doubt if higher-ups will feel the same way, but what's done is done."

Was he worried about being fired? He had told Mathers about having been a chef at fine restaurants. Surely, he could go back to one, so Doro moved to another subject. "I didn't see you when the others were going through the cars. Did you stay in your compartment?"

"Of course not," he shot back. "I came here to make coffee and lay out a snack."

The response surprised Doro. "For the workers."

"Yes," Andre replied. "Being roused in the middle of the night is unpleasant. Some coffee and cookies help. Those who went out in the rain were especially appreciative."

"How kind of you to think of them," Aggie said.

A slight nod was the chef's reply.

Although the surly man's benevolence surprised Doro, she took it in stride. Perhaps there was a nicer side to the high-strung chef, but she wondered why he had not revealed his activities earlier. For a moment, Doro weighed whether or not to ask. Finally, she went on to a more crucial question. "What time did you come here?"

"After two-thirty. I stayed until nearly four o'clock," he replied. "I went right back to sleep because I needed to be back by six o'clock."

"When you got here at two-thirty, the door was locked?" Aggie made the inquiry.

He nodded. "Yes. Joshua and Clyde had just come back before I left, so I told them to lock up."

As Doro jotted more notes, she considered the time frame. "Do you know if Joshua and Clyde went back to their bunks?" Both had indicated they had, but had they told the truth?

"I assume so," the chef replied.

"If they did, Joshua arrived back before you did. Around ten before six."

"That's what he said," the chef muttered.

"You don't believe him?" Doro studied the man's face. Was he pushing attention from himself to the young waiter? Or did he know something more?

"Mathers humiliated him last evening, and it wasn't the first time," the chef replied.

Uneasiness filled Doro. "The professor travels fairly often, but I wouldn't think Joshua would frequently cross paths with him."

Andre shrugged. "A few times was enough to upset the boy. Joshua wishes to rise above his lowly station. Since Mathers is friends with a railroad big wig, he lorded it over the kid. Getting people to do his bidding made the professor feel powerful."

"But you didn't jump to his tune," Doro suggested.

"No, I didn't. I'm a trained chef, and I could go elsewhere."

The comment made Doro wonder why he stayed with the railroad. Not that chefs on trains weren't top-notch. Many were, and the menus revealed as much. "Do you prefer this job?" she asked, being careful not to pry.

"It has advantages and disadvantages," the chef said.

Aggie smiled. "The advantages must outweigh the disadvantages, or you wouldn't stay on."

As he turned toward her, Andre folded his arms across his chest. "My wife, children, and in-laws are in Kansas City, and my elderly parents are in Colorado Springs. My father's been ailing for a couple of years, and my wife's mother has been ill much longer. Moving wouldn't allow me to check on both sides of our family. By working on the trains, I can be in both places every couple of weeks."

Amazement hit Doro hard. The arrogant chef was also a concerned son and son-in-law.

"That can't be easy," Aggie mused.

He ran one hand over his weary features. "Some trips are more trying than others. Most passengers are agreeable. Only a few aren't."

"And Professor Mathers was one of the few." Aggie spoke in a soft, but compelling, voice.

"He was," Andre agreed. "He was demanding. Unfortunately, he had an unsophisticated palate, which made him unable to appreciate more delicate dishes. That's where we first crossed swords. Our menus have variety, but he sampled very few entrees. Steak, potatoes, green beans, tomatoes, bread and butter. He ordered that combination whenever possible but added what he called 'a Frenchie item' occasionally. And critiqued each one with vengeance." A harsh breath left the chef. "Cantaloupe pie is not French fare. It's a recipe used on the Texas and Pacific Railroad, and I got it from one of their chefs. Mathers blathered on-and-on about it during his last trip with us. I planned to serve it tonight, so I'm sure he would've complained again."

"I've never heard of it," Aggie said, "but it sounds good."

Andre smiled. "Refreshing on a hot day. But the professor didn't care about anything unusual. I believe he only ordered such items, so he could whine."

"We witnessed him being difficult in the train station before we left," Doro added. "And during the dinner hour on board."

The chef's expression grew contrite. "I apologize for last night's scene in the dining room, but I cannot abide the man. This trip, I had more responsibilities than usual because this car was added in the Springs."

"I can see how that increased your duties," Doro said. "As for Mathers, others have similar feelings toward him."

"An understatement, I'm sure. I heard him arguing with two passengers, his belittling of Joshua, and the squabble with Clyde," Andre said. "Awful, awful man."

The exchange between the waiter and the professor had been far worse than a squabble, but Doro used the observation to ask a question. "Why does Clyde hate Mathers?"

"I'm not privy to the waiters' personal feelings," the chef replied.

If he had not glanced away, Doro might have believed him. "You have no idea why Clyde accused the professor of taking something away from him?"

The chef's narrow shoulders bounced up and down. "As I said, I know nothing of Clyde's emotional state."

"We met Mrs. O'Brien, whose husband was a conductor for years," Doro observed.

Andre's expression softened. "And a good man. I was sorry to hear of his passing."

"You worked with him?" Aggie asked.

"No, he retired long before I started working on the trains. He and his wife traveled several times a year, and I'd see them occasionally," the chef replied. "Fine folks."

Since Andre seemed to like both O'Briens, Doro built on that. "She mentioned Clyde's son leaving school when he lost his scholarship. He went to work in a rail yard to earn money, so he could go back. Since the boy went to Pikeley College, where the professor taught, we wonder if Clyde's hatred of Mathers had something to do with Custis."

Andre's gaze shifted to a point behind Doro and Aggie. "The boy was killed in a terrible accident, but I know little about him. I started working for the railroad only a few years ago, and I didn't have many runs with Clyde before the boy died. Unlike many railroaders, I don't spend much time with other workers, because I have family in need of attention. And I don't listen to gossip, either."

Frustration filled Doro. She shot a gaze at her friend, who gave a slight nod.

"Is there anyone else among the crew who has argued with the professor in the past?" Aggie inquired.

"No one comes to mind. The brakeman and flagman still on board wouldn't have crossed paths with him," the chef responded.

"What about Mr. Sayers?" Aggie posed the question.

"This is his first trip as a conductor," Andre replied.

"Couldn't he have interacted with Professor Mathers in another role?" As she spoke, Doro realized they knew little about the conductor's previous positions.

"He was a flagman for a few years and a stationmaster after that. Or so I've been told," Andre replied. "Following the deaths of his wife and son, he didn't want to stay in one place for long. He may have to go back to another position if he isn't more assertive. Crews will push a weak conductor around."

"What happened to them?" Aggie, her voice soft with sympathy, asked.

"Fell victim to Spanish flu back in 1920," Andre said. "When I mentioned my in-laws and their illnesses keeping my wife with them, he told me about his own losses."

Although Doro felt a surge of sympathy for Sayers, she focused on another of the chef's comments. "You tried to take advantage of the conductor's inexperience earlier."

A rueful smile touched the man's mouth. "My only excuse was getting very little sleep. Finding a dead man in my kitchen didn't help."

"I'm sure it didn't." Doro looked at the draped body. "I'm sorry we can't move him, but a lawman needs to see the scene."

"I understand," Andre murmured. "If you don't have other questions, I could use a nap before lunch."

"You didn't see anyone on your way to the dining car early this morning?" Doro asked.

He shook his head. "Some of the crew, but that's all."

Doro flipped the notepad shut. "Thanks for your help."

He nodded to both young women. "Now, if you'll leave, I'll lock up. We don't want anyone coming into this car, under the circumstances."

"Certainly," Aggie readily agreed.

Doro led the way back to their drawing room. When the chef passed them to go to his compartment, she turned to Aggie. "What do you think?"

"He's not as dreadful as I figured, but we have no way of knowing if he lied about when he left the kitchen or if the waiters were still there. It's his word only."

"My assessment, too. Andre has decency in him, but he was furious with Professor Mathers. On top of that, several people reported that he's high-strung and hot-tempered, which we've witnessed. If Mathers demanded food service amid a crisis, I can picture Andre stabbing him."

"Unfortunately, so can I."

Chapter Six

On the way to their drawing room, Doro and Aggie bumped into Grayson Bailey. The young man had dark circles under his red-rimmed eyes. Although everyone had been disturbed in the night, he seemed unusually drawn and pale and tense.

"Good morning," Doro said, injecting as much cheer as possible into her tone.

He released a pouf sound. "Far from good, if you ask me. Being stuck in the middle of nowhere when I need to get home...it's awful. I wish I could've gone ahead with the rest of the train."

Uneasiness gripped Doro. While wanting to get home was understandable, he sounded edgy and upset. Yesterday, he had discussed his father's death calmly. Why the change? "We'll be going on in a few hours."

He drove his fingers through his hair. "I suppose so."

His surly attitude increased Doro's interest in questioning him. Before she did, she made an observation. "The accident didn't occur until after two o'clock. We'd slept several hours before then, but you look like you got little rest."

Bailey's puffy eyes became slits. "Some of us don't go to bed with the chickens."

Doro's sympathy for the graduate student wavered before she resurrected it. Grayson Bailey seemed sincerely upset over Luann marrying Professor Mathers, and his grief over his father's death was deep and understandable. But he was not admitting to sleeping soundly when other passengers were awakened by knocking and noise. Why? Because booze had caused his deep slumber? "Did you and your friend spend the evening in the club car?" Would he tell the truth?

With one hand, he rubbed both eyes. "We played cards and had a few..." His voice trailed off.

He did not need to say alcohol had been consumed. Not only was he obviously hung over, Clyde had alluded to liquor on the train. Because drinking bootlegged booze did not relate to the murder, Doro avoided any reference to it. Instead, she focused on his lodgings. "You and Phineas Spieth have a compartment, not just berths?"

"Yep. Phineas' family has money, and he insisted on paying for a small space for us. Said I'd get more rest, which I need to face what lays ahead." Grayson bowed his head. "My mother and sisters will be distraught, not to mention worried. My father had a good job, but his illness kept him from working this past year. I wanted to go home and help, but I've got one more term before I get my master's degree. Then, I can teach at a college or find work in a business. Either would pay decently."

Doro was surprised at how much Grayson had revealed. Was he trying to distract them from where he and his friend had been in the early morning hours? "You must've gone back to your compartment before the decoupling, since the club car is in the main part of the train."

"I did," Gray agreed. "I didn't hear anything until a half-hour ago. Even then, I woke on my own."

That seemed to mesh with what Clyde had said, so Doro asked another question. "Did Phineas answer?"

"I suppose," he replied, "because I was the worse for wear."

Drunk was a more succinct explanation. "Do you know who came to the door?"

Color surged into his face. "Not when I was asleep." His voice took on a hard edge. "Sorry to be grumpy."

"Understandable," Aggie said.

Gray's terse responses were understandable for several plausible reasons: his father's death, his loss of Luann, and his current condition. Although Doro had never been *worse for wear,* as Gray was, she had seen college boys in similar straits.

"Thanks, Professor Darwine." He shifted from one foot to the other. "I want to apologize for my behavior last evening at dinner. And for Phineas' outburst, too. Both of us acted out of character."

For a moment, Doro studied his expression and found sincerity. Or a veneer of it. After she and Aggie accepted his regrets, Doro asked, "Where are you going now?"

"To the dining car for coffee," he replied.

Aggie clasped her hands in front of her. "I'm afraid breakfast service is over, but you're welcome in our drawing room. We have a little electric pot and tea bags. No coffee, though."

Since Doro wanted to talk with Gray, she readily agreed. "We have scones from yesterday morning, too." When his stomach growled, they all chuckled. "Come in. This is our door."

Doro tapped before inching the door open. "Gram, we brought a guest."

"Come in," Rose McLaren called out.

Doro glanced around the compartment. "Where is Mrs. O'Brien?"

"She went to get some of her things, since she'll be staying with us," her grandmother replied. "The conductor was coming from the caboose, and we ran into him. He escorted her, and he'll help bring her bags back. After he takes her to the caboose to see the brakeman and flagman. They both knew her husband well."

Relief filled Doro as the last statement registered. They had a little time to question Grayson. But not much.

After formally introducing Gray to her grandmother, Doro prepared tea and scones. While she went about the task, Aggie and Gray sat down at the table with Gramma Rose.

Gray cleared his throat. "I've apologized to Professors Banyon and Darwine for my behavior in the dining car last night, and I'd like to apologize to you, too, ma'am. I acted abominably."

Gramma Rose patted his arm. "Thank you, but it's understandable. Professor Mathers wasn't a nice man. Although I hadn't met him until yesterday, we saw his wife on several occasions." She shook her head. "The girl, and she is young, seemed shy. When we went to their home for lunch, the servants were in charge. Or so it appeared. She went along with them."

Inwardly, Doro beamed. Her grandmother was an asset to the investigation. Making a benign comment could open the door for a deeper exchange, and Gramma Rose was an expert.

"Luann can be spirited," Gray murmured, "but Mathers keeps her captive in that big house, and the staff serves as her jailers."

His words painted an ugly picture, but Doro could not disagree. Luann Truman Mathers had appeared to be ill-at-ease in her own home. While any murder was terrible, at least the girl was free to have a decent life. Doro wanted to ask about the man she'd seen that day in June. With little time, she had to focus on the murder. But had Grayson or Phineas been the furtive figure? Or might Gray know who it was? For now, Doro pushed those questions to the recesses of her mind. Perhaps she could deftly weave them in later. "Has anyone knocked on your door since early this morning?"

Confusion clouded his gaze. "No, why would they?"

The three women looked at one another before Doro replied. Did Gray Bailey know about the stabbing? If not, he was putting up a good front. "Professor Mathers was found murdered around dawn."

"Murdered?" Bailey's eyes went wide. "How? Where?"

Although he looked and sounded shaken, Doro knew outward appearances could be deceiving. "The kitchen staff discovered his body when they started the breakfast shift."

The young man did not move or speak for several moments. "From what we heard last night, he always got a snack in the pre-dawn hours. Maybe he had apoplexy or a heart attack. He wasn't young or trim."

Again, Doro could not be sure if Grayson was sincere or dissembling. "We're sure it was murder."

After a moment, Gray looked at Aggie and Gramma Rose. "Is that for certain?"

Doro understood his doubt because, despite being an amateur sleuth, her first thoughts had not turned to homicide. Even now, hours later, shock remained with her.

"I didn't see the body," Rose said, "but Doro and Aggie did, as did some of the crew. From what I've heard, there's no doubt in my mind."

"He was stabbed," Aggie added in a solemn tone.

When Gray turned to her, Doro nodded. "Mathers was killed with a knife."

Color ebbed from his face. "I see." After clearing his throat, he went on. "Was it a robbery? Mathers had an expensive gold pocket watch. He pulled it out as often as possible, at least he did whenever I saw him."

"The watch and chain were next to him," Doro replied, "so theft isn't a likely motive. Dr. Cartwright, a passenger, examined the body," Doro added.

"Lots of men have pocket knives," Grayson said.

"Dr. Cartwright is fairly certain the murder weapon was a kitchen knife, probably cleaned and replaced in a drawer from what we saw. No knives are missing, and there was a soiled cloth left on the counter near the knife drawer," Doro told him.

"I see," the young man murmured.

As Doro studied Gray's handsome face, she wondered how much more to tell him. Not too much, but a few more facts might lead to him revealing himself—if he was guilty. "A railroad security man may come with the repair crew, just to ensure the coupler wasn't vandalized. I doubt if he'll bring a fingerprint kit, but the law in the next big town should have the right equipment. I asked if the kitchen crew could use the chef's knives until then. He wasn't happy, but at least the other knives won't have additional prints on them, although I'm doubtful any will be found, in any case."

Grayson Bailey nodded. "Because of the soiled cloth."

"It seems like a significant clue," Aggie put in.

The young man was quiet for a moment. "If the killer wiped the blade and hilt clean before leaving the knife and the rag behind, is it possible to get fingerprints off cloth? As an experienced sleuth, you must know."

His knowledge about prints gave Doro pause. No one else had mentioned them. Why had Bailey? Because he was more knowledgeable than others? Or because he'd wiped away all traces of his own prints? "No, it isn't." Doro folded her hands in her lap.

"It was just a thought." A bleak expression shadowed Bailey's handsome face. "I wish I was in the Springs. Poor Luann is all alone. The staff won't help her."

Gramma Rose cleared her throat. "I noticed the butler and housekeeper told Mrs. Mathers how and when tea would be served, instead of the other way around."

"We all saw that Luann deferred to the help, even the maids," Doro added.

A harrumph left Gray. "I'm not surprised. The professor undoubtedly had them spying on Luann. Now that the old goat is dead, I hope she fires all of them and hires people who will see to her needs." Silence echoed in the compartment for a long moment. "I hated the man, but I didn't kill him," Grayson insisted. "I wouldn't do that."

"But you threatened him," Doro pointed out.

Grayson's dark brows rose. "What are you talking about?"

"In the station, you said he was a problem that needed to be solved, and you knew how to do it," Doro replied.

He shrugged. "I said that to get a rise out of him. Mathers thought he was smarter than everyone else. A self-identified scientific genius. The man was intelligent, but not as sharp as some of his students, which he didn't like."

"Students like you," Aggie suggested.

A smile touched Grayson's firm lips. "I don't like to brag, but I've always grasped tough material quickly. That annoyed Mathers. However, I only took one course from him. As a transient student, I could've enrolled in several others, but he's not a good teacher, and he wasn't up-to-date, either."

"Your attention to his wife annoyed him, too." The comment was out before Doro considered the wisdom of voicing it, but Grayson's reaction provided more food for thought.

"I knew her before he did." Gray fingered the rim of his cup. "I met Luann at her family home when I first came to Colorado Springs as an undergraduate. She was seventeen, and I was eighteen. Her father often invited students for dinner. I took several classes with him as a transient. After a time, Luann and I began stepping out."

"You two were seriously courting?" Doro asked.

A bleak expression blanketed his handsome face. "We hadn't gotten that far. We were young, and I hadn't completed my studies."

As Doro studied Grayson's expression, she noted bittersweet longing. Had it been one-sided? Had Luann preferred the older, richer man? Rather than asking, she made an observation. "Luann chose Professor Mathers, though."

Gray released a humorless laugh. "No choice involved. When his health deteriorated, Dr. Truman told me Mathers promised to look out for Luann, but I know he didn't expect them to marry."

For a moment, Doro mulled over the comment. "Did Dr. Truman think Mathers would take Luann as his ward?" Her father had hinted at the possibility, but Grayson might know.

Grayson nodded. "At the wake, Luann told me Mathers was handling her father's affairs and looking out for her." His jaw tightened. "Looking out for himself is more to the point."

"How long after Dr. Truman's death did Luann and Mathers marry?" Aggie inquired.

He gritted his teeth until a muscle in his jaw twitched. "Four months. Everyone who knew either of them was shocked, and many were appalled."

"You were one of the latter," Doro said with certainty.

"I was both." Grayson drove his fingers through his hair. "Luann and I spoke before I went home for the holidays. We agreed about waiting to court until the mourning period for her father ended. I was only away for two weeks. Fourteen days. When I got back, she had married Mathers."

The anguish in his voice touched Doro, but it also added to his motive. "How did you find out?"

His jaw tightened. "I stopped at my dormitory to drop off my valise and freshen up. My housemother insisted I sit down for a cup of tea." He shook his head as if in disbelief at what had happened. "She knew Luann and I had stepped out before her father died. He invited me to their house many times, at first, because I was so far from home. Later, Luann invited me, with Dr. Truman's blessing." A note of bittersweet longing roughened his voice.

"He approved of you courting his daughter," Doro suggested.

"He did. Luann and I wouldn't have married until I completed my master's degree, because I wanted to have a job teaching first." A rueful smile touched his lips. "Luann didn't want to wait, but she'd never scrimped, and I wanted to provide well for her. A pleasant home with a yard, not a small room in a boardinghouse. That's where I live now."

Sincerity and anguish rang in his voice and, although Doro still saw Gray as a suspect, she felt sorry for him. And for Luann. Did he realize his words could be used against him? "Luann is free to remarry," she pointed out.

Grayson's jaw dropped. "You think I'd kill her husband to free her?"

Doro considered how to respond. Was Grayson a talented actor, or was he sincerely shocked by the suggestion? A second denial might indicate honesty—or not. "Possibly."

Anger flashed in his eyes. "I didn't, and I wouldn't. Mathers was too old for Luann. He cut her off from young people, refused to let her attend college, and expected her to be the perfect hostess. She called herself a bird in a gilded cage—pampered, admired, but not free. But I wouldn't make her life worse by killing the man."

An image of Luann Truman Mathers rose in Doro's mind. The young woman's clothes, although old-fashioned in style, were expensive. And she wore costly, ornate jewelry. The clothing and jewelry were likely chosen by Mathers. "Most college professors make comfortable livings, but they don't keep themselves or their families in the most luxurious attire. Professor and Mrs. Mathers seem to be an exception."

"He inherited a large sum from an uncle, along with the mansion near the Broadmoor Hotel," Gray replied.

A mental image of the home came to Doro, who had not given much thought to how a professor afforded such a grand residence. Knowing Mathers had not earned his fortune added insight into his character—or lack thereof. "As my grandmother said, Luann entertained us several times. It's an impressive home in a wealthy neighborhood. Maybe Luann wanted to live in luxury."

"She certainly was in that house," her grandmother added. "We have nothing so majestic in Sylvania, and the Mathers' place looked to be one of the most expensive in its neighborhood."

Grayson nodded. "I was in that home when I took the course with Mathers. The place is enormous with all the latest conveniences, but dreary. The Truman home was smaller, although not tiny by any means. There was light and liveliness there. Luann kept up her mother's garden. In the summer, every room had vases of flowers. Sunlight poured in during all four seasons.

That's the kind of home I wanted to give her. One where she would flourish." His bittersweet tone accentuated his words.

"The Mathers' mansion was filled with a lot of heavy, elaborate furnishings and accessories," Aggie agreed.

"It had a weighty atmosphere. I noticed that on every visit," Doro observed.

He narrowed his gaze at Doro. "If you saw Luann on more than one occasion, you must've seen how downtrodden she is."

"I saw her several times over the summer. Twice early, and another few more recently, but I'm not sure downtrodden is the right word." Spiritless seemed more descriptive to Doro. And the girl had been nervous after the unidentified figure flitted away. Why?

"Did she act happy and lighthearted to you?" Bailey asked in an accusatory tone.

Doro shook her head. "Not really, but—as my grandmother said—Luann acted shy."

"You didn't see the real Luann. She's funny and feisty." Admiration and something more glowed in his eyes.

Uneasiness crept through Doro. Far too many men treated their wives like children, especially when there was a large age difference. "Perhaps, she would be more animated in less formal settings. Mother invited her for lunch three or four times this summer, and Luann reciprocated with a tea and luncheons. We chatted, of course, but I didn't really get to know her." Not even when Doro had gone alone was Luann carefree and open.

Grayson's lips flattened. "Mathers wouldn't allow anyone to spend much time with her. Your father is a colleague, which is why Luann gets to socialize with your mother. Although even that is limited. Mostly, the professor and Luann entertain his associates—from both Colorado College and Pikeley—and their wives together. She rarely goes out alone."

"And yet you know about her activities," Aggie observed.

Color bloomed in his lean cheeks. "For a while, Luann could attend lectures at the college libraries, and I ran into her a few times. Since the two schools are close to one another, students and others attend meetings at both institutions. When we crossed paths, we only spoke in passing." A defensive note was in his voice.

Doro wondered what the pair had said, but doubted Grayson would reveal details. "How long has it been since you've seen her?"

"Four months," he replied in a glum tone.

If that was true, Grayson Bailey had not been the man Doro had seen in mid-June. But would he admit to visiting the house? Doubtful.

"And you've had no communication during that time?" Gramma Rose asked.

Silently, Doro blessed the older woman, who had a warm way of making inquiries—a talent that Doro sometimes lacked.

A long moment passed before Grayson responded. "A mutual friend passed notes for us. He's still a student of Mathers and was invited to their home on a regular basis."

"I see," Doro murmured. "What does he look like?"

Bailey frowned. "Why do you need to know?"

Although his tone had a caustic edge, Doro explained herself. "I visited with Luann one day in June. She went into the house for something while I waited in the garden. A short time later,

I saw a young man leaving from the library side of the house. Luann didn't mention having a visitor when she returned, so I wondered who he was." Doro described the fellow.

Bailey massaged his temples, as if warding off a headache. "It had to be Xavier Connors. He saw Luann often, since he's been invited, along with other graduate students, to meals at Mathers' house. After Luann stopped coming to the library programs, I asked Xavier if she was all right. I was afraid she'd fallen ill. That was in May, so he checked on her."

"I see. What did Mr. Connors tell you?" Doro asked.

Gray's jaw tightened. "That Mathers forbid her to go to any more events. Or any place alone. Either he or one of the maids goes with her now. Went with her, that is. Evidently, he'd heard she and I sat together a few times."

"Did Luann reveal that to your friend?" Gramma Rose inquired.

Gray nodded. "He was seated next to her at dinner twice, so they chatted. She said little else, but Xavier saw how unhappy she looked. And she wanted to know about me. How I was, and so on."

Despite keeping Gray as a suspect, Doro felt sympathy for the young couple. Not that they were still a couple. How could they be when Luann had been married for nearly three years? "Your friend shared all this recently?"

"He wrote to me back in late June, probably following his last visit, which you saw."

Another memory came to Doro's mind. "The professor told us that papers had come up missing from his library. Would your friend or other students have been responsible?"

Bailey snorted derisively. "No one stole from him, so he made that up, like he did a lot of things." He paused briefly before continuing. "Mathers being on this train was pure happenstance. Bad happenstance, but I definitely didn't plan to be going home again so soon. Although Pa has been in poor health for more than a year, no one expected him to pass right off."

Since Doro had been wondering if Grayson followed Mathers to kill him, she felt a stab of guilt. "It is unfortunate, especially since you didn't need an ugly confrontation with him while you're grieving."

"No, I didn't." A humorless laugh escaped him. "The truth is, Xavier told me Mathers was going out of town. I planned to see Luann while he was gone. Xavier was willing to help us meet."

His assertion seemed sensible, but Doro wasn't dropping him as a suspect. Many crimes were not pre-planned, which could be true in this case. "You'll be able to see her when you return to Colorado Springs."

"But she could use support right now, and I'm not there for her. No one is. The staff treats her poorly, as you noted, and I'm guessing Mathers' lawyer will bully her, too." He drove his fingers through his hair. "I'd go back to the Springs from the next station, but Ma and my sisters need me, too. Of course, who knows how long we'll be stuck here?"

"Help will be on the way soon," Gramma Rose said.

"It will," Doro added, "but I wouldn't worry about anyone taking advantage of Luann. Word won't reach Colorado Springs about Professor Mathers' murder until after we're rescued."

"You're right. I hadn't considered that," Gray admitted. "I don't suppose you'll give up the idea of me being the killer, even with my alibi."

While Doro could check on how long Gray and his friend had been in the club car, she had no way of knowing if he had left their compartment later. Due to that fact, she refrained from a direct response. "I'm not a lawman."

His mouth quirked. "Your father told his students about you being an amateur sleuth and a mystery fan, so everyone at Colorado College knows. He said you've solved cases in your hometown."

Since the topic had arisen already, Doro grinned in return. "Four, actually."

A chuckle left Aggie. "One wasn't a serious crime."

Gramma Rose clucked her tongue. "It was serious for you and your future."

"It was," Aggie agreed before summarizing the case for Gray.

"Impressive," he replied. "So, even though you two don't have the law behind you, you're looking into this case. I hope you'll keep digging, because I'll likely be a top suspect to whatever copper shows up."

Disagreeing with his supposition was impossible, because Grayson Bailey was a prime suspect. Doro made another observation. "Passengers are nervous. I'd like to reassure them about their safety. Whatever I learn will be shared with the police and railroad security."

"Good." Gray finished one scone and picked up another. "These are great."

Was regaining his appetite a sign of guilt or innocence? Doro wished she knew. "My parents' housekeeper made them. She packed a picnic basket for us. We ate the sandwiches and fruit yesterday, so we only have scones left. But she put a dozen in."

After a swallow of tea, Gray replied. "This is wonderful. I was starving."

"Young men usually are," Gramma Rose observed.

"Yes, ma'am," he said. "My ma says the same."

The comment reminded Doro of the loss faced by Gray's family. She hoped he was not the murderer, but letting sympathy get the better of her was impermissible. "Where is your friend Phineas?"

"Still sleeping when I left. He drank...er, that is, he was more tired than me," Gray said. "But he stayed later in the club car."

The slight slip revealed what Doro had surmised: the young men had consumed illegal liquor. Although booze had been outlawed for nearly a decade, drinking did not rank with murder as a crime. Not even close. "You two seem to be good friends."

"Real close," Gray agreed. "We often travel to-and-from the Springs together, so we've gotten well-acquainted. We've attended the same school for three years, so Phineas and I cross paths often."

"He also knows Professor Mathers," Aggie commented, "and vice-versa, since the professor threatened to interfere with Phineas' thesis being accepted. How could he do such a thing?"

Gray stared into his empty coffee cup. "A lot of students and professors at our school and Pikeley are acquainted, and Phin was a student there for two years."

Since his reply did not address the question, Doro tried another one. "What influence would Mathers have at Colorado College?" When Gray did not answer, she considered possibilities. One jumped to mind. "On rare occasions, I've heard of graduate students being accused of stealing work from others. Even if it's not proven, that can end with a thesis being rejected."

Gray's jaw tightened. "It doesn't happen only to graduate students. Undergraduates can be victims, too."

"You know of cases?" Aggie made the query.

He shrugged. "I've heard gossip. Some from Phin."

Doro glanced from Gramma Rose to Aggie before returning her attention to their guest. "Do you know why he transferred?"

Several seconds passed before Gray looked up. "He wasn't doing as well as his father expected, and they thought a change would help. Since Phineas finished his undergraduate program with honors, and he's gotten all *A's* in graduate school, it turns out they were right."

"You mentioned taking a course from the professor. Did you meet Custis Oscar?" Doro inquired.

Recognition flashed in Gray's gaze before he focused on his teacup. "Was he a student at Pikeley?"

"He was," Aggie replied. "Clyde is his father."

"I see," Gray murmured, but he kept his eyes averted.

Doro exchanged a long look with her friend. Briefly, she debated the wisdom of hammering him with more questions. Since experience had proven that tactic to be futile, Doro made a casual query. "What course did you take with Mathers?"

"Botany. He was supposed to be a foremost authority. As it turns out, his knowledge was behind the times."

"Sometimes tenured faculty don't feel like they have to stay up-to-date," Aggie suggested.

Gray released a long breath. "Mathers would fall into that category."

"Wasn't he going to Chicago to present a paper?" Doro asked. "Surely, he wouldn't have been welcome with dated information."

A snort left Gray. "The paper would've been fresh, but it wouldn't have been based on his work."

Dismay flashed through Doro. "He was presenting another professor's research?"

"Nope. More likely, he stole work from one of his students. He was good at that," Gray replied.

Shock hit Doro hard and, when she looked from Gramma Rose to Aggie, she saw they were equally stunned. "That's what you meant when you said he lied about things."

"Exactly," Gray Bailey said.

"That's a harsh accusation," Doro remarked.

"But it's true, and he did it more than once. Not that he ever got called out for it. Still, plenty of gossip goes around whenever he publishes something, which is less and less often," Gray said.

"If people suspect him of academic dishonesty, why was he welcome in Chicago?" Aggie asked.

"The conference is at a small school, where one of his old friends is the president. The man may not believe Mathers is a cheat. I don't know, but he hasn't presented many papers in the last few years, which should tell you something."

The news told Doro gossip has spread, gossip that probably had roots in facts. "I see," she murmured. "Didn't students complain?"

Gray grimaced. "Sure, but the professor was ready for them. He accused several of plagiarism or cheating on examinations before they had a chance to accuse him. That's hard for a student to refute."

Once again, Doro was taken aback. Professor Mathers' behavior was beyond unprofessional. It was appalling. "Did you know any of the students involved?"

"When I took the course at Pikeley, others warned me about Mathers' behavior, so I didn't take another one." After finishing the scone, he stood up. "Now, if you don't have more questions for me, I'd like to get some rest. I appreciate the hospitality."

Since Gray had provided fuel for continuing the investigation, Doro nodded. After she and Aggie gathered more information, they could talk to him again.

"Please stop by anytime, and bring your friend," Gramma Rose said.

"Thank you." Gray nodded to the young women and hurried out.

When the door clicked shut behind him, Doro sighed. "He offered some interesting details."

"He certainly did," Aggie agreed. "I'd like to know more about Mathers stealing work from students."

"So would I," Doro said.

Gramma Rose nodded. "That's a terrible thing to do. Surely, it isn't common."

"Not at all," Doro assured her. "In fact, I've never heard of a case."

"Even though I haven't, either, it isn't hard to imagine Professor Mathers engaging in such conduct. The man exuded arrogance," Aggie said. "What Gray told us makes me wonder if something happened when Phineas was his student."

Doro pondered the idea for a moment. "Would a freshman or sophomore do research worth publishing or presenting?"

"That's a good question, but Gray didn't want to provide details about exactly why Phineas transferred," Aggie said.

"He certainly didn't," her grandmother agreed. "Getting poor grades is a reason, but why would a student believe he'd do better elsewhere?"

"He wouldn't, unless something personal happened," Doro put in.

Aggie steepled her hands and rested her chin on them. "Phineas was angry with Mathers last night. Very angry."

"He was, and Gray's remarks about students being wrongly accused of cheating are cause for concern, especially since Professor Mathers threatened Phineas." Doro drummed her fingers on the table. "I'm just not sure how he'd influence faculty at another school."

"Me, either," Aggie agreed. "And I wondered about Gray's reference to undergraduates being accused of cheating. When Phineas attended Pikeley, he might've been in one of Mathers' classes. Maybe they locked horns then."

"That's possible," Doro said, "and it would explain why Phineas changed schools."

"It certainly would," her grandmother agreed.

"I'd like to talk with Phineas, but running into him at lunchtime would be less aggressive than seeking him out," Doro observed.

"A good idea. There's no sense in putting him on the defensive before we ask the first question," Aggie added.

Gramma Rose smiled. "You girls are good at sleuthing. Did you learn anything important after I left the dining car?"

Doro summarized the exchanges with Andre, Joshua, and Clyde. "What do you think, Gram?"

The older woman folded her hands in her lap. "The chef must be nicer than I originally figured. At least, he has a concern for his family, and that sounds like a reason to work for the railroad instead of a restaurant or hotel."

"I'd say so," Doro agreed.

"Are you moving him down the suspect list?" Aggie asked.

"I think that's wise. What about the two of you?" Doro looked from her best friend to her grandmother. Both agreed. Another concern rose in her mind. "What about discussing the case in front of Mrs. O'Brien? We've learned a lot from her, and she seems interested in solving the murder. I'm just not sure how much more we should share."

Aggie's lips turned down. "She helped us obtain details. If we learn something big, we don't have to tell her right off, and we can ask her to keep mum, if we do."

"I agree," Gramma Rose put in. "The woman acts genuinely concerned. She isn't gossipy, and she knows some of the crew, which makes them more open to answering questions when she's around. She might even get the conductor on your side."

For several moments, Doro considered the observations. "All right. We can talk about the case, in general, and share some bits and pieces. We might also include her in chats with the crew." She turned to her grandmother. "Will you point out how important it is to be circumspect? She might take the warning better from someone closer to her age."

A chuckle left Gramma Rose. "Mrs. O'Brien has a few years on me, but we old ladies have to stick together."

Doro immediately protested. "I didn't mean you're old."

"But I am, my dear. I am."

Chapter Seven

When Mrs. O'Brien and Mr. Sayers returned, he placed her bags on the extra bed. "It's a good idea for all of you to stick together," the conductor said. His attention riveted on Doro. "Keeping passengers safe is my top priority."

The veiled warning was not lost on Doro, who gathered her composure before responding. "That's good to know."

Although Sayers looked as if he wanted to issue another warning, he nodded. "More rain is coming, but it shouldn't delay the repair crew's arrival."

"Are they coming from Colorado Springs or Dodge City?" Gramma Rose asked.

"I'm not sure, ma'am," he replied. "Now, if you'll excuse me, I want to check on—uh—the professor and grab some food."

After the door closed behind Sayers, Rose gestured to the seat beside her. "Make yourself comfortable, Mrs. O'Brien. Do you enjoy whist?"

"I do," the other woman replied.

Before her grandmother asked the two girls to join the game, Doro suggested a walk through the train. Her friend readily agreed. As soon as they left the compartment, Doro paused. "We're lucky Mrs. O'Brien joined us. Although I don't mind playing whist occasionally, I don't want to spend all afternoon doing it."

"Me, either," Aggie said with a grin. "Your grandmother looked like she wanted to issue another warning, but thought better of it. Probably because she didn't want Mrs. O'Brien more upset."

"Probably so," Doro agreed. "The dining car, with its small kitchen, is the only one ahead of us. Then, there are only three more cars after this one: the regular compartment, the crew sleeping car, and the caboose, so we could amble along and see what's happening. Mr. Sayers was headed the opposite way, so we should have a little time."

A grin tugged at the corner of Aggie's mouth. "To ask questions."

"If we cross paths with people, I'm sure we'll chat." Doro could not keep a lilt of humor from her voice. Aggie knew her well. A walk was never just a walk when a crime had occurred.

"I'm sure we will," Aggie agreed with a trace of asperity.

The friends went through the rest of their car without seeing anyone. When they exited, both looked out the gangway window. Rain made it impossible to see very far. "Mr. Sayers didn't think the repairmen would be delayed, but I wonder if that's wishful thinking."

"Even if they arrive in a timely manner, they can't replace the coupler in this downpour," Aggie observed.

"No, they can't. But let's go on, so we don't run into Sayers while we're out-and-about."

The next carriage also contained compartments. As they passed the doors, the two friends heard voices but nothing related to the murder. Since the sleeper car for crew members followed, they moved along quietly. The waiters had planned to get much needed rest, so the friends continued to the caboose, which was empty.

"I don't think we should snoop in there," Aggie said as soon as Doro opened the door. "It's private. The sign says so."

Doro rolled her eyes. "The men are a few cars away and outside, so this is our best chance to see if there's any evidence here. Since the conductor's desk is right there, I'd like to take a quick peek." She gestured to the battered oak desk in the near corner.

"All right, but hurry."

While her friend waited in the gangway, Doro rushed to search the drawers. Most were filled with detritus. After a last study of the caboose, she rejoined Aggie. "Nothing of interest."

"Let's get out of here before someone catches us," Aggie said.

After a last perusal of the area, Doro followed Aggie across the gangway, through the crew's sleeper car, and back to their drawing room. Both young women were breathless by the time they stopped at the door. Before either spoke, Phineas entered from the opposite end. Dismay flashed across his face. Then, he smiled. "Good day, ladies."

"Hello," Aggie replied.

The young man's initial reaction to seeing them provoked curiosity in Doro. "We missed you at breakfast."

Phineas' smile wavered as he rocked back on his heels and shoved his hands into his pockets. "I had a late night."

"So, we heard from your friend." Doro scrutinized Phineas.

He cleared his throat. "Gray mentioned running into you two and being invited for tea and scones. I could use something myself, since lunch is two hours away."

"We have a couple of scones left," Aggie replied, "and a hot pot to make tea."

"Sounds great," he replied, but his grin still did not match his gaze.

"Come along, and we'll see you get fed." Doro tapped on the door and called out to her grandmother. "We have more company."

Gramma Rose answered with, "Come in, come in." She introduced Mrs. O'Brien to the young man.

"Nice to meet you, ma'am," Phineas said.

The elderly widow returned the greeting with a smile. "It's my pleasure."

After preparing a light snack and handing it to their guest, Doro and Aggie sat at the table while Gramma Rose and Mrs. O'Brien remained on the divan. "Sit down, young man," the latter gestured to the seat across from them.

Phineas hesitated a moment before accepting her offer. "Sorry to bother you, ladies." He took a bite of scone, followed by a swallow of tea.

"It's no bother," Gramma Rose assured him.

"Not at all," the elderly widow agreed. She waved one hand around the compartment. "I'm a guest here, too, but for the rest of the ride. Or at least until the murderer is found." She folded and unfolded her hands. "I'm a tad nervous, but I feel better not being alone."

Phineas laid what was left of his scone on the saucer before draining his cup. "I see."

The banal response seemed odd. "You've heard about Professor Mathers." Doro voiced a statement, not a question.

Phineas blinked as if something was in his eyes. "Gray told me when he came back to our compartment."

His lack of reaction, no surprise or dismay, bothered Doro. "We heard you were one of the professor's students as an undergraduate, but you left Pikeley after a couple of years."

He licked his lips. "I did. Pikeley is an excellent school, although not as well-known or respected as Colorado College. Transferring was a wise decision."

"I'm sure that's true," Aggie put in, "but it's unusual to transfer from one school to another in the same area. Did you change majors?"

Her friend's astute observation pleased, but did not surprise, Doro. Although Aggie was often reserved, she was intelligent and intuitive, and her unassuming manner lowered people's barriers. Would it work with Phineas?

After a moment, he shrugged. "I kept majoring in science, but the professors at Colorado have a different slant. It's a better place for me."

His explanation, which seemed strange, also confirmed that Phineas must have studied with Mathers. But what sort of different slant would anyone have on science? "Aggie and I both went to Michaw College, which is where we work. It's a fine school for us, as students and as professors," Doro said.

Phineas' taut expression relaxed. "I was in two of your father's classes as an undergraduate. He mentioned Michaw a few times and both of you."

Doro grinned. "He loved teaching there, and so do we."

"I hope to find a school that suits me as well. Being a professor is my dream." Phin ran his fingers through his hair. "If Gray and I can be in the same place, we'd be ecstatic. If we can earn doctorates, we'd have more options. But Gray can't afford that, and my father won't pay, so I can't, either."

"Professors having doctorates is becoming more and more common," Doro put in, "but neither Aggie nor I have them. Only a handful of our colleagues do, so you might aim to teach at a smaller school."

The young man nodded. "We will."

"Working with your best friend is wonderful," Aggie put in with a smile. "We're fortunate, and I hope you and Mr. Bailey will be, too."

"We planned to try, but now, I don't know. Gray may be set on staying in Colorado Springs," the young man said.

"Because Mrs. Mathers is now a widow," Gramma Rose said.

Her grandmother's blunt statement did not surprise Doro, but Phineas blanched.

"I...that is, I don't know why I said that. I shouldn't have." Phineas stared into his cup. "He didn't kill Mathers, if that's what you're thinking. And neither did I, for that matter. Neither of us liked the man, but a hundred others could say the same. Maybe a thousand others. Some people respected him, mostly due to his position and wealth. Many more knew what he really was."

"What was that?" Gramma Rose's voice was gentle and cajoling.

The young man's jaw tightened. "An overbearing, arrogant, dishonest boor." Phineas' glance traveled around the group. "Most of his scholarship and most of his writing were based on the work of his students. Some say it was different when he was younger. I don't know. I only know it wasn't that way when I took his classes, and it isn't now." He shifted to the edge of his chair, as if he was ready to rise.

With only a few minutes in the station, Doro's father had not revealed his opinion of Professor Mathers, although his attitude had been civil, not effusive. But the allegations of stealing students' work troubled her. Could it connect to the murder? Gray Bailey had an emotional motive. Did Phineas have an academic one? Unsure, Doro went on to other matters. "What time did you and Gray leave the club car?" As soon as the question was out, she cringed at the lack of transition. But Phineas was about to bolt, and Doro wanted to see if he would confirm his friend's responses.

"Late," the young man replied.

The terse answer increased Doro's skepticism. Why not be specific? To cover up the crime? Or because he'd been intoxicated and did not recall?

Gramma Rose chuckled. "Young Mr. Bailey admitted to imbibing, but that hardly comes as a shock. There are a fair number of bootleggers in our area, which is probably true in many places. It's not stunning that young fellas like yourselves would have a few drinks while gambling."

Color suffused his rounded cheeks. "My father doesn't approve of consuming alcohol, now that it's illegal. He poured his supply out as soon as the Volstead Act passed."

"People could drink what they had," Aggie put in. "The law didn't prohibit that."

"Father is an attorney, and he's interested in running for office. As his son, I have to be on the straight and narrow." Phineas bit off the words like each one tasted bitter.

"What does he think about you wanting to be a professor?" Doro asked.

A guffaw left Phineas. "He's still pressuring me to go to law school, but I love science." His expression grew forlorn. "If I don't get a position right after graduation, he'll cut off all financial assistance unless I follow in his footsteps."

"I'm sure you'll find a job," Aggie said.

"I hope so." Phineas stood up. "Gray will wonder where I am. Thank you for the tea and scone."

The women barely got their farewells out before he was gone. When the door closed behind Phineas, Doro slumped back into her chair. "I wanted to ask more questions, especially about Custis, but working them in was difficult."

"Phineas' conversation was fairly superficial, and he seemed hesitant to say a lot," Aggie observed. "Maybe admitting he consumed booze was the reason, but I wouldn't eliminate him as a suspect."

Since her friend's observation mirrored Doro's impression, she nodded. "What about you, Gram? What do you think?"

The older woman tapped the book on her lap. "I don't disagree with anything either of you have said. Phineas evidently relies on family money for his living expenses, which increases his dependency. For a young man his age, that has to be difficult. Most of his peers are already working."

"Hmm," Doro murmured. "I hadn't thought of it that way, but you're right. Gray told us Phineas paid for their compartment, since his family is well-to-do."

"That was kind," Mrs. O'Brien observed.

"It was, but I wonder if he often helps his friends that way," Aggie said. "He acts rather unsure of himself. Like wondering if he can find a teaching position. He must be a decent student, or wouldn't be in a master's program."

"Or consider a doctorate," Gramma Rose said.

Doro clasped her hands. "That's true. What bothers me most is the talk about Mathers using his students' work and passing it off as his own. I'd have been furious if that had happened to me."

"Me, too," Aggie agreed. "It seems like Mathers hid his academic dishonesty by accusing his students of being the plagiarizers, which would be even more aggravating."

"Both Gray and Phineas hinted at or stated that idea," Doro added. "If Phineas was accused, his father would be angry."

Aggie nodded. "Last evening, it sounded like Mathers wanted to interfere with Phineas' thesis. What if the professor planned to say the thesis was based on stolen work?"

For several moments, Doro considered the idea. "Even an accusation could cause trouble for Phineas. From the way he spoke, his father might use any excuse to get him into law school."

Gramma Rose pursed her lips. "Could he be admitted with a plagiarism accusation hanging over his head?"

"An excellent point, because it could be an impediment." Doro grinned. "I'm glad we have you working with us."

Her grandmother beamed. "It's intriguing to discuss clues and suspects. Even better than reading a mystery."

"I agree," Mrs. O'Brien added. "In light of what young Phineas said, I wonder about what happened to Custis, who was smart as a whip. When he was at our house, he mentioned doing extra research before he lost his scholarship. Seemed odd he'd lose out when he'd been chosen to take on special assignments."

The observation put a knot in Doro's stomach. "Somehow, we have to find out why he lost the grant."

"Asking Phineas outright isn't likely to work," Aggie suggested.

"No, it won't. He'd clam up completely," Doro said.

"Just like in mystery books," the widow observed.

"Do you enjoy reading whodunits?" Aggie asked.

Mrs. O'Brien nodded. "Oh, my, yes. My husband enjoyed Sherlock Holmes, and he picked up many of those books in his travels. When he was away, I spent all my free time reading. Now, I'm working on Agatha Christie's mysteries. Such good stories."

"We love her work, too," Doro said.

"Doro teaches a course on mystery novels," Aggie said. "Students enjoy it tremendously."

Mrs. O'Brien clasped her hands together. "I can imagine. No wonder you girls have become detectives."

"I only read the books and help Doro," Aggie said. "She's the real sleuth."

"Aggie teaches and writes poetry," Gramma Rose added. "Both of them are accomplished young ladies."

"Sharing wonderful mystery books with students is a joy. I always include at least one I haven't read myself, so we can solve it together," Doro told the widow.

"Working through clues keeps the mind sharp," Mrs. O'Brien said. "I suppose it's even more challenging with real life mysteries."

"It is. Although I'm always sorry when there's a crime, solving them is satisfying," Doro put in.

A frown accentuated the wrinkles on Mrs. O'Brien's forehead. "It's a shame Mr. Sayers doesn't support you investigating. But he's right about keeping passengers safe."

"He is," Gramma Rose said before looking straight at Doro. "You invited Phineas to join us for a reason."

Doro cleared her throat. "He missed breakfast."

Gramma Rose rolled her eyes, as a snort of laughter escaped Aggie. Meanwhile, Mrs. O'Brien peered at Doro over her spectacles. "You asked some pointed questions."

Clearly, Doro was not kidding any of these women. The invitation to Phineas had stemmed from wanting a whack at questioning him. "It doesn't hurt to ask."

"I hope not," the widow said in a worried tone. "But I feel like I've missed some things."

After explaining the one-time relationship between Luann Mathers and Grayson Bailey, Doro followed with her opinion.

"Gray has a solid motive, and Phineas might, too. We don't have enough details about him."

"His anger must stem from his freshman and sophomore years at Pikeley," Gramma Rose suggested.

Aggie nodded. "That seems likely."

After a moment, Doro made another observation. "It's such a small school that he had to know Custis."

"I'm racking my brain for any mention of a Phineas or a Spieth. Custis never brought a friend with him to visit us, and we usually talked about his father and other railroaders. I wish I could help," Mrs. O'Brien said.

"Maybe something will come to you later," Aggie said.

The elderly widow sighed. "I hope so, my dear."

After fetching her notebook and pencil, Doro jotted a few notes. Since Mrs. O'Brien was proving to be an asset, Doro decided the woman's perspective might prove even more useful. "Even though the conductor doesn't want us asking a lot of questions, we could discuss the case. Sort of like if we were all reading the same book." She hoped the idea sounded benign, because she was dying to go over her ideas.

"That wouldn't hurt anything." Mrs. O'Brien smiled. "In fact, I'd like to hear how you girls approach a case."

Although Gramma Rose looked more skeptical, she nodded. "Just talking is safe."

The caveat was clear, so Doro began with the simplest facts. "Phineas, Gray, Clyde, and Chef Andre all have long-term resentment toward the professor."

"In addition, all four of them had altercations with Mathers last night," Aggie said. "The professor berated Joshua, who didn't talk back."

"The young waiter might harbor antipathy, since he had no outward reaction to the professor's ranting," Gramma Rose pointed out. "Not that I want to believe such a nice young man is a killer."

Doro rolled the pencil between her hands. "That's a good assessment, and I don't want to believe it, either."

"I can't believe he'd harm anyone myself," Mrs. O'Brien murmured. "But I don't always figure out who committed crimes in books."

"I doubt if any of us do," Gramma Rose added.

Laughter left Aggie. "Doro does."

"Not always," Doro insisted, but her friend was right. She almost always figured out whodunit before the end of a book.

Aggie shrugged. "To get back to this situation, I agree with all of you. Unfortunately, Doro and I have learned that sometimes people act out of character."

"Just like in a book," the elderly widow said. "I've never been sure if authors stick to facts or embellish."

Thinking of her own novel, Doro offered insight. "Most writers aim to be as accurate as possible with details. If a character acts oddly, he or she needs a powerful reason. Of course, that's often somewhat murky to readers."

"But hints are given," the widow said.

A grin lit Aggie's face. "Subtle hints are best, since I like a challenge."

Gramma Rose's blue eyes sparkled. "I'm no amateur detective, but I love solving mysteries in books. A mix of subtle hints and stronger ones is helpful to me."

Because her grandmother was, like Doro, an avid fan of whodunits, Rose McLaren was well aware of how cases were solved. Fiction did not always align with reality, but it came close. "You're sharp, and I appreciate your contributions." Doro turned to Mrs. O'Brien. "We'll be happy to have your involvement, too."

"We will," Aggie said with a grin.

Gramma Rose chuckled as she focused on Doro. "You're a top-notch amateur sleuth, and Aggie is on par with you."

"Not really, but I help as I can," Aggie said.

Their praise lifted Doro's spirits, but the current case still had her puzzled. How she wanted to solve it before a lawman came on the scene. Mr. Sayers' lack of support galled her, but so did Dr. Cartwright's reluctant backing. "You're a big help. As for our suspects, I'd put Joshua down the list. We won't eliminate him, but he seems the least likely perpetrator to me."

"To me, too," Aggie said. "We definitely need more details. Talking with Grayson Bailey emphasized the close connection between him and Luann Mathers. A thwarted romance is a powerful motive."

"And Gray was furious with Mathers," Doro said. "Phineas was, too. We can assume it relates to when he was a student of Mathers, but we need details."

"Do you believe the professor used Phineas' work as his own? Would a freshman or sophomore have a report or research worth stealing?" Gramma Rose asked.

"It's possible, but not probable," Doro replied. "At least not in my experience."

"I agree," Aggie said. "The professor would be more likely to steal from a senior or graduate student. However, Phineas was irate, so there's something we don't know."

"Gray mentioned Phineas getting lower grades at Pikeley. If they were from Mathers, that could be a motive. Especially since Mr. Spieth expects excellence from his son," Gramma Rose put in.

Doro rolled her pencils between her palms. "Phineas might've lost his allowance for a while as a result. Something else we'd need to find out." For a moment, she studied her notes. "I'd sure like to eliminate another suspect."

"That'd be useful. Right now, we have five." Aggie provided the list. "Phineas, Grayson, and Clyde would be my top choices, with Chef Andre and Joshua being down the list."

Gramma Rose and Mrs. O'Brien agreed, and so did Doro before continuing with her ideas on getting more information. "We didn't find anything in the caboose, but we might if we search the kitchen."

Her grandmother frowned. "You went in the caboose?"

The question made Doro hurry to cover up. "Only me, and only for a few minutes. Aggie stood lookout. We weren't in any peril."

The older woman studied the two younger ladies. "Why do I think you've downplayed the danger in your previous investigations?"

After exchanging a look with her best friend, Doro forced a smile. "I wouldn't say we were in danger." She would not admit they had been. "Even with the lost exam, Aggie and I had help. Lately, Wade and Ev have been involved." Her comments were subterfuge, not reality, especially in regard to their last investigation.

"That's right," Aggie agreed.

"Your young men were out of action during most of the May case," Rose observed, studying the two friends. "That left you two on your own."

The first statement needed correction, and the second required refutation. "Ev isn't my young man, and both he and Wade provided help during the case," Doro said. Her grandmother didn't need to know the lawmen had been too sick to lend physical aid.

"Are your young men are with the police?" Mrs. O'Brien asked with avid interest.

After explaining their exact jobs, Doro reiterated her relationship—or lack thereof—with Ev. "The security officer and I share ownership of a puppy."

A snort left Gramma Rose, while the other older lady looked pensive before making an observation. "My husband and I grew up on the same block. I always maintained we were just neighbors, but I was sweet on him as far back as I remember. He took a little longer to be interested in me."

Aggie grinned. "Sometimes, it's the girl who takes longer to figure things out."

Heat scorched Doro's cheeks as she struggled for something to say that would end the speculation. She was still thinking when her friend spoke.

Aggie supported part of Doro's response. "We talked to them as soon as they were able. Of course, they made the arrest."

Gramma Rose's expression grew contemplative. "I won't pose direct queries because when the constable dropped you off at my house, he was careful in how he answered my questions about the case. I doubt if either of you will admit as much."

Aggie bit her lower lip. "You didn't ask Wade many questions."

A knowing smile touched Rose McLaren's lips. "We chatted on the porch while you got lemonade and cookies."

Realization dawned on Aggie's face. "Oh."

Gramma Rose turned to Doro. "The constable mentioned you having Aggie call him when you were chasing after the poisoner. Alone."

Dismay knotted Doro's insides. After a moment, she regained control. Her grandmother had known only bits of the story about the culprit who had poisoned Wade and Ev. But Rose McLaren evidently possessed more bits than Doro knew. "You didn't mention that to Mother and Dad." It was a statement and a question.

"No, because they'd worry more than they do now," her grandmother replied.

"But you won't worry." Doro proposed the idea in a tentative tone.

A shrug moved her grandmother's narrow shoulders. "I fret, dear. About both of you, but Aggie is more circumspect, while you're adventurous. The balance makes you a fine team. And usually, you have your young men working with you."

Doro opened her mouth to object to the repeated use of the phrase *young men*, but Gramma Rose lifted one hand. "You're focused on becoming the head librarian and always have been. At next week's meeting, the trustees may vote to employ working wives. That would eliminate part of your hesitance to step out with Officer Mallow, wouldn't it?"

After her initial surprise at her grandmother's bold question, Doro turned to Aggie, who put both hands up. Clearly, her friend and her grandmother had discussed her friendship, such as it was, with Ev. "I'd like to focus on this case."

Her grandmother put her hand over her mouth, but a sound similar to a chuckle left her. "Of course, dear."

Mrs. O'Brien looked on with undisguised fascination. Luckily, she remained silent.

Although rattled, Doro studied her notes. Unfortunately, Ev's handsome face rose in her mind. With determination, she thrust all thoughts of him aside. "We've named the suspects, so let's discuss clues and challenges. Clyde insists his grudge with Mathers is none of our business. But we know something happened between them." She glanced at the widow. "He was upset when we asked."

The widow clasped her hands in her lap. "I'm not surprised. Losing Custis in that terrible accident devastated both Clyde and his wife. After their boy's funeral, Annabelle told me about Clyde feeling guilty for not providing better for his family. With more money, Custis could've continued his schooling, so his father is angry with the professor. But I don't have details."

"It's hard for students whose families aren't well-off," Aggie put in. "I couldn't have attended college without a scholarship."

Doro knew her friend was thinking about how she had nearly suffered the same fate as Custis. "I wish more young people had the opportunity to attend a university." She sighed. "I also wish we knew if Professor Mathers had anything to do with Custis losing his funding."

"I wish I could help more," Mrs. O'Brien said, "but I have no details."

"We understand," Aggie said. "Do you think other crewmen might?"

The widow scrunched her brow, as if in deep concentration. "Both the brakeman and the flagman, Mr. Rogers and Mr. Smithers, have been with the railroad for many years." She smiled. "They were kind enough to check on me, since they worked a number of runs with my husband. Anyhow, they've surely known Clyde a long time, so they might be able to help you."

After making a note, Doro thanked the woman. How would she question the two crewmen without Sayers knowing? She'd find a way. "Another point is Chef Andre stating he knows nothing about his waiters' personal matters. Does that ring true to you, Mrs. O'Brien? You said railroaders are close-knit. Would that extend to the chef?"

"Some are friendlier than others," the widow replied. "But everyone is acquainted, so I'd think he has some idea of what was between Clyde and the professor."

"Aggie and I will see about talking with the brakeman and flagman after lunch. With the utmost discretion."

"Very wise," Mrs. O'Brien said. "Although they aren't among your suspects, the murderer is apt to be watching the two of you."

"As I said, we'll be cautious." But she was not sure if she added the reassurance for the older women, or for herself. During past cases, the killer had not been stranded in a confined area with them. And, despite her earlier comments, Doro knew well that she and Aggie did not have Wade and Ev to help.

Chapter Eight

After further conversation, Doro and Aggie decided to pose casual questions at lunch. That strategy provided the additional benefit of Gramma Rose and Mrs. O'Brien observing the exchanges. Later, they could all talk again—if they gleaned information. Would they? And what about talking with the other passengers? How could she and Aggie query them on the sly?

A short time later, Doro led the way to the dining car. When the group arrived, only one table was occupied. "Let's sit close to the kitchen door," Doro suggested. She didn't need to say they could eavesdrop on the staff from that vantage point, but they could.

Gramma Rose sat on the window side, while Aggie and Doro took the aisle seats. Within moments, Joshua approached them.

"Good afternoon, ladies." His glum expression did not match the greeting. "I'm sorry that we still got a limited menu. Once we're underway again, it'll be back to normal."

With one hand, Rose McLaren gestured at the tabletop. "You've made the settings elegant, and I'm sure the offerings will be wonderful."

"Chef Andre insisted we follow our typical procedures." Joshua studied the table. "We got some clean linens left, but not many. Most are in the bigger dining car in the other part of the train. Of course, we can wash the dishes, silverware, and so forth. Starched tablecloths aren't as easy to come by, since we can't get to the main supply."

The young man's babbling about linens seemed useless to Doro. Was there a reason? Or was Joshua nervous? When she studied his expression, Doro noted his gaze darting around the car. Was he looking for someone? If so, who? Then and there, she resolved to remain at the table as long as possible. With so few cars stranded, needing to relinquish seats would not be an issue. Although many of the passengers in the cars ahead of them had eaten in the main dining car, some had been in this one the previous evening. None would be now. "The tables look elegant, and I'm sure that took a lot of work, along with everything else you have to do. Were you able to get a nap?"

Joshua's gaze went to Doro. "An hour. Chef Andre woke us up."

A harrumph interrupted, and Doro turned to Clyde, who was standing at the next table. His stern countenance added weight to his words. "Andre don't care about nobody beneath him. Just like the professor. So hoity-toity, but the old guy got his due."

A silent interlude followed. Although Mathers had been a lout, he did not deserve to be stabbed. What made the older waiter assert such a thing? Momentarily stymied, Doro held her tongue while resolving to find out why Clyde hated Mathers.

Luckily, Mrs. O'Brien stepped into the breach. "I missed last evening's arguments, but you've seen Professor Mathers before this trip, I guess. Was he traveling the line before my husband retired?"

When he focused on the widow, Clyde lost some of his anger. "Maybe so, but I don't know that Mr. O'Brien ever met the man. Of course, your husband was a great conductor. Everyone—passengers and crewmen—liked and respected him."

Mrs. O'Brien smiled. "How long had you and the professor been at odds?" the widow inquired in a conversational tone.

His expression hardened. "Not long, but he was a nasty piece of work. Plenty of folks will say the same."

The widow had made a narrow in-road. Now, Doro needed to press forward. "He was rude to you last night." Not that Clyde had not given as good as he got, but she was trying to be subtle.

"Sure, cuz I'm a lowly waiter. At the advanced age of forty-two, I oughta do better—according to him. But not much better. He don't believe in folks getting above themselves." Clyde bit each word off like bitter bits of lemon.

The waiter's assertions made little sense. "Did you talk with the professor about a different job?" Doro asked.

He looked at her with obvious skepticism. "Course not. I knowed him back when my boy..."

Joshua broke in. "We need to see to all these tables. I'll take care of the ladies."

For a moment, Clyde looked like he might object. Then, a flush rose in his cheeks. "Sure thing," he said before moving on.

Joshua took the orders and delivered them ten minutes later. While she ate, Doro took part in the casual conversation, but her mind whirled with possibilities. As with previous cases, clues and suspects were plentiful. But they did not have telling evidence, and there were too many suspects. Thinking back, the situation was nothing new. Investigations were usually rough at first. With determination, they could succeed before a lawman showed up. And that was Doro's goal.

***

After the meal, Doro followed the other three women back to the drawing room compartment. After they were all seated, her grandmother spoke. "Aren't you going to get your notes out and add what we learned?"

"We didn't find out much," Doro replied. Her spirits were sagging, due to fatigue and frustration. "Interviewing folks is next to impossible when the man in charge wants Aggie and me to behave like nice young women."

Both of the older ladies snorted with laughter. "You girls seem quite nice to me," Mrs. O'Brien observed. "But I understand what you mean."

"Look," Aggie said, pointing out the window. "There's someone coming on horseback."

Doro went to look out. "That's odd."

"Could help come from the north?" Gramma Rose asked.

"I wouldn't think so," Mrs. O'Brien said. "I've ridden this section many times, and my husband made the trip on a regular basis. Some small towns and ranches are in the area. Most have a telegraph office, so maybe word went out when the train was at the next whistle stop. The stationmaster might've wired places in the area. It's what my husband would've done, when he was a stationmaster. That was many years ago." A wistful expression fell over the women's lined face. "We spent the first two years of our marriage at a whistle stop town." She smiled. "I was mighty glad when we moved back to the Springs, since we were raised there. Lots bigger."

Was the rider a lawman? Doro wondered. If so, their investigation might end before it really got started. "Let's head to the gangway vestibule, so we can find out while he's here."

Aggie jumped to her feet.

"Hurry back, girls. I'm curious," Gramma Rose added with a smile.

"I am, too," Mrs. O'Brien tacked on.

Doro and Aggie rushed to the gangway, where Sayers was already descending. With outside steps in place, the two young women were able to follow.

The rider doffed his hat when he caught sight of the young women. "Ladies."

Sayers glanced at them and back to the horseman. "Can I help you, sir?"

The man, of muscular build and middle years, shook his head. "Nope, but I've got some information for you. The telegraph operator up in Tyson, that's about seven miles to the north, asked if I'd ride down and let you know about the tracks washing out a few miles west of here."

Sayers ran one hand over his face. "In that patch where they're low?"

"Yep," the rider said. "Heavy flooding took them out in that big storm." He jerked his thumb toward the west. "No help coming from there soon. Your engineer heard the news when he got to the next station going east. That's a small one. No repair crew or extra engine, so he sent word up the line. They wired saying not to expect workmen until tomorrow afternoon, at the earliest. A derailment farther down the way is tying up a lot of crews."

"That's not good news, because we also need a lawman," the conductor, his face pale, stated. "We got a murder victim on the floor of our kitchen."

The rider frowned. "I didn't hear about that, and there's no sheriff up my way and not any towns closer than Tyson. Word was a railroad security man will come with the repair crew because your engineer found the broken coupler odd. If we had a telephone at my place, I'd call up the line and let them know. But we don't have none yet."

That information did not surprise Doro, since not everyone outside Michaw had a telephone. Some looked at the device like they did automobiles: newfangled contraptions.

"My chef and his staff have to fix meals, and a body in their way isn't good," Sayers said.

"You could move the man into your cooler," the rider replied.

"We wanted to preserve the crime scene," Doro said.

"Understandable," the man said as he glanced her way. "And you are?"

After introducing herself and Aggie, Doro offered their experience as amateur sleuths. "I was in the kitchen this morning."

"I see," the cowboy said, with a glint in his gaze. "My wife and daughters are avid mystery readers. Too bad our ranch isn't closer, since they'd love to hear about your cases."

"How far is your ranch?" Doro asked.

"Almost four miles to the northeast." He pointed to a bluff in the distance. "Out that way."

"I wish we could meet them," Doro said. She also wished the ranch was closer, since the murderer was still on the loose. Having a haven nearby would ease minds. To cloak her anxiety, she asked a question. "Do you enjoy whodunits?"

A deep chuckle rumbled out of his barrel chest. "Don't have much extra time, except in the winter. Then, I'm usually catching up with bookwork. But I solved a few cases myself back when I spent two years as a deputy marshal. That was before I married."

"And you believe moving the body is all right?" Doro inquired.

"If help wasn't delayed, I'd say to leave him. As it is, a good lawman won't need to see the body in place. Just mark where it was, if you can." The rancher frowned. "Not sure about a railroad security man knowing a lot. If I didn't need to get back to my ranch, I'd look. My men are out on the range with the cattle. I don't like leaving my wife, our two daughters, and the housekeeper alone for too long. The West isn't as wild as when I was young, but you never know when some desperado will come along. It happened at another ranch in these parts recently. Don't want my womenfolk held hostage."

Doro had read a few dime novels set in the Old West as a girl, and ranch life had seemed exciting. Being isolated and a target for outlaws did not.

"I don't blame you," the conductor said. "Thanks for taking the time to ride over, and for the advice on the body."

"If the law asks who advised you, my name's Carlton Menzing. I'm known in these parts." His gaze flickered to Doro and Aggie. "You two gathering evidence? That might be helpful to the lawman who finally investigates."

The suggestion buoyed Doro's spirits. "Mr. Sayers doesn't want us involved." Out of the corner of her eye, Doro saw the conductor shift from one foot to the other and back.

"I don't want them getting hurt," the conductor put in, "which isn't quite the same."

That had not been his full rationale, but Doro did not contradict him. "The train seems safe, especially since we keep our compartment locked. Besides, many folks think women are incapable of a hard task like investigating a crime." A glance at Sayers revealed the man's face to be beet red.

"My wife and girls are bright as copper pennies. They could solve crimes as well as any man." Menzing stared at Sayers. "Surely, you feel the same, sir."

"Well, I...that is. Uh..." The conductor's voice trailed off. "Like I said, I don't want them getting hurt."

The cowboy shrugged. "Sounds like they have substantial experience, and they could glean details while people's memories are fresh. As for danger, locking their compartment is enough.

You might have your crewmen take turns walking the corridors at night. That oughta be sufficient for now."

Sayers sputtered a bit more before agreeing. "Yep, that's a good idea. Since the repair crew and security man should be here tomorrow, we'll have only tonight to stand guard."

The conductor's concession seemed grudging. Doro hoped whoever came was as accepting of a woman's involvement as this rancher. "What a wonderful idea," she said.

"It is," Aggie agreed.

"All right." The conductor turned back to the rider. "Again, thanks for coming out here."

"I'm sorry you had to ride so far," Doro said.

A grin took decades from Menzing's lined face. "Spent most of my life in the saddle, and an extra couple of hours don't hurt my horse or me none. No roads close enough to get an automobile over here. Not that I fancy them myself. We got a truck at the ranch. My wife and girls love driving it." He patted his mount. "I prefer Brownie."

His comment reminded Doro that not everyone thought cars were an improvement over horses. Since she adored her vehicle, Doro did not agree.

"I appreciate you telling us the news," Sayers said.

The man again touched his hat brim. "Good luck to you. If the lawman gives you trouble about moving the body, tell him I advised it. Likely, we know each other, at least by name." Then, he rode off.

Although Sayers did not look at the two young women, he addressed them. "I'll have the crew move the professor and tell the passengers that we'll be stuck a little longer than planned."

"Is it common for tracks to wash out?" Aggie asked.

"Not common, but it happens, especially when there's been lots of rain," he replied. "Now, I better see to the body and the news. Andre won't be happy about a corpse in his cooler."

"I'm sure he won't, but it's probably best to move Professor Mathers, under the circumstances," Doro observed. She cleared her throat. Besides, it wouldn't be worse than a body on the floor. "Can we assume you no longer object to us interviewing passengers?"

When the conductor met her gaze, resignation was written on his features. "If a former deputy marshal thinks it's a good idea, I won't stand in the way." Then, he turned on his heel and headed toward the train.

Doro noted him stopping to talk with Gray and Phineas, who were standing fifteen feet away. Had they heard the entire exchange with the rancher? Doro watched as the trio conversed before boarding the train without backward glances.

Doro turned to Aggie. "We have permission to investigate and more time to solve the case, but additional complications."

Aggie scanned the horizon. "It's a little scary being out here with no towns or people nearby. I can't imagine living on a remote ranch. The farms around Michaw seem too far from town to me. But I'm a city girl."

"Not as much as you used to be," Doro pointed. "At this point, you're almost like a native Michawan."

A chuckle left Aggie. "That's a funny name, and I've never heard it before."

"Michawian?" Doro suggested.

"Just as funny."

Doro laughed, too. "Maybe Michawite. We really need some noun to describe the residents. Toledo has Toledoans and Sylvania has Sylvanians. Michaw doesn't have a name, and I've always thought it should."

"Some towns have names that lend themselves to a term for residents," Aggie said. "But we have more important matters to handle."

A tad of humor lightened the situation, so Doro replied with that in mind. "We do, but I'll keep ideas in the back of my mind."

"A good place for them," her friend said with a chuckle.

"Your point is well taken." Doro opened the door to their car. "Let's tell Gramma Rose and Mrs. O'Brien what we learned."

A few minutes later, the young women got settled in the drawing room and explained the rider's mission. "So, we won't be going anyplace for another day," Doro said to sum up.

"It could be much worse. We have comfortable accommodations, so another day won't matter," Gramma Rose said.

"Your accommodations are lovely, and I'm glad one of the crewmen will stand watch tonight," Mrs. O'Brien said.

"It will help us sleep better," Aggie said.

"True." Although she had not been as concerned as the others, Doro wasn't always a sound sleeper. Waking up in the night happened far too often. Now, if she roused at some point, she'd feel safe and sound. "Let's discuss what to do next." She retrieved her notepad and pencil.

"It's too bad the knife wasn't clearly identified. You mentioned fingerprints being important in solving the murder of your colleague last fall," Gramma Rose said to Doro.

"How fascinating," Mrs. O'Brien added. "Have you taken fingerprints?"

"I watched Ev take the prints, and it was absorbing. He even let me do a set," Doro said. As soon as the statement was out, she regretted it. Bringing up Ev had come without forethought. Exactly what that meant, Doro did not examine.

"How nice of him to further your sleuthing skills," Gramma Rose observed with a smile. "I look forward to meeting him."

Since Doro typically traveled to Sylvania to see her grandmother, and not vice versa, she had been able to keep the two of them apart. Although Rose McLaren was not a busybody, her interest in Doro and Ev—not that such a coupling existed—was evident.

"Maybe we could have a small party for Doro's birthday," Aggie said. "We celebrated in Colorado, but we have to do something on the day itself. Wade and his children would enjoy that, and Ev could come, too."

Doro stared at her friend. "We celebrated with my parents two nights ago."

"What a wonderful idea," Gramma Rose, acting as if she had not heard Doro, said with unbridled enthusiasm.

Since she loved festivities, Doro did not want to dismiss the plan, but being careful about responding was wise. "Ev might be busy, but a small group, including Wade, his mother, and his children would be fun."

Both Aggie and Rose chuckled. "Definitely Ev," they said in tandem.

Rose turned to the other widow. "I wish you lived near us. You'd enjoy the group and the party."

"I love parties," Mrs. O'Brien remarked before focusing on Doro. "And how fun for you to include your young man."

Doro resisted repeating that, while Ev was a young man, he was not hers. Besides, considering their uneasy parting in May, she was not at all sure Ev would want to join in her birthday celebration, so Doro tabled the discussion. "We can talk about celebrating after the train is moving again. Right now, I'd like to meet with the brakeman and the flagman. They might be in the caboose. We could get vital evidence, and there's time before supper. We can chat with other passengers then."

"Let's go now, so we can freshen up before heading to the dining car," Aggie suggested.

"Once again, we'll be eagerly waiting for news," Gramma Rose added.

"We certainly will," Mrs. O'Brien put in.

"I hope we get some," Doro replied, before she and Aggie went to find the two crewmen.

Chapter Nine

When the young women reached the caboose moments later, Doro rapped on the door.

"Who is it?" a gruff male voice called.

"Doro Banyon and Aggie Darwine. Could we chat with you?" Since she didn't recognize the voice, Doro figured it was the flagman, whom she had not met. The brakeman had an unusually high voice, but this man had a deep baritone.

A moment's hesitation preceded his response. "Come on in."

Before entering the caboose, Doro raised crossed fingers to Aggie, who returned the gesture. Then, the two young women went ahead.

With a smile on her face, Doro nodded to the flagman. "We're sorry to bother you."

"No bother, miss," the man said. "Sayers just told us about the two of you investigating the professor's murder. I'm Micah Smithers, by the way."

"It's nice to meet you, Mr. Smithers, and to see you again, Mr. Rogers," Doro said.

"No mister needed. Al or Rogers is good," the brakeman replied. "I don't know no more than I did this morning."

The flagman nodded. "I've heard about the murder, but I got no clues to give you."

"You might know something and not realize it. That often happens during investigations," Aggie put in.

"Fire away," Rogers replied in a resigned voice.

"But sit down first." Smithers gestured to two chairs near the door.

Doro and Aggie settled in the seats before exchanging a glance. Doro gave her friend a slight nod, and Aggie moved the conversation forward.

"You both must've been outside after the decoupling," Aggie suggested.

"Yep," Rogers agreed. "I woke up right after it happened. If you've ridden the rails as long as I have, you know when a train stops dead, ya gotta dress right away."

"Do you sleep in the caboose?" Doro asked after glancing around. "I see two cots."

Rogers nodded. "We do, just in case we're needed when we get to a station late. That way, we don't bother the others in the sleeper car. Since this is a long train, at least it was before the accident, it's mostly kitchen staff bunking in the next car. They got to get up real early, so they don't need to have their sleep disturbed."

"I see," Doro murmured. "I noticed eight bunks in that car, but there are two waiters sleeping in them, right?"

"As far as the kitchen workers, yep," Smithers said. "But more would be there if the rest of the train hadn't gone ahead. If we had a railroad security officer, he'd sleep there, too."

"Is it standard to have a security officer?" Aggie asked.

"Not so much anymore, although there was a guy riding with us this time," Smithers replied. "The days of train robberies are long gone. If a big shot is on board, we'd have someone. Or if there's something real valuable. Sometimes, for other reasons. But there's always an extra bunk available. Sometimes, a second brakeman sleeps down this way, but like I said, this was a long train, so there's another sleeper for the crew behind the engine."

"Interesting," Doro murmured. The logistics provided more food for thought, but she pressed on to the matter of Clyde's son. "Trying to unravel the case is challenging, so I hope you can help us." She looked from one man to the other.

Both nodded. "Neither of us knowed the professor. Haven't heard nothing good about him, but got no cause to do him harm," Smithers said.

"Me, neither," Rogers chipped in.

Aggie rushed to offer reassurance. "We don't suspect either of you."

"Far from it," Doro added. "But we've heard some things that brought up more questions. Unfortunately, no one has answers." Or, more to the point, if anyone knew details, they were not sharing them.

"And you think we do?" Rogers asked in a clearly skeptical.

"Maybe so," Doro replied.

"About what?" Rogers, his brow furrowed, made an additional query.

"Do you know Clyde well?" Doro inquired.

Both men shrugged, but Rogers answered in short order. "I been on runs with him over the years. We started about the same time. Can't say I know him well, but we chat in passing. He was off to war for a couple of years, though."

Doro turned to Smithers. "Are you acquainted with him?"

"A little, but I knew his boy better, although not for long," the flagman replied.

Anticipation rippled through Doro, and a glance at Aggie revealed her friend felt the same way. "How did you meet his son?"

A grim expression blanketed Smithers's broad face. "After he left college, Custis took a job with the railroad. I was working the train yards at the time, and we were at the same station for a few months, which was about all the kid worked before he died." He shook his head. "Terrible accident."

"We heard about his death," Doro murmured.

"Did he ever say why he left school?" Aggie asked.

Smithers ran a hand over his face. "Didn't talk about it much, but the kid wasn't happy in the train yard. From time-to-time, someone would ask why a smart guy like him would give up his education to bread his back on the railroad."

"What did he say?" Aggie asked.

"That he had no choice because a teacher stole his work, and the man complained it were just the opposite," the brakeman.

"Someone accused Custis of plagiarism," Doro murmured with sad certainty. More pieces of the puzzle were appearing, but how would they fit together?

"Accused him of what?" Smithers, clearly confused, asked.

"Cheating," Aggie supplied.

The flag man nodded. "Yep, the boy wouldn't say no more, though. I asked Clyde about it once, and he got real upset. That was after Custis got killed."

"He didn't tell you who accused his son?" Even though it was a question, Doro had her suspicions. Strong ones.

"Never did," Smithers said. "All I know is the man were a teacher. Thought better of them folks myself, but I only went through the sixth grade."

Rogers shifted restlessly before speaking. "I never told no one about something that happened some months back, and maybe I shouldn't now. Clyde's a good man and what happened to his boy were wrong."

Doro wanted to reassure the man. But how could she? What if he knew something that made Clyde a stronger suspect? "We'll find out, sooner or later." At least she hoped they would.

Smithers turned to Rogers. "I don't know what it is, but it'd be better if you tell these ladies. They can figure out if it's important. If it ain't, no one else needs to know." He looked at Doro and Aggie. "Right?"

"That's right," Doro said. "We won't spread news that'll hurt anyone unnecessarily, but we need to get to the truth, or the killer may go free, possibly to murder again." The last phrase might loosen Rogers' tongue.

A harsh breath left Rogers as he leaned forward and braced his elbows on his knees. "I was on a run with Clyde last winter. A blizzard stranded the train, and we had to stop overnight in a little town in Colorado. Joshua, Clyde, and me shared a room in the local boardinghouse." A slight smile touched his mouth.

"Since we weren't working, we had a little something to warm us up."

Despite Prohibition, liquor was everywhere, so Doro made no comment on the illegality of their actions. What interested her far more was Joshua's presence and what Clyde had revealed. "Did Clyde talk about Custis?"

"He sure did. When the story was out, I felt real bad for him," Rogers said. "Such a terrible thing."

When the man did not continue, Doro wondered if he would avoid providing details, as Joshua had. There was only one way to find out. "What did he say?"

Rogers bent his head. "Custis did good in college and wanted to get more schooling. He dreamed about teaching in college. Just hearing Clyde talk about the boy, I knew he was real proud. Then, Custis got into some bad professor's special class, or something."

Aggie provided the correct title. "A seminar."

"Right," Rogers said. "I don't know much about how colleges operate, but Custis worked on a big project for his final grade. According to Clyde, the professor kept saying how it needed to be improved, so the kid burned the midnight oil for weeks. Just before Christmas vacation, he turned in what he had so the teacher could go over it. Instead, by the time Custis got back a few weeks later, the professor had passed the boy's work off as his own."

Although she had suspected something similar, disgust had Doro's stomach knotting. "Did Custis try to straighten things out?" She knew fighting a professor's word would be difficult for a student, but many would try.

"When Custis accused the professor of stealing his work, the man made his life miserable. Said Custis was a terrible student, who cheated more than once. The result was the boy getting expelled only a few months before graduation." Rogers leaned back in his chair and released a shuddering breath.

"That's awful," Aggie said. "Custis must've been an outstanding student, if his work was good enough to steal."

The man nodded. "His father told Josh and me that Custis graduated first in high school class and got all *A's* in college until he ran into that professor."

"He was a good boy, from what I saw working with him," Smithers agreed, "but he never said nothing about why he left school."

Clearly, Mathers was the professor in question, so Clyde's antipathy toward him was understandable. But had he killed the man? Doro did not have enough information to decide. "We only heard Custis left school and died later."

Smithers nodded. "In a freak accident in the train yard. I wasn't working there at the time, but we all heard how upset Clyde and his wife were."

"What a heartbreaking loss for them," Aggie said, her voice soft with sympathy.

A long exhalation left Rogers. "I can't imagine losing none of my brood. I saw Clyde after his boy's death, and he was half-sick with grief."

Although she had no children, Doro empathized. The holes left in his parents' hearts would never heal. "How did Custis end up working for the railroad? Couldn't he have finished school elsewhere?" According to Mrs. O'Brien, money was the reason, but double-checking details was important because hearsay was not always correct.

"Clyde and his wife couldn't afford to pay no tuition, and Custis weren't able to get another scholarship," the brakeman replied, his voice rough with suppressed emotion. "He planned to work until he got enough money to finish and then, go on to higher schooling. Then, the accident happened."

"To graduate school," Doro offered as clarification.

"Yes, miss," he agreed.

"How long ago was that?" Aggie asked.

"Last summer was when he was working in the yard. I guess he talked about it. At least that's what some of the men were saying," Smithers replied.

The information corroborated what they already knew and reminded Doro that a year would not mute the profound grief of losing a child. "Did either of you hear the argument between Professor Mathers and Clyde last evening?"

The flagman and the brakeman looked at one another for several moments before Rogers answered. "I heard about it in the kitchen this morning before you came, Miss Banyon. Sorry, Professor Banyon."

Doro put up one hand. "Please call me Doro." She only insisted on her title with men like Sayers.

"That wouldn't be proper, but I appreciate the thought," Rogers said. "Anyhow, that's the first I knew they ever crossed paths."

"Did you know?" Doro asked the flagman.

"Rogers told me about last night just a while ago," Smithers replied. "As for other times, Clyde talked about running into the professor not long after Custis died."

"But he talked a lot more the night of the blizzard because he was drunk," Aggie suggested.

"Yep." Rogers' lips thinned into a harsh line. "When Clyde confronted Mathers after Custis died, Mathers insisted he hadn't stolen the boy's work, said the kid was lazy, didn't deserve a scholarship, and the railroad was the right place for him."

For several moments, Doro absorbed the awful lies, while Aggie seemed to do the same. "Last night's confrontation is understandable, considering what happened with Clyde's son," Doro said.

"It sure is," Aggie agreed. "Did Mathers and Clyde often cross paths?"

Rogers shook his head. "As far as I know, only the time right after Custis died and last night. But maybe more often. Hard to say."

The answer gave more weight to Clyde as a suspect, which saddened Doro. Killing the professor would not bring Custis back and, if Clyde was found guilty, his wife would suffer even more. Although justice was her aim in every investigation, she hated to think this might end with the waiter behind bars. Or worse.

"I hope you don't think Clyde killed that professor," Rogers said.

Aggie offered a benign expression. "We're gathering evidence, not making accusations."

The man looked upset. "Maybe I shouldn't have repeated what Clyde said when he was drunk. That makes a man blurt out things he wouldn't say otherwise."

Liquor loosened tongues but the saying *in wine, truth* came to Doro's mind. "Did Clyde threaten the professor that night?"

Rogers bowed his head. "He said Mathers would get what was coming to him, but he didn't say nothing about getting even himself."

"Good," Aggie said.

"But he's a suspect." Smithers spoke with certainty.

"He was and still is." Doro made the confirmation. "And so are several others."

"Chef Andre among them?" Rogers asked.

Doro rose from her chair. The chef was farther down the list, but the crewmen did not need to know. "We shouldn't share information about who is under scrutiny, but we're grateful you spoke with us. Now, we'll leave you in peace."

Aggie seconded Doro's comments, and the pair left the caboose. Neither of the young women spoke until they reached their car. "I didn't expect to hear so much," Aggie said.

"Neither did I," Doro said, "and I wonder why Joshua didn't share it, since he was in the same room with Rogers and Clyde."

"Joshua works side-by-side with Clyde, and they seem to know each other well and like each other. We heard Joshua lost his parents at a young age, so he may look at Clyde as a father figure. That'd make it hard for Joshua to reveal information that puts a shadow over Clyde."

The observation was insightful. "Since Clyde lost his son, he may feel fatherly toward Joshua, so they'd protect each other. I still plan to talk with Joshua again."

"A fine idea," Aggie said. "When you reveal what Rogers told us, Joshua may cooperate."

"I hope so," Doro murmured, "and I also hope Clyde isn't the killer. He and his wife have had more than their share of grief."

"They have," Aggie said, her own voice soft with sorrow.

"Let's tell Gramma Rose and Mrs. O'Brien how things went. I'd rather catch up with the other passengers in the dining car than knock on their doors."

"Agreed. With last night's events, some folks may be napping."

Chapter Ten

A s soon as Doro and Aggie stepped into the drawing
room, a smile spread across Rose McLaren's face. "Sit
down and tell us all," the older woman urged.

"Please do," Mrs. O'Brien added with enthusiasm.

After the young women seated themselves, Doro repeated
Rogers' revelations.

As she listened, Gramma Rose's eyes grew wide. "You uncov-
ered many details, and none of them help Clyde."

"They sure don't," Aggie agreed. "Unfortunately, as far as we
know now, he has one of the most powerful motives—avenging
his son."

Mrs. O'Brien laid her hands on her cheeks. "I hate to believe
Clyde would do such a thing."

"We all do, I imagine," Gramma Rose put in.

As Doro pulled out her notepad and pencil, she considered
the suspects again. "I agree. Besides, losing the love of one's life
is equally strong to me."

Aggie nodded. "We won't dismiss Gray, because you're right."

"His friend may have a formidable reason, too," Gramma Rose reminded them.

"True," Doro said. "The additional incident of Mathers stealing a student's work gives credence to Phineas' assertions. Even though he didn't come right out and accuse Mathers, the intent was strong."

"From what we witnessed last night, Mathers understood Phineas' threat," Aggie observed.

"I'm not sorry I missed that," Mrs. O'Brien murmured.

"It wasn't pleasant," Gramma Rose said before addressing Doro and Aggie. "The entire exchange is clearer now that you have more information. At this point, can we rule out anyone?"

During the silence that fell, Doro studied her list. "Chef Andre's motive seems weakest. As a chef, he's heard plenty of complaints and, although no one enjoys being criticized, he couldn't possibly go after every unhappy passenger."

"It seems like the chef is quick to anger, and he doesn't care what passengers like Mathers think," Aggie added. "He seems quite secure in his abilities, so I agree his motive isn't as strong as the others."

A chuckle left Doro. "The man doesn't lack self-confidence."

"I agree with that," Gramma Rose said.

"True of many chefs," Mrs. O'Brien added. "My husband often remarked about some being high-strung, but it's a hard job with a lot of pressure."

"It is, and Andre has family struggles," Aggie observed.

"What about Joshua?" Gramma Rose asked. "He didn't tell you about last winter's snowstorm tête-à-tête, but that doesn't mean he knew about or took part in the killing."

"It doesn't, but he and Clyde seem close," Aggie said. "From what we've discovered, Joshua must've joined the railroad about the time Clyde's son died. That might've encouraged a father-son relationship."

"You could be right," Gramma Rose said.

"As I told all of you, railroaders often become like family, so that wouldn't surprise me," Mrs. O'Brien added.

Doro nodded. "We'll ask him about that. If we can meet with him alone, I'd love to know why he didn't admit Clyde had it in for Mathers."

"Maybe Joshua doesn't know if Clyde killed Mathers. If he's uncertain, he might hide the details," Gramma Rose said.

Doro tapped her pencil against the notepad before writing more down. "We've got plenty left to uncover, but I'm almost ready to move Joshua off my list. He hasn't got a decent motive."

"True," Aggie put in. "Covering up for Clyde isn't the same as murder."

The others agreed.

"Which leaves Grayson, Phineas, and Clyde vying for first place." Gramma Rose flushed. "Not vying for it in the sense they want it."

"We know what you meant," Aggie assured her.

"We do," Doro agreed. "Which means we're down to three solid suspects. We're making progress." More pieces of the puzzle were falling into place. Now, they needed the key components.

****

Doro and Aggie, hoping to intercept Joshua, went to the dining car ahead of Gramma Rose and Mrs. O'Brien. Luck was with them because the young waiter was setting tables by himself. When he caught sight of the two women, Joshua froze.

"The meal won't be served for twenty minutes," he blurted out. "You'd be more comfortable in your drawing room."

His assertion did not sway Doro, who figured Joshua wanted to avoid more questions. "We'll be fine here." She gestured to a table already fitted out. "We can sit at that one."

An expression akin to a pout descended on his youthful features. "I need to set all the tables by myself."

"We won't get in your way," Aggie assured him.

"We certainly won't," Doro agreed, "but why are you working alone? Where's Clyde?"

Joshua shifted from one foot to the other. "He doesn't feel good, so he's resting."

"Won't it be difficult for you to serve the passengers alone?" Aggie asked.

"Clyde will help later," Joshua said. "Now, I need to get back to work."

As the young waiter turned away, Doro spoke again. "Just a moment, please."

He looked back. "I'm busy, miss." Frustration and annoyance were in his voice.

"We have a couple of questions," Aggie said. "I promise, they won't take long."

"You had questions before," the young man retorted. "How many do ya got?"

"We have a couple more because we've learned additional details," Aggie replied in her usual placid and pleasant voice.

A harsh breath rattled out of him. "All right, but hurry. I don't want to get in no trouble with the chef."

"We don't want that, either," Doro replied with sincerity. "What we wonder about is Clyde's son."

Color ebbed from the young waiter's face. "I didn't know him or nothing about him."

"That's not true," Aggie murmured.

Joshua's jaw went rigid. "You calling me a liar?"

One corner of Aggie's mouth lifted in a slight smile. "No, I think you're a loyal friend, who wants to protect a father figure."

For a long moment, Joshua simply stared at her. When the boy did not respond, Doro did. "You met Clyde shortly after his son died, and he took you under his wing. Since you're without family, you got close to him, close enough to hear his troubles." Although the comments were primarily supposition, Doro wanted to test the possibilities.

A bleak expression descended on Joshua's face before he bowed his head. With one hand, he rubbed his neck. "It's hard when kin dies."

"Losing loved ones is terrible," Aggie said. "I know because my parents are gone, too."

That revelation earned a nod from Joshua. "It's bad. Real bad."

"So, you were sympathetic to Clyde when you heard about his boy dying," Doro suggested.

He looked from Doro to Aggie. "He and his missus were grieving hard for Custis, and I was sorrowing for my aunt. We had loss in common, but what's that got to do with anything?" Joshua asked, his features carefully schooled.

"Maybe a lot," Doro replied. The boy was not giving much ground. "Aggie and I spoke with the brakeman and flagman a little while ago. Mr. Rogers had some interesting details to share."

Alarm darkened Joshua's gaze before he glanced away. "I don't know him very well."

Doro let several moments pass before commenting. "You and Clyde shared a room with him last winter when your train was stranded during a blizzard."

The waiter's dark lashes fluttered down. "Clyde got drunk. He didn't know what he was saying."

Although sympathy for Joshua filled Doro, she could not drop the topic. "What he said was the truth, wasn't it?"

Joshua met her gaze. "Maybe. How can I know for sure?"

Doro glanced at Aggie, who rolled her eyes. Could they get a straight answer from the young waiter? Although she hated to accuse Joshua, doing so might be the best bet. "Since you and Clyde became close, did you consider helping him get even with Professor Mathers?"

Joshua's jaw dropped. "Get even? What do ya mean?"

"I think you know exactly what I mean." Doro maintained a calm demeanor. Hurling accusations was not her style, but

Joshua had to know more than he was admitting. She could not allow him to continue obstructing the investigation.

The boy swallowed convulsively. "I wouldn't kill nobody, and neither would Clyde."

Doro hesitated a heartbeat before pushing on. "Mr. Rogers said Clyde's son Custis studied with Mathers, and the two clashed." Since she wanted to hear Joshua's slant, Doro did not mention the charge of plagiarism.

Joshua's nostrils flared with a sharp intake of breath. "They didn't clash. Mathers stole Custis' work and used it like it were his own. When Custis found out, he asked the professor to do the right thing. But the old guy refused and turned things around."

"By accusing Custis of stealing work," Aggie said.

Defeat shadowed the young waiter's features. "Yep. Mathers spread it far and wide. Not only did Custis get expelled, he couldn't find another scholarship because the professor blackened his name." Joshua bit off each word as if it tasted foul. "Clyde was furious, but he couldn't afford tuition for Custis, which made him feel awful. Then, the accident happened, and Custis got hurt real bad."

Since Doro knew that barely described the incident, she rushed on. "According to Mr. Rogers, Clyde wanted Mathers to get what he deserved." She took care to use the same wording as the brakeman, because it did not explicitly implicate the older waiter. How would Joshua react?

"Clyde didn't kill him," the young waiter blurted out. "He wouldn't do nothing like that, and he didn't talk about murder. He only hoped the professor got what was coming to him."

"Which could be construed as a threat," Aggie said.

"But it wasn't," Joshua insisted. He looked from Aggie to Doro. "I know you want to solve the murder, but don't pin it on him just cuz he had reason to hate that professor."

"We would never do that," Doro told him. "Aggie and I are interested in identifying the killer, not simply solving the crime by targeting just anyone."

"That's right," Aggie added. "We want to bring the guilty party to justice, not pursue an innocent man."

Joshua rubbed the back of his neck before responding. "All right. I guess I believe you, but I don't know no more than I already said. Clyde says his son didn't cheat, but Mathers made sure Custis got expelled."

"Probably to cover his own misdeeds," Aggie observed.

"That seems likely," Doro agreed before focusing on the young waiter. Joshua's admissions added credence to the theory, but that did not exonerate Clyde. "If you have any other information, you'd do well to tell us. You won't help Clyde by hiding facts, which will surely come out later."

"I don't know no more, and I really gotta get back to work."

"Of course," Aggie said. "Thank you for speaking with us."

After the young waiter moved away, Doro looked around the dining car. "A few passengers are coming in. Let's chat with them and see what they know."

Within ten minutes, Doro and Aggie had spoken with the newlyweds, Mr. and Mrs. Smith, who knew next to nothing about last night's rows and cared little about the murder, except to murmur passing sympathy. The middle-aged couple, Mrs. and Mrs. Gensen, and her mother, Mrs. Warren, did not have information, either, although they were more profuse in their condolences and concerns. The retired army officer, Colonel Ledke, was the last to arrive, and his attitude was dismissive, at best. Although he did not say the two young women ought to have husbands and children, he was unimpressed by their *snooping*, as he called it. Mr. Boggun and his son had no additional details, but they extended their good wishes for Doro and Aggie to crack the case.

Gramma Rose and Mrs. O'Brien entered the car as Doro and Aggie were about to find a table. The two friends helped the older women into window seats before seating themselves.

Since Doro did not want to alert other passengers, she modulated her voice. "We talked to some of the people here and learned nothing. However, we got confirmation of information from Joshua."

"And some fresh insight," Aggie added.

Rose immediately looked interested. "What did he say?"

After summarizing the conversation, Doro asked, "What do you think?"

Rose put one hand to her cheek. "The boy is close to Clyde, as we figured, but having him say so is key. That means he wouldn't want to reveal any negative information. But he confirmed what Rogers told you, so Joshua was honest to that extent."

"He was, and nothing we know pinpoints Clyde," Doro said. "But he remains among my three top suspects, along with Gray and Phineas."

A glum expression shadowed Mrs. O'Brien's face. "I'm afraid you may be right."

Rose patted the other widow's hand. "The murderer could still be someone else."

Although that seemed increasingly unlikely, Doro nodded, and Aggie followed suit.

"What's next?" Aggie asked.

"Finding out more about Phineas," Doro replied. "We know what Gray's motive would be, and we can guess Phineas left Pikeley because of Mathers, although the exact reason remains to be seen."

"Sometimes, students change colleges for no dramatic purpose. Maybe Phineas did poorly in Mathers' classes, and it's as simple as that." Aggie offered the idea.

"You could be right," Doro observed. "The only way to find out is to chat with him more."

"He wasn't all that amenable to talking," Gramma Rose pointed out. "He left our drawing room quickly and without finishing his scone."

When Doro looked down the aisle, she saw the two graduate students enter the car. "They're here."

"There's an empty table across from us," Aggie said without turning to look at the men herself. "Why don't you wave them over?"

"Wonderful idea," Gramma Rose said with enthusiasm.

Since Doro agreed, she lifted her hand. Gray and Phineas exchanged a few words before coming toward her.

"Good evening, ladies," Gray said.

Phineas offered a nod. "I see you're still practicing strength in numbers."

"I'm lucky to be included with this lovely group," Mrs. O'Brien said.

"We enjoy the company," Gramma Rose added, "and sticking together is a good idea."

"Probably so, although I doubt if the killer will strike again. The murder had to be personal," Phineas stated.

"Unfortunately, that seems to be most likely." Gramma Rose gestured toward the nearby vacant table. "Why don't you sit over there? That way, we can chat."

Only a moment's hesitation preceded the men's acceptance. After they settled into chairs, Gray shifted to face the ladies. "We overheard the conversation with the rancher and Sayers." A glint shone in his gaze. "How is the investigation going now that you have the conductor's okay?"

"We're learning a little more, but not a lot." Doro realized it sounded like she was hedging, but she was. Both men were suspects, so discretion was advisable.

A smirk moved Phineas' lips. "Here, we thought you were a top-notch amateur sleuth."

Although the remark was made in an amused tone, his expression telegraphed hauteur.

"The murder occurred about twelve hours ago," Aggie pointed out, her tone more clipped than usual. "Few serious crimes are solved in such a short time."

"Of course they aren't." Gray shot his friend a quelling glare.

To move the conversation to less shaky ground, Doro provided some news. "We found out the train is stuck here until tomorrow afternoon, but you might've heard all the conversation."

"We stepped outside not long after you two did," Gray replied.

"Some fresh air was needed," Phineas added.

Doro did not comment on the casual remark. Instead, she focused on details. "It was kind of him to ride out here and tell us, since he was in a hurry to get home."

"Too bad he didn't have the ranch truck with him. I wanted to ask him about driving back for us, but Gray didn't agree. We need to get on our way." Phineas scowled at his friend.

"We didn't need to put the man out by asking him to motor back here and take us elsewhere," his friend said. "You wanted him to drive us to another town where we could buy a vehicle. No place in this area is big enough to find a car from what we've heard."

A rough sigh left Phineas. "It was a passing thought. What I can't figure out is why can't an engine and crew come from the other direction?"

"You must've heard what we did. The train yard in Colorado Springs has men to make the repairs. Going east, the next big station is Kansas City. The Springs is much closer so, even with the tracks out, help will get here faster from there," Doro replied. "Besides, crews to the east are tied up with a derailment."

One of his shoulders bobbed up and down. "It's an imposition," Phineas said.

"None of us is happy, but we have to make the best of the situation," Gramma Rose put in.

"These things happen," Mrs. O'Brien added. "The crews do the best they can."

"Of course they do," Gray said.

Phineas' scowl only intensified. "Gray needs to get home. His mother and sisters will fret about him."

"I'm sure reports of the decoupling have spread," Doro said.

"That's likely the case, so my family must know by now," Grayson put in. He looked and sounded annoyed with his friend.

"From what we overheard, no lawman is coming down from the nearest hick town," Phineas said.

"That next town is too small for a sheriff," Mrs. O'Brien commented.

"Besides, no one knows about the murder except those of us on the train," Aggie said. "The rancher has no way to pass word along,"

"Hard to believe some folks are still without telephones," Phineas muttered.

"It's not rare. Even in cities, not everyone has one. It's a luxury some can't afford," Mrs. O'Brien pointed out.

Phineas' features softened. "You're right." He turned to Doro. "It sounds like a security guard will come with the repair crew."

"From what we know, yes." Doro scrutinized Phineas. Was he relieved that no lawman would arrive soon? That contradicted his displeasure with being stuck. Once again, she considered his relationship with Mathers. How could they learn more?

"Probably standard procedure," Phineas said.

Although Phineas was not providing an opening, Doro aimed to create one. "I first met Professor Mathers in the train station, and he seemed old-fashioned and opinionated. I had the impression he believed women shouldn't be in college." Since that was true, it might evoke an exchange that led to genuine clues.

A snort left Phineas. "When I attended Pikeley, I took four courses from him. He often made derogatory remarks about the female professors. Said they ought to have husbands and children to tend."

Gray frowned. "He would've never succeeded at Colorado College, since married women teach there."

"It's known as a progressive school, which is one of the rea sons my father took a position there," Doro put in.

"Your dad makes it sound like Michaw is progressive, too," Gray said.

"But not as much as Colorado," Aggie observed.

Doro knew Aggie was thinking about her future. Wade wanted to court and wed, but Aggie felt uncertain. Doro did not blame her. Surrendering a wonderful career for marriage would not be easy. For Doro, it seemed impossible.

"How do you mean?" Gray asked.

Doro snapped out of her reverie. "The school's current policy is to not employ married women, but the trustees are meeting soon, and they'll discuss a change."

"If they're like Mathers, they won't change," Phineas said. "That old coot belittled female students and scholarship students, too. Especially the brightest ones."

The last comment set Doro to thinking. Had Phineas and Custis been classmates? They would've been about the same age. Asking outright seemed like a poor strategy, so Doro tried a circuitous route to the truth. "Some male professors don't think women belong in college, but what did he have against those with scholarships?"

"He's a snob, who inherited a lot of money. Mathers thought that made him better than others," Phineas replied. "But he wasn't better. He wasn't as good a teacher as most professors, and he was lazy, too."

Aggie re-entered the exchange. "When we visited with Luann, she mentioned the professor doing research but said he was losing interest in teaching. Wasn't he well-respected for both at one time?"

Gray's gaze narrowed on the women. "He's told her that, I'm sure. Years ago, Mathers was an active researcher, but recently, he's been accused of stealing his students' work. Luann may not know, since he keeps her away from all but a few people."

"He's been accused because he has stolen work from several students," Phineas added. "If he wasn't wealthy and influential, he would've been fired long ago. He donates money to the college, which keeps the administration from scrutinizing him."

"They may not want to believe he'd do such a thing," Gray pointed out. Phineas made no response.

"Do you know someone whose research was stolen?" Gramma Rose asked.

"Yep," Phineas replied. "I've heard about three cases. One was a coed, and she left school without confronting Mathers, but she told some of us. Mostly as a warning to be careful. She was a senior, who worked as a lab assistant."

"What happened to her after she left Pikeley?" Aggie inquired. "Do you know?"

"She went to a girls' school," Phineas said, "and on to graduate school at the same place."

"Good for her," Rose said with enthusiasm. "But it's sad that man drove her away from Pikeley."

"He drove a few of us away," Phineas said. "I didn't like the way he treated the scholarship boys or the girls, and I told him so. Stupid of me, because he marked all my papers as barely passing. My father was furious and didn't believe my accusations. He threatened to cut off my funds, but after I transferred, my grades went up."

"Did the professor steal your work?" Aggie asked.

"No. He only stole from upperclassmen," Phineas explained. "They do more extensive research."

"The professor picked on you because you defended other students," Doro said.

"Pretty much. As time went on, he got worse and worse. Always nitpicking my schoolwork. He even criticized my clothes. Of course, his attire was stylish before the war, so he's no judge of fashion." Phineas' voice rang with censure, while anger flashed like flame in his gaze. "The old coot even called me *freckles.* But he won't be now, and I'm..."

Before his friend could finish, Gray spoke. "Mathers wasn't a nice man. He made life miserable for plenty of people. Colleagues and students and others."

"Others like Luann," Doro murmured.

Gray briefly bowed his head. When he glanced up, regret lined his face. "Yeah. Like Luann."

Further conversation was cut-off by the waiters bringing appetizers to the tables. After being served, Phineas nodded to the women. "We'll let you chat among yourselves."

Wanting to avoid rudeness, Doro saw no option but to agree. "Enjoy your meals." How could they find out if Phineas had known Custis? Was she getting stuck on the point? Maybe it had no bearing on the murder. Who could say for sure?

Chapter Eleven

Although Doro hoped to re-engage with Gray and Phineas, the pair left the dining car before the women had finished dinner. Frustration filled her. More dribs and drabs of information helped, but not as much as she needed.

When dessert was served, Aggie made a suggestion. "Why don't we take cupcakes to Grayson and Phineas?" She glanced at Joshua. "Are there enough for us to get extras?"

"Sure. I didn't figure on them two leaving before dessert was served. Last night, they mentioned how they love sweets," the young waiter replied.

"Really?" Aggie murmured.

"Most young fellows enjoy treats, so it's a wonderful idea for you girls to take cupcakes to them," Gramma Rose added.

"I'll put several on a plate," Joshua replied.

"Thank you, young man," Mrs. O'Brien said. "It's kind of you to help, but that's what makes a fine railroader."

Joshua beamed. "Yes, ma'am. Can I get you anything else?"

The widow shook her head. "No, but it was a wonderful meal with excellent service."

Doro, amazed at the young man's sudden change in demeanor, watched him go. Clearly, Mrs. O'Brien had reached into his heart with her comments about doing a good job. Sincere praise could lift spirits.

Within moments, he was back. Doro accepted the cupcakes, and the four women went to their drawing room. "Why don't you two go ahead with the desserts?" Gramma Rose said. "Perhaps, you'll have a moment to chat with the boys. They took off a little too soon for my liking. Not saying they wanted to evade questions, but Grayson cut off Phineas, just as he was speaking freely."

Her grandmother's last remark made Doro smile. Rose McLaren might be an armchair detective, but she was a good one. "I noticed that, too."

"We all did," Aggie added, "which makes us a fine team."

"You girls do the legwork, and I lend an ear," Gramma Rose said. Amusement sparkled in her blue eyes. "Which suits me well at my age. Mrs. O'Brien has added her own expertise."

"I haven't done much," the widow insisted, but her smile was bright.

"It's working together that moves a case forward," Doro observed. "Now, let's go, Aggie."

"I'm ready," the other young woman replied.

After the two friends left their drawing room, they headed to the far end of the next car, where Grayson and Phineas were staying. Doro was about to knock when Phineas' voice, louder than normal, reached her.

"Thanks for hushing me up, before I said too much at dinner," Phineas was saying. "Mathers still gets to me, and I lose my temper. No need to alert the two amateur detectives." A chuckle rumbled through the door.

"It's not funny," Gray said, his voice grim. "Dr. Banyon says his daughter is a top-notch amateur sleuth. After seeing her and her friend in action, I believe him. They asked pointed questions, ones that made me look bad. I hated the old coot, but I didn't kill him."

"I know that," Phineas said with verve. "They'll back off soon. Plenty of people detested him, and several are on this train. Remember the chef's rage at him? And both waiters? The older one was downright nasty, and all of them have access to the kitchen knives and the kitchen. They have to be the top suspects. Maybe the young waiter helped the old one, who's got a valid grievance, for sure."

Several seconds of silence passed before Grayson spoke. "How do you mean? From what I heard, Clyde's upset over Custis losing his scholarship and working in the rail yard. But would his father commit murder because of it? From what you said after the funeral, Mrs. Oscar is devastated. Why would her husband make matters worse?"

"Maybe he got carried away." Phineas spoke in a hurried tone. "It's just that he sounded furious. If he crossed paths with Mathers, and the old man was nasty, Clyde might've lost control."

Realization hit Doro hard. When she glanced at her friend, Aggie had much the same reaction. Both Gray and Phin had known Custis. How well? And what did it mean in terms of the murder? Although she wanted to ask for Aggie's opinion, Doro did not want to get caught eavesdropping, so she kept silent.

"Maybe," Gray replied. "Maybe not. As far as the waiters and the chef being suspects, you and I are, too. Let's not forget that."

"I don't forget it for a single moment," Phineas muttered. "I hope this train gets moving soon. Being stuck here as sitting ducks for two amateur sleuths is a dead bore. Mathers wasn't worth all the effort they're putting into finding his killer. He's gone, and I say good riddance."

"Phin, don't talk like that. It makes you sound guilty."

"You know better," his friend replied in a cajoling tone.

Again, a period of quiet ensued. "Do I?" Gray asked in a barely audible voice.

A guffaw sounded through the door. "Of course you do. The two of us imbibed too much in the club car, so we came back here and collapsed into our beds."

"I came back before you," Grayson said.

"Sure, and you were sound asleep when I got here."

"But I don't know when you got back or if you went right to bed. Or if you got up and went out again."

"I was drunk," Phineas replied in a clipped tone. "Remember, I didn't rise when you did this morning. I slept in."

"Which isn't proof that you didn't leave our compartment after word came about the decoupling."

"What are you saying? That I did something to Mathers? How would I know he went to the kitchen? Or what time he went?" Phineas' voice rose with each word.

"Last year, you and I took different trains home for summer vacation. When you wrote to me, you mentioned Mathers being a passenger, too. You said he bothered the kitchen staff for a snack every night around three-thirty to four o'clock, and he said the same last evening. We both heard him."

"What kind of friend makes a murder accusation?" Phineas asked.

"No accusation, just some troubling facts."

"I can't believe you. We've known each other for four years."

"We have," Grayson agreed, "and you've carped about Mathers the entire time."

"What about you? The past three years, you've been a lovelorn sop because the old lecher married your sweetheart, so don't tell me you care about him being dead."

"I'll shed no tears for the man, but I didn't want him murdered." Seconds of silence ticked away before Gray spoke again. "You mentioned supporting scholarship students. That was news to me. You knew Custis, but how well?"

"Not much better than you. We were in classes when I went to Pikeley, but I didn't see much of him after that."

"You went to his funeral."

Again, silence ensued. "With some other guys from Pikeley. It wasn't far from my house."

"If you say so."

"I can't believe you suspect me." Disbelief and hurt filled Phineas' voice.

"Sorry. I'm worried about my family and Luann," Gray muttered. "And about being a suspect myself."

When Phineas replied, he sounded less strident. "Understandable. Besides, the chef and the waiters are better suspects than either of us. A lawman will see that, even if those two nosey girls don't. As soon as this train gets moving, you and I can be on our way to your father's funeral. No one will hold us up for that. Until then, we'll lie low and stay away from the two snoops."

"We'll need to answer questions when a sheriff or railroad security officer comes on board."

"We can talk with the law on our way back to Colorado Springs. Besides, by then, the killer will've been found," Phineas insisted.

"You're probably right," Gray agreed. "Let's steer clear of the women. I shouldn't have admitted so much about Luann and me."

"You love the girl," Phineas put in.

"I do." Gray's voice was soft with emotion.

When a lull ensued, Aggie jerked her thumb toward the opposite end of the carriage. Doro nodded, and they scurried down the aisle and back to their own compartment. As soon as they entered, Gramma Rose raised her eyebrows. "They didn't want the cupcakes?"

After dropping into the nearest chair, while Aggie joined Rose on the settee, Doro put the sweets on the table next to her. She followed by revealing what they had overheard.

One of Rose's hands flew to cover her mouth. "How interesting."

"Very much so," Mrs. O'Brien, seated in a chair, added.

"I felt the same way," Aggie agreed. "Interesting and unsettling."

"Both are true, but what we heard doesn't point us in any certain direction," Doro began, "but Gray sounds suspicious of Phineas, which is troubling."

"He did, before they both indicated we're annoying them," Aggie put in. "Gray is sorry he was honest about his relationship with Luann Mathers, too."

"And he suggested staying away from us," Doro added.

"Oh, my," her grandmother murmured. "Because you two are so astute."

"Thanks, Gram, but the word used was annoying." Doro drummed her fingers on the table. "But why are we annoying to them? Because they're skeptical about our skills, or because one or both is guilty, and they're afraid we'll learn the truth?"

"Although it could be either one, I believe they're fretting about you two solving the case, and identifying one of them as the killer," her grandmother observed. "Drinking last night is interesting. Evidently, Phineas brought his own liquor. Perhaps that's true for all passengers. That way, the railroad isn't violating the law."

"But they're providing mixers like soda," Aggie said.

"Which isn't illegal," Doro pointed out. "I don't know much about liquor, since Mother and Dad seldom drank, even before Prohibition, and I was still in high school when it went into effect in Ohio."

Gramma Rose folded her hands in her lap. "No one in our family was a heavy drinker, although your grandfather and I had a few spirits in the house before Ohio went dry. Vodka has no smell, and it's clear. Perhaps Phineas pretended to drink that, but really had water."

"Why pretend to get drunk?" Doro asked. "He couldn't have known ahead about the decoupling, could he?"

"It hardly seems so," Mrs. O'Brien said.

"Are you thinking he planned to kill the professor before we left Colorado Springs?" her grandmother asked. "Remember, the train pulled into the station shortly before we boarded. Some folks got off, and others got on. With cars being added, plenty of workers were in the train yard. Someone surely would've seen tampering."

"Maybe it's far-fetched, but could a worker have vandalized the coupler?" Doro asked.

Aggie pressed one finger to her forehead. "If others were nearby, wouldn't that be hard to hide?"

"I'd imagine so," Mrs. O'Brien agreed.

"You would know better than we do," Doro said. "Besides, Phineas couldn't have known Professor Mathers was on the same train."

"So, if he's guilty," Aggie said, "he got the idea on the trip. The same with Gray and Clyde."

Doro leaned back in her chair. "Gray and Phineas heard the professor mention his overnight snack, and it didn't come as a surprise to Phin, since he traveled on the same train as Mathers in the spring. Others have alluded to him going around the same time. Clyde would realize as much."

"Which shines a bright light on him," Aggie said.

"It does, but anyone might've heard him going to the kitchen," Doro said. "We know Gray was sound asleep, since Phineas answered the door when word came about the decoupling."

"And he was drunk or feigning it," Aggie added.

"That's all troubling, but it isn't enough proof to accuse any of them," Doro said.

A long exhalation left Aggie. "No, it isn't. Knowing who else was in the club car could yield clues."

"I agree, but some probably had compartments in the cars that went on, and we can't ask the bartender because he's not in this part of the train, either," Doro said.

"Mostly men, probably all men, would've been in the club car late," Gramma Rose said. "In thinking back over those in the dining car today, we saw several men besides Grayson and Phineas."

Doro nodded. "Although Aggie and I spoke with them, we didn't ask about being in the club car last night. If we hurry back, we might catch some of them."

"I didn't see the doctor and his wife in the dining car this evening," Aggie observed. "They must've gone down after we left. Starting with him might help."

"Maybe so," Doro murmured. "Maybe we could go back to see if they're eating now."

"What excuse do we have to return?" Aggie asked.

For a moment, Doro considered ideas. "We could say the cupcakes were so delicious, we wondered if any were left."

"They were wonderful," her grandmother put in.

"Indeed," Mrs. O'Brien added with a smile. "Even though, we have several here, no one else needs to know.

Aggie grinned in response. "Then, that will be our excuse."

Since dinner service would end soon, the two friends hurried to the dining car. When they stepped inside, Doro nodded to a couple at a table near the kitchen door. "That's Dr. Cartwright. I'll stop and greet him, which should provide an opening."

Aggie grinned. "Knowing you, it will."

Doro smiled and continued on. As they drew closer to the Cartwrights, the physician noticed the young women and stood up. "Professor Banyon, good evening." His gaze strayed to Aggie. "This must be your friend and partner."

After Doro introduced Aggie, the doctor's wife spoke. "I'm Eliza Cartwright, and Myles told me about the two of you being amateur sleuths. I love reading mysteries." The plump blonde gestured to the empty chairs at their table. "Please sit down. I'd love to hear what you've discovered about Professor Mathers' passing."

Although her husband looked less enthusiastic, he nodded. "Please join us."

Doro and Aggie expressed their thanks after sitting down. Before the conversation continued, Clyde appeared. "Thought you two ate already."

His gruff tone signaled a lack of welcome. Did the waiter know he was a prime suspect? Probably so, since Joshua could have warned him. "We did, but we wanted to visit with the Cartwrights."

After Clyde scowled and went on, Doro turned to Mrs. Cartwright. "We've gotten a little information." Revealing every detail was unwise. The doctor's wife was chatty, maybe gossipy, and Doro wanted to be cautious. "You might be able to help us with one thing, Dr. Cartwright."

He paused in cutting his meat. "How so?"

"We heard some men were in the club car late last night," Doro replied.

Several moments passed before he replied. "I was there until a little after eleven o'clock, since a few of us played bridge. Some of the younger fellows stayed on. What would that have to do with the murder? Only three of us who were in the car got left behind after the decoupling. Bailey, Spieth, and me."

Still keeping caution in mind, Doro phrased her response with care. "Part of what we heard related to drinking alcohol. Was it served from the bar?"

"Of course not," he hurried to say. "The railroad wouldn't break the law."

"So, no one was drinking," Aggie suggested.

Dr. Cartwright laid his knife and fork down. "Some folks carry their own flasks. After all, the Volstead Act didn't outlaw drinking liquor that was already on hand."

Since Prohibition had been in effect for a decade, people having alcohol around for that length of time was unlikely. Doro withheld comment and focused on gleaning pertinent information. "Then, a few of the men were drinking."

"A few," he agreed.

"Were any of them intoxicated?" Aggie asked.

The physician shrugged. "A couple might've had a bit too much."

Because the man was being circumspect, Doro felt forced to be blunt. "Was Phineas Spieth one of them?"

"Is he one of your suspects?" Mrs. Cartwright asked. "We heard the argument between the professor and him last night. And there's the friend who also berated poor Mr. Mathers."

Aggie smiled. "We aren't pinpointing suspects. The law will do that. We're only gathering information."

"Oh. I see." Mrs. Cartwright looked like a kid who had just been told the sweet shop was out of candy.

Although Doro had been about to issue a caveat that they could not share privileged details, she admired her friend's quick thinking. "Once the train gets rolling, we'll be at a large station within a few hours. The local lawman and railroad security will work together." If she and Aggie did not identify the killer first.

"As it should be," Dr. Cartwright said.

Doro bit her tongue to keep from telling the physician that she and Aggie probably had more experience in sleuthing than most small-town constables or railroad security officers. As for a big copper, he might know more. She reiterated her question. "What about Phineas? Was he intoxicated?"

"He constantly had a glass in his hand, but I'm not sure he wasn't pretending to be worse off than he actually was. Young Mr. Spieth was playing cards, and a ploy among some gamblers is to feign inebriation. To give their competitors a false sense of security," Cartwright said. "Just speculation, but he placed some big bets. I can say that for sure."

"Interesting," Doro murmured. No one she knew gambled, so the idea of pretending drunkenness to win was new to her. "Did it seem like Mr. Spieth was a regular gambler?"

"He certainly knew all the forms of poker," the physician replied, "so it was far from his first foray into wagering."

"Mr. Bailey wasn't taking part in the poker game?" Aggie asked.

"He played one game and sat out afterward," Cartwright said.

Again, Doro tucked the detail away before posing a question. "Did Phineas and Grayson Bailey leave the club car together?" Could the doctor confirm what she and Aggie had overheard?

"No, young Bailey's luck wasn't good, which is why he quit," the doctor replied, "and he looked the worse for wear. He left before I did, in fact."

Which had been relatively early, according to what Doro and Aggie had overheard. "So, you have no idea how late Phineas stayed?"

"No, I don't," Cartwright said. "He was playing with men staying in the cars ahead, so I don't know who would have more information."

Disappointment laid like a lump in Doro's belly. A solid answer was not apt to arise this evening. But she and Aggie had tried. And they'd gotten confirmation of Gray's comments. That was one step forward.

After bidding the Cartwrights farewell, Doro and Aggie picked up a couple of cupcakes and returned to their drawing room. As soon as they entered, Gramma Rose laid down her book. "What did you learn?" she asked in an eager voice.

"Only a little," Doro replied before summarizing their conversation with the Cartwrights.

"Sounds like Phineas feigned drunkenness, as we suspected," her grandmother observed.

"It does, which Gray insinuated," Aggie agreed, "but that may not be verifiable until the other card players are questioned."

"Dr. Cartwright's suggestion that Phineas wanted to fool his competitors seems valid," Doro observed. "I wonder if Gray pretended to be in a drunken stupor when Phineas was awake. Maybe he was waiting for an opportunity to find and kill Mathers."

Aggie chewed on her lower lip. "Maybe so. What we over-heard indicated he was accusing Phineas, but guilty parties sometimes do that."

"I wouldn't lose sight of either as a suspect," Gramma Rose said. "Or of Clyde."

For a moment, Doro reflected on the possibilities. "We won't. We can talk to Phineas again, but we'll need to be careful. I don't want either him or Gray to know we overheard them."

"Or let them know we asked Dr. Cartwright about them," Aggie added.

"Or that." Doro paused before continuing. 'Maybe we should talk with the two separately, if we find an opportunity."

"That's wise, dear," her grandmother said. "Some sort of opportunity will arise."

"If the weather is better tomorrow, people will go outside, so we could approach Gray and Phineas," Doro said.

"I agree," Gramma Rose added. "If the two of you split up to talk with others, they might, as well."

Doro smiled. "That's a sound strategy." And maybe one that would garner real results.

"I hope so," Mrs. O'Brien put in. "Mysteries in books seems simpler."

A tap at their door interrupted, and Doro opened it to find the conductor in the hallway. "Good evening."

He touched the brim of his cap. "I'll be taking the first watch. My flagman and brakeman will follow, so don't fret if you hear footsteps."

All four women offered their gratitude.

Sayers gave a slight nod. "We'll miss a little sleep, but if our passengers rest better, that's what's important. We'll spend most of our time in the two passenger cars, but we can walk through the crew's sleeping car and the dining car, too."

After he left, the three women readied for bed, but Doro remained awake well into the night. Pieces of the puzzles were coming together, but several open spots remained. Big spots.

***

Doro tossed and turned all night. Every time she woke, clues filled her mind. But, as hard as she tried, they did not yet form a full picture. Finally, at five-thirty, she rose and dressed. Not wanting to wake the others, she picked up her notepad, pencil, and a flashlight before going to the dining car. Within the next half-hour or so, the staff would arrive. Perhaps, she could get coffee and a roll. In the meantime, she would go over her notes.

As she stepped into the corridor, Doro looked up-and-down. The crewman on duty must be in another car, or he might be getting coffee himself. In either case, she felt safe venturing out.

On her way, she made a mental review. Three solid suspects remained. Eliminating one would move the investigation forward. But which one? Clyde Oscar had a powerful motive, access to the means, and a wide window of opportunity. Gray Bailey and Phineas Spieth had motives and means, but not familiarity with the kitchen. Did one of them possess a knife? Or could they have waited for Mathers and, after he unlocked the kitchen, followed him and dug out a blade? That seemed most likely. Both were young and agile, so outmaneuvering the older, bulkier man was possible. But the waiter had that advantage, too. As she tiptoed along, Doro considered various angles and possibilities. So much pointed toward Clyde.

Only dim lights were on in the dining car, while the door to the kitchen was shut and most likely locked. Doro sat at a table close to the gangway and kitty-corner from the kitchen entrance. She would see anyone entering from the adjacent car, although only a crew member was apt to come into the area so early. If Joshua came early, as he had the previous day, he might make coffee, which sounded wonderful after Doro's restless night. Or another crewman could stop by. She wanted to thank them for losing more sleep on behalf of the passengers. Although Doro had not fretted, she wouldn't have ventured out of the compartment without security in place. Pluck was a fine trait. Foolishness was not.

While holding the flashlight beam on her notes, she scanned them. Nothing substantial pointed to one of the three in particular. Clyde was the most reticent to talk. Was that an indicator of guilt? Possibly. But the overheard conversation between Gray and Phineas was also unsettling.

The sound of a door opening drew her attention, and Doro swiveled to see Phineas—a bundle slung over his shoulder—coming out of the kitchen. "I thought the door was locked," she observed, surprised by his appearance. "Did one of the crewmen let you in? Maybe for coffee?"

He stopped in his tracks. "What are you doing here? Breakfast won't be served for nearly two hours."

The question did not address her observation, but Doro was more troubled by Phineas' grim expression. And what was in his satchel? Suddenly, her insides knotted. "I wanted to look at my notes without disturbing my grandmother, Mrs. O'Brien, and my friend. They'll be down soon, though."

A smirk curved his lips. "At this hour? There's no reason for you to be here unless you didn't want to wake them up with your light."

While his comment hit the mark, she would not admit it. "No, I just wanted to get out of their way, so they can dress."

"You're lying. They're all sound asleep, as is everyone else." As he spoke, Phineas came to Doro's table. She wanted to stand up, but he was crowding her. Doro looked at the door to the gangway. "Have you seen whoever's on duty right now?"

A chortle escaped him. "I did. Rogers and I crossed paths in the gangway vestibule between the passenger cars."

Her heart rate accelerated. "Where is he?"

"Resting in a bunk in the crew car."

"Resting?" Doro knew that was not true, but she hesitated to voice what was.

Phineas snorted. "After a knock on the head, he was easy to move. Poor fool never saw it coming. He was telling me how we're all safe from the murderer. I suppose he thinks it's Clyde. Well, probably not now."

Doro swallowed convulsively to get saliva into her dry throat. "Mr. Rogers isn't dead?"

Phineas shook his head. "Nope." He laid one hand next to the place setting. Before she knew what was happening, he grabbed a napkin and shoved it into her mouth. Doro started to pull it out, but he drew a pistol from his jacket pocket. "Do as I say, and you won't get hurt. Now, stand up."

As shock momentarily froze her in place, Doro stared into the barrel of the gun. Surely, he wouldn't shoot her because a gunshot could bring others to the car. She swallowed hard over the rising lump of fear in her throat. Never, not even when she and Aggie had been tied up in a dank cellar, had Doro felt so helpless. Why hadn't she considered the killer attacking the crewman on guard duty? Not that anyone else had.

"Get up," he barked.

As he moved to give her leeway, Phineas jabbed her between the shoulders with the gun, so Doro stumbled to her feet and moved forward. Her shock was slowly ebbing, but no escape plan replaced it. What could she do? What should she do?

"Put your hands behind your back and keep them there." Phineas laid the gun aside, but well out of Doro's reach, before digging into his pack. "Good thing I found some rope in the kitchen. I didn't think I'd need it so soon, but turns out I do." A guffaw left him.

Within moments, Doro felt a rope go around her wrists. As she did, Doro tried to jab him with her elbow, but Phineas pulled tight enough that the hemp dug into her skin and her shoulders were strained by being yanked back. Pain shot up both arms, and she bit back a moan.

"Don't try anything funny again. I've killed once. A second time won't make any difference."

Unable to speak, Doro nodded. But terror stalked her. What was he going to do? Take her outside and leave her in the ditch? No, that was too close. Someone would find her quickly. Was he going someplace and hauling her along? But they were in the middle of nowhere. Where could they go on foot?

Her mental meanderings were interrupted by another jab from the gun barrel. "We're going to the far end of the car and getting off, so move."

With little choice, Doro walked in front of him, which was not easy. Her breathing was hampered by the gag, and her balance was affected by being bound. When they got to the gangway, he jumped off and pulled her down. Unable to catch herself, Doro tumbled to her knees. More pain jolted through her. Before she could react, he jerked her to her feet.

"It's not long until dawn, and I want to be far away from this train by then."

Doro tried to talk through the cloth, but her words were garbled. Where were they going? The closest town was seven miles away. Surely, he didn't expect to walk that far. With the weapon at her back, Doro moved ahead. The faint pre-dawn light made seeing the uneven ground difficult, and she stumbled more than once. They had traversed several hundred yards when, breathless, she stopped.

"We need to keep moving," he muttered.

Again, she tried to speak.

"I guess we're far enough that no one will hear you scream," Phineas said, as he pulled out the napkin.

For several moments, Doro sucked in breath after breath. When she was no longer winded, she asked, "Where are we going and why?"

A chortle escaped him. "You know why. As for where, the rancher who rode out yesterday said his place is four miles to the northeast. He was kind enough to point in the right direction. We can make it there in a couple of hours, if you don't dawdle, and I'll make sure you don't."

"Why go there?"

"Too many questions. Move along." Phineas pointed the gun at her. "Maybe I should revert to my original plan, take a hostage at the ranch, and leave you here."

Doro cast a glance over her shoulder. In the distance, the train cars looked like toys, but sound carried in open areas. The last thought had her turning to Phineas. "If you shoot me, people on the train will hear, and the men will catch up with you before you get far."

"I doubt it," he replied. "Besides, I don't need to shoot you. I could tie you to a tree and leave you for someone—or something—to find."

A shudder ripped through her. What kinds of wild animals roamed the area? Doro had no idea, but she didn't want to find out. After releasing a pent-up breath, she turned and began walking again.

"Smart girl," Phineas remarked in an amused tone.

Since saving her breath seemed wise, Doro did not respond. Remaining silent did not keep her mind from swirling. According to what Phin had said, his plan had been to kidnap someone at the ranch because of Mr. Menzing's revelation. But the man had disclosed more. One by one, the points rolled through Doro's mind. His hands were out on the range, and he'd be the only man there with his wife, daughters, and housekeeper. If Phin nabbed one of the women, the rancher wouldn't fight back. Besides, her captor had plenty of rope, so he could bind several people. Another point was him mentioning only one vehicle, which Phin had brought up with Gray. Clearly, Phin planned to take it. Even if the rancher could follow, he'd have to ride to the nearest town to alert authorities. Would he leave his family? Could all the women go with him?

Considering the likely scenarios did nothing to quell Doro's anxiety. Phin could get a long way before the law caught up. Although she wanted to ask if he planned to keep her with him, Doro figured he was unlikely to answer. Besides, with fatigue dragging on her, she needed to save her breath for walking. But that didn't keep more questions from surfacing in her mind. How long would it be before someone went to the dining car and found her notepad? When the conductor realized Doro was missing, he'd send men out, wouldn't he? Putting the pieces together would take time. Too much time? Doro was not sure.

Chapter Twelve

Although she hoped help was coming, Doro did not look back. Instead, she kept putting one foot in front of the other for what seemed like endless minutes. At least the ground was flat, but heavy rains had made it soft so tromping along with her hands bound was a sore trial. Her tightly roped wrists hurt while her feet ached and several toes burned. Blisters must be forming. At home, she walked almost everywhere around Michaw. But there were sidewalks and well-worn paths, which made progress easier. Much easier. Images of her beloved hometown swam in Doro's head. Every storefront was familiar—the bakery, the general store, the diner, the apothecary, the newspaper, the candy shop, the bank, the barbershop, the dress boutique, and the constable's office.

Tears pricked the backs of her eyes, and she blinked quickly to keep them at bay. Was Ev in the office right now? No, it wasn't much after seven o'clock in Ohio, so he wouldn't have left his campus apartment yet. Unless he was walking Tee. How

Doro ached to see both of them again. Would she? Ev's face swam before her tired eyes. What would he say to do in this situation? *Avoid taking chances*, but it was too late. Staying in the compartment would have been wise, but how could she have known Phineas would attack one of the crewmen? Would Ev have pointed out that possibility? If so, would he chastise her for being foolish? Would he get a chance? Although she disliked his highhandedness at times, Doro would welcome the sound of his voice and the sight of his face now. But he was far away, and she was on her own. Somehow, she had to get away from Phineas.

As the sun rose, fingers of light spread over the plains. Up ahead was a stand of trees. If she escaped soon, Doro might elude Phineas long enough for the men from the train to catch up. Surely, they were coming. It was only a matter of time, wasn't it?

Sweat ran down her neck and pooled around her locket. The jewelry piece was her good luck charm. Would it keep her safe now? Touching it would offer solace, but she couldn't with hands bound behind her. Nor could she wipe away the perspiration. Doro moved her head and shoulders to stop the steady trickles, but to no avail. The front and back of her blouse were soaked. Everything hurt. Her head. Her throat. Her lungs. Her wrists were on fire from the rope cutting into them. Misery held her in its unforgiving grasp.

Since she needed her breath to keep going, Doro did not speak again for a half-hour. By then, her confidence about being followed and found had lagged. Why weren't men coming from the train? Didn't they realize she was missing?

After what seemed like an eternity, but might have been thirty minutes, Doro could no longer stand the silence or her uncertainty. "Where will you head once we have transportation?"

Moments passed before Phineas responded. "To Mexico. No one will track me down there. Too much trouble."

Mexico. If she disappeared across the border, would anyone ever find her? Or maybe Phineas would dump her long before then. Her pulse raced with dread and, although Doro was not sure she wanted answers, she asked the questions clouding her mind. "What about me? Are you taking me across the border with you?"

"It depends," he muttered.

The ambivalent answer only increased her fear. "It's a long way from here to Mexico."

"Yep, it is."

If Phineas wanted to keep her upset and on edge, he was employing the right tactics. Still, she had other questions. Would he answer? "Did you plan to pin the murder on Clyde?"

"No," Phin shot back. "He and his wife have suffered too much already."

The burning emotion in his voice caught Doro off-guard. Had she finally slipped past Phineas' guard? "Because their son died."

"Mathers ruined Custis' life and drove him to his death." The words came out shotgun fashion, fast and furious. "But Clyde is like Gray. Unable to commit murder."

"You were able to do it," she said, taking a sidelong glance at him. Doro wanted to know more about Custis, and they had time to talk. If only she could get Phin to continue.

When he glanced at Doro, fury flashed like wildfire in Phineas' gaze. "That old goat made plenty of people miserable. Custis died because of him. Luann was trapped in a loveless marriage. Gray was heartbroken."

"And you had to change schools, which upset your father enough to cut your allowance," Doro said. "Did that affect your gambling?" For long moments, she feared he would clam up again. But it seemed the dam holding him back had broken, and a floodtide rolled out.

"You are shrewd, professor. Without ample funds, I got in a pinch for a while. All because of Mathers. Gambling debts can pile up quickly, and I owed a couple of guys who didn't enjoy waiting." He grimaced. "I took the brunt of their anger."

The actual cause of his trouble was his gambling habit, not a lack of allowance, but she did not comment. "Being in financial straits was only part of your anger at Mathers. He drove you away from Pikeley and accused you of cheating. Custis, too. Were you two friends?" What she and Aggie had overheard certainly indicated as much.

"Custis was a fine friend and a bright student. We worked on a project together when I was at Pikeley. By the time Mathers stole his research and published it under his name, I had transferred. But I went to Mathers to help Custis. That made the old man ever angrier. Custis would've gone far without Mathers in his life."

Sadness filled Doro, but she pressed for more information. "You transferred but Custis couldn't." They were walking at a steady pace, so Doro was able to maintain her balance and stay abreast of Phineas, whose expression was increasingly morose.

"I wanted him to change schools back when I did, but Mathers wasn't giving him so much trouble then."

Several moments of silence passed while Doro considered Phineas' revelations. "What about Mathers' threats to keep you from getting your master's degree?" Doro asked, even though that seemed like a dubious prospect. "What would your father have said if that happened?"

"The professor might've tried, but my degree is in sight. It's more likely he'd interfere with Gray and me getting jobs at the same college, especially in Colorado. We could've gone back east, where Mathers is unknown, but Gray wanted to be close to Luann, even if he only saw her in passing." Phineas stopped to face Doro. "You won't believe me, but I didn't kill the professor just for myself. I wanted to avenge Custis and help Gray. And keep the old goat from hurting anyone else."

Doro's heart turned over because Phineas sounded sincere. Maybe he believed what he said. "Murder isn't the right way to exact justice."

He snorted. "What would be in this case? No one has kept him from stealing students' work. He was probably still doing it. And what about Luann? He could've lived another thirty years, so she and Gray would never have a life together."

His reasoning was faulty, and his action was appalling, but Doro could not argue with the facts. "Did you plan to kill Mathers when you boarded the train?"

One of his shoulders rose and fell. "After the confrontation at the train station, I started thinking about it. When he shot off his big mouth in the dining car, I couldn't stop mulling over ideas on how to do it."

A shiver rippled through Doro. Phineas had planned the murder in advance. "Mathers confirming to Sayers that he'd want his usual pre-dawn snack gave you a place and timeframe."

"Yep." Phineas looked back, and so did Doro. "I don't trust Gray not to get some men and follow us. We need to move on."

When he started forward, Doro stayed in place. "This part doesn't seem so well thought out. You had time to get to the kitchen when Mathers was there, and you probably watched for him. That would've been easy, because Gray was really drunk, which made him fall into a deep sleep. You were faking drunkenness."

"All true." He swiveled back to face her. "You've done a lot of investigating."

"Some," she replied.

"I didn't figure on getting caught, and I wouldn't have if you two women weren't so persistent."

"We narrowed the suspects down, but we hadn't decided on you."

"Not yet, but I heard too much about your sleuthing abilities from your father. As for deciding to escape through the ranch, it was in my mind ever since the cowboy came yesterday. Not an ideal solution, but I don't want to be executed for murder."

Another issue came to Doro's mind. "What about the knife? Did you have one with you?"

"Nope, but there are plenty in the kitchen, and a handy towel to wipe it clean."

"You knew fingerprints wouldn't show up on cloth."

"I majored in science," he said with a snort. "Let's go."

This time when Phineas began walking, Doro did, too, although not quickly. "What will you do if people come after us, or if the rancher won't let you have a vehicle? Or if the crewmen catch up with us."

"I'll cross those bridges if I come to them."

The answer was not satisfying.

***

Doro and Phineas trod on for another half-hour before fatigue and thirst and anxiety wore her down. She was not sure which of the three was the worst, but the pain radiating through her took first place. From time-to-time, Doro had glanced back but going through a sparse copse of trees hampered her perspective. Although she had hoped to escape through the woods, the ground was uneven, so tripping was far too likely. Surely, help was on the way. Faith was necessary. Faith and endurance. The latter was draining away, and the former was weakening.

"Do you still have water?" Doro asked through parched lips.

Phineas paused and reached into his jacket to extract a flask. "Not a lot, but it should see us through." He took several swallows before putting it to her mouth.

Doro drank greedily. "Thanks."

After a nod, he slipped it back into his pocket. "We need to keep moving."

"Could you loosen the ropes? They're digging into my wrists." Although Doro could not see her hands, she felt sure the skin was being rubbed raw.

"I'm not taking a chance on you going for my gun, especially when the train crew shows up, and I figure that could be any time."

After he started forward again, Doro trudged behind him. Staying next to Phineas no longer mattered. Saving enough strength to fight or run when the time came did. But would an opening occur? And where was help? When she glanced back, her captor did, too. Several figures were visible in the distance, and hope leaped inside Doro.

Phin turned, too. "Keep moving or I'll put a bullet in you."

Doro doubted he would, since she was better as a prisoner than a victim. "If you shoot me, they'll shoot you."

"I've got enough bullets to shoot them, if I must." Phineas glanced ahead. "There are some rocks not far from us. We can stake out a place there." He snatched back the canteen and pointed the gun at her. "Move."

With few options, Doro did as she was ordered. Most of the area was dead flat, but the hill offered a place to hide. As level as the rest of the area was, she would not be able to slip away undetected. What were her options? None came to mind.

Five minutes later, they were ensconced in the outcropping some twelve feet above the ground. Seven men from the train were closing the distance. Although she could not pick out individuals, Doro figured Gray, Sayers, Smithers, Cartwright, and the waiters were in the group. Maybe Chef Andre was one of them. But one crewman must have remained behind. The one felled by Phineas? Most likely. Not that it mattered who was coming to rescue her. Two appeared to have rifles, whose range was greater than Phineas' hand gun, slung over their shoulders.

How soon would they be within firing range? And what would happen when they were?

Dismay filled Doro. The men would not take advantage of the long guns' great range when she was next to Phineas. What would they do? What could she do? After a sidelong glance at Phineas, who was focused on the men, Doro decided she only had one course of action. When he was distracted, she had to kick out and hope to throw him off-balance. Since she was sitting on one of the rocks, that was possible. Fresh sweat broke out across her upper lip, and her pulse pounded in her ears. Taking deep breaths became a challenge.

As the minutes passed like hours, Doro thought again about Ev. Why had she parted with him on bad terms? What if she never got a chance to fix the fissure between them? Regret, bone-deep and heart-wide, gripped her. Resolve followed. Should she be lucky enough to escape with her life, Doro planned to clear the air when she saw him again. How that would happen, she could work out later because the group of men were getting closer.

When they stopped sixty yards away, she held her breath. Although she had little knowledge about firearms, Doro figured rifle shells could reach the stony perch, but bullets from Phineas' handgun would not travel so far.

"Let Professor Banyon go, Spieth," Sayers called out.

"Don't come any closer," Phineas shouted. "I can't be executed more than once, so I'll kill her if you take one more step."

Despite the sun beating down on her, a chill rippled through Doro. She would not let him shoot her without a fight. She might die trying, but she would try. With her heart nearly beating out of her chest, she watched him turn to his left and away from her. Cartwright and Gray came closer. If one of them engaged Phineas in conversation, she might have an opening.

"Stay back, Gray. If you get too close, I'll shoot you, too," the killer yelled.

"We're friends." Gray moved methodically toward them.

Doro narrowed her gaze on the young man, but she saw no trace of a weapon. Surely, he was armed. The growing lump in her throat threatened to make swallowing impossible.

Phineas gripped the gun with both hands. "I don't want to hurt you, so stop."

"I can't do that," his friend said, as he continued to amble toward the rocks. "Put the gun down and let the professor go. You don't really want to hurt her. She's done nothing to you. Or me. Or Custis. Or Luann."

Phineas, focused on the approaching men, scanned the group before looking back at Gray. When he hesitated, Doro kicked both of her feet into his back. As a groan left him, she booted him again. He fell forward and rolled to his side, while the gun skittered across the rocks. For long moments, Doro felt disconnected from the present. With determination, she fought through the fog threatening to suck her in. "Hurry. He's down, and he dropped the gun," she yelled to the men.

All seven men darted toward the rocks. As they did, Doro kicked the gun out of Phineas' reach and jumped away from him, as best she could. The next few minutes passed in a blur, as she looked on with growing gratitude. It was over. She was fine. While Gray untied her, Sayers and Rogers bound Phineas' hands behind him. She wondered how he'd like walking like that, because it wasn't easy.

"Professor Banyon, let me look at your wrists when we get back to the train," Dr. Cartwright said. "The skin is raw in places."

For the first time, Doro glanced at her hands. During the few minutes Phineas had been disabled and bound, adrenaline had kept the discomfort at bay. Now, pain again seared her abraded flesh. Nausea roiled inside her, because her skin looked as terrible as it felt. "All right," someone murmured. It took several moments for Doro to realize the two words had come from her. But her voice sounded far away.

***

The next several minutes passed quickly. After the doctor handed a canteen to her, Doro drank her fill, which helped her feel more rooted in the present. After murmuring her thanks to Cartwright, Doro let him help her up. When she wobbled, his brow furrowed with concern. "Are you able to walk back?"

"I'll be fine," she replied, although weakness assailed her. What alternative was there? At least she no longer felt like passing out.

"We brought plenty of water," the physician said, "so, let me know when you want more."

"Maybe now." After draining half of it, Doro returned the container. "I'll be fine now." Had she said that already? She was not sure.

"If you get faint or weary, let us know. We're not in a rush," Cartwright said. "When we get back to the train, remember that I want to put antiseptic on the wounds."

Doro nodded because it seemed like the right thing to do, but she did not recall the idea being mentioned already. Evidently, she needed more than water.

Gray Bailey fell into step beside her during the return trek. While she was grateful for his reassuring presence, Doro wished it was Ev at her side. The thought presented a new slant on her goals and dreams, as did her reverie while being held captive. Apprehension and excitement danced along her nerve ends. She had plenty of time before talking with Ev. Surely, she would come up with the right approach. After all, after reading Doro's mystery, her mother had called her a wonderful wordsmith. Now, to use that ability in talking, not just writing.

Gray's voice interrupted her contemplation. "I'm sorry. I meant to monitor Phineas, but I fell asleep."

She slanted a glance at him. His eyelids were drooping, which provided a clue. "Do you think Phineas drugged you?"

Surprise flashed across his face before dismay replaced it. "He brought a flask of cold tea from the dining car late last night. Since he drank some, I didn't see any problem with having it myself. I'm sorry."

"It's not your fault," she hurried to assure him. "Or anyone else's. I probably shouldn't have left our drawing room, but everyone was still asleep. I didn't want to disturb them, so I went to the dining car to look over my notes. I felt safe because one of the crew should've been on duty."

"Rogers had the early watch."

Frustration again filled her. "I don't know why I didn't think about the killer going on the attack again."

"I didn't figure on a guard being hit. None of us men did, and we all feel bad about that, but Phin evidently engaged the man in conversation. They chatted for a few minutes. When Rogers turned away, Phin clobbered him with the gun butt."

The words drew an ugly picture. "Is Mr. Rogers all right?"

"He's got a nasty headache, which is why he didn't come along. Otherwise, Cartwright says the man should be fine in a day or two. Mrs. O'Brien is checking on him periodically."

"That's a relief."

"He was real sorry about you being kidnapped."

She waved a hand in the air. "Not his fault."

"We were all terribly worried when we realized Phin was gone and so were you." A rough sigh left him. "And after that, we found Mr. Rogers in a bunk. You must've been gone for twenty or thirty minutes by then."

"You really rushed to catch up," Doro observed.

"We had to."

For a moment, she considered what Gray had revealed. "How did you know which way we went?"

"The wet ground held decent footprints. Once we saw some, Mr. Sayers wondered if Phin was headed to the nearest ranch. Four miles is a tough trek over soft ground, but we all agreed Phin might've headed there to get the truck."

"That was his plan, and it might've worked." Again, Doro shivered. Would Phineas have killed her or abandoned her to die? She would never know for sure.

Gray shoved his hands into his jacket pockets. "I had no idea he was considering murder. Maybe I shouldn't have talked about Luann marrying Mathers, and how badly it upset me."

His deep remorse evoked Doro's response. "You didn't know he was so angry at Mathers. No one did."

"No, but after the fact, I had an uneasy feeling he might be involved in the murder."

"I know." After admitting she and Aggie had overheard the two friends, Doro finished by saying, "He was high on our list, but he wasn't alone."

"I was right up there, too, wasn't I?"

Only a moment passed before Doro owned up to the truth. "You were for a while, because you had an excellent motive."

"And a clear one," Gray added. "Meanwhile, I didn't know how close Clyde's son and Phin were. Or how furious Phin was. I still can't believe he took you as a hostage."

"He was as surprised to see me as I was to see him," Doro murmured.

"I can imagine."

"But it was a foolish escape attempt."

Gray shrugged. "I'm not sure about that. Without you being missing, no one would've suspected Phineas was gone for a while, because I'd still be sleeping, and Mr. Rogers might not have woken up so soon, either." A yawn put an exclamation point on the assertion.

"I was lucky," she murmured.

"You made some of your own luck by attacking him. Otherwise, I'm not sure what we would've done. We hoped he'd surrender without a fuss, but..." His voice trailed off.

A long breath left Doro. "I hoped he would, but Phineas realized he was trapped. Taking me as a hostage was a last resort, although he would've taken one of the rancher's daughters."

"You were in the wrong place at the wrong time," Gray said.

Since his comment was true, Doro nodded.

The conductor joined them. "Spieth admitted his plan to head to the nearby ranch. A foolish idea. Four miles over uneven ground is an ordeal."

Doro agreed. "We probably didn't make it over two, and it wasn't easy."

"Luckily, you've got a good head on your shoulders, Professor Banyon," Sayers said.

Using her title signaled his respect, which Doro appreciated. "Thank you for acting quickly, Mr. Sayers. Thanks to all of you. I couldn't have walked much farther."

"Having your hands bound behind your back made it darn hard, I'm sure," Gray muttered. He focused on his friend, who was being marched along with a man on either side, and two behind him. "Phineas will find that out for himself now."

"What will happen when we get back on the train? Do you have a secure place to hold him?" Doro asked the conductor.

"We'll lock him up in the caboose with a couple of us outside. Help should arrive later today. Once we get hooked up, we'll involve the law in the next town, but the security man can take charge until then," Sayers replied. "Since we don't know exactly where we were when Spieth killed Mathers, the railroad will handle the case. Maybe bring in U.S. marshals. It depends on how the bigwigs want it handled, I suppose."

"As long as he stands trials for both killing and kidnapping, that's what matters," Gray said.

Although Doro agreed that justice was important, she dreaded the thought of testifying—especially when it would mean another trip. As much as she enjoyed spending time with her parents, Doro was ready to be home. And Michaw was home.

***

As they got close to the train, Doro saw Aggie and Gramma Rose outside. Her best friend was pacing back and forth, but her grandmother was seated in a chair. When she was only twenty yards away, Doro saw relief cross both beloved faces. Despite being weary and dirty, she darted forward. Both Aggie and Gramma Rose, who stood up, welcomed Doro with open arms.

"Are you all right?" her grandmother asked as she stepped back to survey Doro.

"Worn out, but I'm not hurt," Doro replied.

"We were so worried," Aggie said.

Remorse flashed through Doro. "I'm sorry. It never occurred to me that Phineas would attack one of the crewmen."

"Or to any of the rest of us, for that matter," Rose said. "The men were equally surprised when they figured it out. Luckily, Mr. Rogers is resting comfortably, and Mrs. O'Brien is tending to him."

"He feels terrible about letting Phineas get away," Aggie added. "We've told him not to fret."

"Good," Doro said. "I certainly don't blame him."

After scanning her friend's face, Aggie said, "You must be exhausted. Let's go to our drawing room, so you can clean up and rest."

"That sounds lovely," Doro murmured.

Before the women reboarded the train, Mr. Sayers joined them. "We'll get Spieth under lock and key. If you ladies want refreshments, Joshua or Clyde will bring them to your compartment as soon as possible. Then, take it easy for a while."

"We all need to rest. You two have been up since the pre-dawn hours, haven't you?" Doro asked her grandmother and best friend.

Aggie nodded. "We couldn't go back to sleep after finding out you and Phineas were both missing."

"We certainly couldn't," her grandmother added before turning to the conductor. "Some refreshments would be lovely, but I hope all of you get a break, too. You must be exhausted."

A weary smile touched his lips. "We'll manage until the next station. Then, I'll ask for my crew to be relieved. And me, too."

Before going to their quarters, the women agreed the crew deserved time off. By the time, Doro bathed and changed, Dr. Cartwright arrived. "He tied those ropes really tight," the man observed as he cleaned both wrists, applied antiseptic powder, and wrapped them in bandages.

Doro fought to keep from flinching, but her raw skin stung. When Cartwright finished, she thanked him.

He nodded. "Keep the bandages on overnight. I'll leave the powder with more gauze and tape. Carefully wash the skin before bed tonight and in the morning. If there's any sign of infection, call for me immediately. If not, rewrap your wrists. Follow the same procedure for the next two days and have your doctor look when you get home." Just as Cartwright rose to his feet, a knock sounded at the door.

When Gramma Rose opened it, Joshua stepped inside with refreshments. After both men left, the women settled at the table.

"What a nice array of food," Aggie said.

As soon as the first bite of fruit hit her mouth, Doro realized the extent of her hunger. The ham sandwiches, cantaloupe pie, and coffee tasted and smelled wonderful. Doro inhaled deeply. The hot brew was a great pick-me-up. "I'm surprised Andre made a pie this morning."

"While we were waiting and worrying, he brought us some melon and tea," Aggie said. "He mentioned making the pie since the melon was close to being overripe. Besides, he said it's a crew favorite, and the men deserved a treat. Us, too."

"This is heavenly. Cool, creamy, and sweet." Doro took another bite of the delightful concoction before posing a query. "Are all the passengers getting pie?"

"No, only the three of us and Mrs. O'Brien, since there isn't enough melon for more than two pies," Gramma Rose replied with a smile. "She's sitting with Mr. Rogers until he feels better. Andre knew we were concerned, and you had a long trek under difficult circumstances, so we're recipients of a special delight."

Doro did not say how trying the journey had been. More than once, she had wondered about making it back to the train. More than once, she had wondered if she would ever see Ev again. Now, she would. But what could she say to heal the breach between them? The question returned, but no answer followed. Three months was a long time. Maybe he wouldn't forgive her for leaving town with little notice. Or for rejecting his offer of stepping out. Aggie's voice broke into Doro's troubled thoughts.

"Are you all right?" her friend asked.

"Of course. I was just thinking," Doro replied without saying about whom. Her mind returned to Ev over and over, which had to be significant. "I'm grateful to the men for coming after me."

"So are we," Aggie said. After eating the rest of her pie, she put the dish down. "It is wonderful, so I'll have to try making it myself."

"You're a fine cook and baker, so I'm sure you can," Doro said. Would Ev like the creamy concoction? Probably so, since he had a sweet tooth. Could she make it for him? And maybe take one when she picked up Tee? A dessert could ease her way.

Aggie's voice broke into her thoughts. "Did Phineas plan to kill Mathers all along? Or didn't he say?"

Doro shook off the last of her reverie about Ev. She'd have time to consider her options before arriving home. Two more days to mull over ideas, maybe three, since he would not be at the station to meet her. "He claims the idea came to him after the decoupling, which may be true." She twirled her fork in her fingers. "Phineas had several reasons for hating Mathers." After repeating what the killer had told her, she finished with, "He and Custis were friendly, like Phineas was with Gray. That was part of his motive. His low grades and having his allowance slashed was the key to his original anger. Evidently, he's been gambling for years. And not always winning. Having fewer funds kept his habit in check, and that resulted from Mathers giving his work low marks."

"Which he didn't like?" Aggie asked.

"Not at all," Doro replied. "Mathers' other victims gave Phineas more excuses to hate the man. The same with the professor forcing Luann into marriage. The confrontations over the past couple of days were probably the last straws. But he'll be brought to justice."

Aggie posed another question. "Will we need to testify?"

"I suppose so, especially me. He'll be charged with kidnapping and murder, I think, but I'm not sure. That won't be for a while, though," Doro murmured.

"So, we can go home for now," her grandmother suggested. "At least we can when the repair crew arrives."

"We can start planning Doro's party, after some rest," Aggie added. "It'll be so much fun for Wade's children and for the adults, especially certain ones."

Heat scorched Doro's cheeks as she took another sip of tea. As she considered her thoughts while being held hostage, Doro realized she had not once pictured the library or focused on her dream of being the head librarian. Her career had not come to mind at all. Only Ev had.

Chapter Thirteen

B y late Thursday, the repair crew reached the train, fixed the coupler, and pulled the cars back to the nearest siding, where a new engine was attached to the dining car so they could be on their way. Word reached the women that the security officer had checked the coupler and taken charge of Phineas Spieth. The man spoke with Doro about her ordeal before reviewing the key elements of the investigation with both young women. He was grateful for their work on the case, which left Doro smiling.

Hours later, they pulled into Kansas City. Sayers got off and summoned the police. Again, the Michaw women were interviewed with Doro fielding most of the questions. The lawmen assured them that Phineas Spieth would be held in the local jail until railroad officials determined how to proceed. The city's mortician would see to Mathers, whose body would be sent back to Colorado Springs. Before leaving the women, Sayers shared other information. "I've checked the train schedules. We got you on one heading to Chicago in an hour. There's another one going east out of there tomorrow in the early afternoon, so you'll only have a short layover."

Relief filled Doro. "I wondered if we'd be stuck in Kansas City or Chicago for a spell. Since it's late already, I thought we might need a hotel."

"So did I," Gramma Rose added. "Thank you for going to that trouble, sir," Gramma Rose said.

After offering her gratitude, Aggie brought up a concern. "We'll be a day late getting home, so we need to send a telegram or call Wade."

"I can handle that for you," Sayers said. "Jot down the information, and I'll do it right off."

Aggie hurriedly wrote a note and handed it to the conductor. "We appreciate you going to so much trouble for us."

"No trouble, ma'am. A porter will get your bags in short order," he replied before bidding them goodbye and moving on.

"That was kind," Doro said.

A knock at their door interrupted. When Aggie answered, she ushered Grayson Bailey in.

He swept off his hat. "Again, I'm sorry for the trouble. I guess I didn't know Phineas as well as I figured."

"When people attempt to hide their true character, we can't fault ourselves," Gramma Rose told him.

"I suppose, but it's hard knowing your best friend is a killer and a kidnapper," he murmured. "We may meet again at the trial, but I'll be heading back to Colorado Springs after my father's funeral. I won't be attending Mathers' service, and I'll wait to call on Luann."

"That's wise," Doro said. "Perhaps you'll seek my mother's counsel on what the right timing would be."

"A good idea," the young man said. "Safe travels the rest of your way home."

"Before you go, I have a question for you," Doro said.

Gray nodded. "Go ahead."

"What about the coupler being broken?" Doro asked. "Is the cause known?"

"I spoke in passing with the railroad security officer, and he believes the coupler was damaged in the train yard, mostly due to rushing to add more cars and jockey other ones around," Gray said.

"So, no foul play," Doro said. The man had not yet studied the coupler when she had spoken to him.

"Nope. But he'll get an alert out about checking the couplers carefully. Now, I best be on my way. We may meet again at Phineas' trial. Or when you visit Colorado Springs again. In any case, I hope it's under happier circumstances." He touched the brim of his hat and moved on.

After Doro shut the door behind Gray, she released a pent-up breath. "I sincerely hope nothing else happens before we get to Sylvania."

"It won't," her grandmother assured her. "In about a day, we'll all be home."

Aggie clasped her hands in front of her and put them to her chin. "I can hardly wait."

"Neither can I," Doro agreed. "Neither can I."

Mrs. O'Brien also said her goodbyes before leaving the train. "Thank you for sharing your compartment and your company.

When you're in the Springs again, I hope you'll call on me. I live on Lake Street."

Although Doro was not sure if Aggie would travel to Colorado in the future, she accepted the invitation. "We'd love to visit, and I'll write my mother with your name and neighborhood. She can call. She'd enjoy meeting you."

"How nice," the widow said. "Now, I must go. My niece will be waiting."

Mr. Boggun and his son approached the group just as Mrs. O'Brien was walking away. Both expressed their congratulations on Doro and Aggie solving the case. Dr. and Mrs. Cartwright did the same, as did the other passengers, even the starched-up retired army officer.

***

As the women were stepping off the train, Joshua and Clyde stopped them. Doro and Aggie apologized for suspecting them.

Clyde, his expression grim, put up both hands. "I had plenty of motive, but I couldn't do no such a thing, if for no other reason than I won't leave my wife alone to grieve for two menfolk. I'm not sorry Mathers is dead, but murder is ugly, and I'll testify, if I have to."

"Me, too," Joshua said.

"I thought you stayed at a boardinghouse back up the line," Doro said, as a memory hit her. "Will you take another train back?"

"No, miss. Clyde invited me to stay with him and his missus," the boy replied.

A genuine smile lit Clyde's face. "On a permanent basis. I'll know she'll agree, because she's met Joshua and likes him real well."

"How wonderful," Gramma Rose said.

Doro and Aggie added their good wishes to the two men.

Doro gripped her valise. "At least something good came out of all this."

"I have a hunch something else positive will result, too," her grandmother observed.

"Luann and Grayson getting back together?" Aggie asked.

Gramma Rose nodded. "You gave him good advice, Doro. Your mother will see to it he doesn't act inappropriately. Moving slowly, although he may want to rush, will be better in the long run. Julia can invite them to dinner, when the time is right. A low-key social occasion can provide a wholesome opportunity."

"It certainly can," Aggie added. "A dinner, a luncheon, a birthday party. They're all nice venues for potential sweethearts to socialize without pressure."

Silently, Doro agreed.

***

When their next train pulled into Chicago late the following morning, the three women were packed and ready to get off. With a two-hour layover, they planned to have lunch and shop near the terminal. The beautiful stores were a draw for Gramma Rose, while Doro and Aggie enjoyed browsing.

After leaving their baggage with a porter, they sought a nearby diner before stopping at several shops. By the time they returned, their next train was only thirty minutes from departure.

"I'm going to sit on the platform," Gramma Rose said.

"All right. I want to get a newspaper at the stand," Aggie observed.

"I'll go along," Doro put in. "Gram, we'll meet you in fifteen minutes."

The two friends went to the newsstand. While Aggie sorted through the papers, Doro looked around. Abruptly, her gaze fixed on a man some forty feet away. She was only vaguely aware when Aggie joined her.

"What's wrong?" Aggie asked. "You look like you saw a ghost."

Doro's gaze followed the male figure as he hurried along the tracks before stopping next to a shorter man. The urge to follow was strong, but she resisted. Surely, her eyes had deceived her. Doro pivoted to face Aggie. "I thought I saw someone I know."

"In Chicago? Who?"

Conflicting urges hit Doro. Should she reveal her supposition? Maybe hearing Aggie poo-poo the possibility would help Doro dismiss it. She gestured to where the man, partially obscured by the crowd, stood beside another fellow. "That guy looks a little like Ev." Doro injected a note of amusement into her voice. "You know how my imagination is. Vivid."

Aggie turned toward the two, who now stood fifty feet away. For long moments, she stared at them. When she faced Doro again, Aggie appeared to be perplexed. "It is Ev."

The statement sent Doro's heart to her heels. "It can't be."

"Look again."

After doing what her friend advised, Doro could no longer deny the obvious. The tall, lean figure was Ev. Her heart pounded so hard, she feared it would bounce out of her body. "What is he doing here? His sister lives near Cleveland, and he has no other family. Why would he come to Chicago?"

"To visit a friend," Aggie suggested in a tentative tone.

As she continued to watch Ev with the other man, Doro remembered a conversation from May. "Ev said he might be gone for a few days during summer vacation, and he let me know Tee would stay with Wade and his family."

"Wade mentioned that, and the children were excited at the prospect," Aggie said. "But Ev was still in Michaw when Gramma Rose and I left a month ago."

Doro turned toward her friend. "He hadn't mentioned leaving?"

"Not to me, but things can change in a month," Aggie replied. "Why not go over and talk to him? There's no reason not to, is there?"

Thinking back to when she had dropped Tee off, Doro battled additional uneasiness. Two reasons came to mind, and she hadn't shared either with her best friend. First, at their last encounter, she'd told Ev about leaving for Colorado two weeks earlier than planned—an announcement that had added to the stiffness between them. Second, when Doro had stepped into his kitchenette, she found the remnants of a beautiful May basket—one that had surely been meant for her because she had admired it in his presence. One that she had not received due to her haste to escape Michaw...and the temptation presented by Everett Mallow.

"Doro, you didn't part on bad terms, did you?"

Although she still didn't want to admit details, Doro couldn't lie. "Not exactly bad." Not good, either.

"There's more to the story, I'm sure. Ignoring him for almost a week before you took off early to see your parents was bad enough. If you did nothing to resolve your differences, I can see how facing him could be difficult." Aggie glanced at her wristwatch. "We've got less than a half-hour to board our train. Go talk to him now."

Doro hesitated only seconds before nodding. "I'll join you and Gramma on the platform in a few minutes," she said before heading toward where Ev and the stranger were still deep in conversation. Weaving her way through the crowd, Doro kept her attention on Ev, so she knew the moment he saw her.

His gray eyes, wide with surprise, stayed on her until she stopped in front of him. "Doro."

Her name came out as a breathless murmur. "Hello, Ev. How nice to run into you." As soon as the words were out, Doro chastised herself for the inane remark. *Nice* did not describe her feelings. Surprise, curiosity, dismay, and more—much more—did. Those words remained stuck in her throat.

"Nice to see you, too," he replied, but his tone did not match his words. He sounded uneasy.

Doro glanced at the other man, who barely came to Ev's shoulder. Despite his lack of height, he cut an imposing figure. Clad in a charcoal gray three-piece suit, starched white shirt, black bow tie, and highly polished wingtips, he appeared to be a businessman. When Ev did not introduce them, Doro smiled. "I'm Dorothea Banyon. Mr. Mallow and I both work at Michaw College."

"How lovely to meet you, Miss Banyon," he said with a nod.

"It's Professor Banyon," Ev put in, his voice as strained as his expression.

The other man smiled. "Pardon me. I didn't know. In any case, it's nice to make your acquaintance." He paused a heartbeat before continuing. "I'm Agent Lowery Canton. I used to work with Ev, too."

As the news hit her like an icy shower, a chill rippled through Doro. Ev had been a Prohibition agent before coming to Michaw. Surely, he wasn't going back to the Bureau. "I see." She glanced at Ev, whose jaw was taut with tension. "Do you live in Chicago, Agent Canton?"

"I'm here temporarily. I'll be returning to Toledo soon," the man replied.

A glance at Ev revealed the rigidity had not left him. If anything, the muscle twitching in his square jaw indicated his strain had increased. But why? Due to his reason for being here? Since Ev was unlikely to answer her questions, Doro focused on the agent. "What brings you to Chicago?" Perhaps, Ev was there for the same reason. He was clad similarly: dark gray suit, black tie, starched white shirt, and black wingtips. The overall look was more formal than his typical attire, but just as appealing.

When Doro sucked in a long breath, his scent was mesmerizing. His jaw was devoid of whiskers, so the pleasant aroma of allspice, citrus, and hints of something else hit her. Warmth spread through Doro, since she could not recall ever noting the fragrance surrounding him. But he wasn't always freshly shaven. Determinedly, she focused on the other man.

Something flickered in Canton's dark eyes, while a slight smile played across his lips. "Some personal matters." He touched the brim of his hat. "Nice to meet you, Professor. Ev, I'll see you outside." With that, the agent strode away.

Doro watched him leave before turning again to Ev, whose expression remained wary and guarded. When he said nothing, impatience got the better of her. "I suppose you're here for personal business, too." Although she injected a note of levity, Doro wanted to know why Ev was in Chicago with his former boss. Their last exchange, in May, had not boded well for their future. Doro had thought she was all right with that. Now, she knew better. What if she was too late? What if Ev had already decided to leave Michaw and take his old job? Could she convince him to stay? Should she? When he simply gazed at her, Doro clasped her pocketbook with both hands. "I'm sorry. What you do and where you go is none of my concern. It's just that..." As the right words failed to follow, her voice trailed off.

"Just what, Doro?" His voice was rough with suppressed emotion. "You left for Colorado two weeks early, with a day's notice. After that, I didn't figure you cared where I went or what I did."

Both his tone and expression were tense, which made responding tricky. "I should've given you more time to heal without needing to care for Tee."

A harrumph left him. "I love Tee, and it was no trouble to take her sooner than planned. That's not what I mean, and you know it."

When emotion flared in his gaze, Doro thought she understood what he meant, and hope bloomed inside her. But what should she say? That she most certainly cared what he did, where he was, how he felt. As she searched her mind for the perfect explanation, the one that would make up for her May departure, Doro grasped her pocketbook handles tighter and lifted it in front of her like it was a shield.

Dismay crossed his face. "What happened to your wrists?" His voice was soft and low, as he gently clasped her forearms and scrutinized the skin beneath her cuffs, which had ridden up.

Drat. She should have reapplied the bandages. Doro cleared her throat. There was no time to describe the murder and ensuing events, so she presented a summary. "A man was stabbed to death on the train. Since there was no lawman on board, Aggie and I investigated."

His gaze again met hers. "And the killer went after you."

"Not exactly." Doro shifted restlessly. Explaining how she had been taken hostage would take time, and she needed to be on the train to Sylvania in short order.

"These are rope burns, so someone tied your hands." Ev released his hold and stepped back. "Don't I deserve to hear the truth?"

The question, rough and ragged, nearly shattered her soul. "Of course, you do. It's a long story, and neither of us has time for the entire tale. But you're right about me being bound by the killer. It all turned out fine, as you can see." She offered a smile of reassurance, but his expression did not lighten.

Ev ran one hand over his face. "Thank heavens for that. Unfortunately, you're right, we don't have time for more, but I want to hear the entire story when I get back."

"I'll be happy to tell you." Although he might not be happy to hear her tell it, since Ev could be overprotective. In the past, Doro had resented his tendency to smother her. Now, his protection did not seem like a bad thing. She would have welcomed it when Phineas had jabbed a gun in her back and taken her as a hostage.

When a passerby jostled them, Ev took Doro by the arm. "You all right?"

"Sure," she murmured, but even through her sleeve, Doro felt the heat from his hand.

The tension drained from him as, with his free hand, he touched her cloche. "Your hat is askew."

"I didn't know," she murmured.

A grin lit his expression as he adjusted her headwear. "It wasn't before that minor collision. Now, it's fine." As he stepped back, Ev scanned her from head-to-toe. "Your travel outfit is quite stylish. Not that you aren't usually."

His comment was kind because Doro typically thought little about fashion. At least she hadn't until Ev had commented on her party costume last fall. Since then, she had gotten more interested in looking nice. This morning, she had donned the ensemble with the faint hope of seeing Ev later. Now, she was. "Aggie, Gramma Rose, Mother, and I went shopping several times. Everyone agreed my wardrobe needed sprucing up. This outfit is one we had made in the Springs." The dropped waist dress—a light blue and navy print—was topped with a matching three-quarters length jacket. Both were in a travel-friendly treated cotton, a new fabric from the dressmaker. A navy cloche with a pink flower and navy t-strap shoes completed the look. Suddenly, Doro was happy she had worn it. Happy Ev was seeing her in it and appreciating the view.

"You had a pleasant summer?" he asked.

"I enjoyed being with my parents, and it was wonderful when Gramma Rose and Aggie came."

For a moment, he gazed down at her. "You aren't planning to move to Colorado?"

"No, not at all." Her answer was honest.

"Good." Ev cleared his throat. "That is, it's good you enjoyed your trip."

Was he blushing? Doro hoped it was because he was glad that she didn't plan to leave Michaw. Before she could comment, he spoke again.

"You've been gone all summer, so you may not have heard the gossip going around campus."

The comment piqued Doro's interest. "What gossip? Aggie didn't mention any important news."

He drove his fingers through his cropped brown hair. "It started in earnest about three weeks ago. A couple of the more progressive trustees were in Michaw meeting with President Adams. Word has it that allowing married women to work at the college will pass at the next board meeting. Married women with children, too."

Joy spiraled through Doro. She could hardly wait to tell Aggie. "Truly?"

"Mrs. Jones told me in confidence, but I'm sure she wouldn't mind you knowing."

Doro had known Violet Jones, the president's secretary, and one of her mother's best friends, all her life. If she passed on a rumor, it was based on facts. "Aggie will be thrilled."

"Wade is." Ev swallowed hard enough to cause his Adam's apple to bob. "What about you? How do you feel?"

Doro felt a lump form in her throat. How did she feel? As she looked into Ev's quicksilver gaze, her heart stutter-stepped. Since girlhood, Doro had believed she would never have her own family, due to her career aspirations. Now, things were changing. Burying her feelings for him was no longer sensible or possible.

"Your silence speaks loudly," he muttered. "If you'll excuse me, Lowery is waiting."

When he turned away, Doro grabbed the sleeve of his jacket. "Wait."

He did not face her as he spoke. "Why?" His arm went rigid beneath her grasp.

"It's a surprise. A shock, really. I hoped the board would change the policy, but I never thought they'd do it so quickly or so completely. But I think it's wonderful." She did not remark on her thoughts—mostly about him—after being kidnapped. That could come later.

Slowly, Ev pivoted to face her. His face was a mask of uncertainty. "You're happy for Aggie and Wade."

A kaleidoscope of butterflies took flight in Doro's stomach. "I am, but it's also good news for all other women at the college."

"All other women," he repeated. "Does that include you?"

Doro only allowed his question to hang in the air for seconds. After a deep breath, she nodded. "It does. It most definitely does."

His handsome features glowed with a smile. "I'll be back home in a few days, maybe a week. Not much longer. I'd wait to ask, but I've waited so long now. Maybe you'd like to go to Sylvania for a movie? We could have dinner before or after."

Hope and joy and excitement spun through Doro. Although she could not recall ever feeling giddy, she did at the moment. "I'd like that."

"So would I." After a glance at his watch, Ev shrugged. "I really should go."

Alarm replaced anticipation. "Does Agent Canton want you to go back to the Prohibition Bureau?"

"He'd like that, but it won't happen." With one hand, Ev rubbed his neck as if to dispel the tension there. "I'm in town because the Bureau thinks booze is being transported along Chicago Pike from Toledo to here. Since Michaw is only a few miles north of the road, Lowery wondered what I know. He's meeting with other agents and asked me to join them."

"Because you know something important," Doro murmured. She looked around before continuing in a whisper. "Mr. and Mrs. Fulton are involved, aren't they?"

A harsh exhalation escaped him. "I can't reveal bureau business, but you're a fine amateur sleuth. One with plenty of insight, and we've talked about the Fultons, more than once."

"We have," she agreed, reading between the lines. The couple had worked for a widow, whose husband had been suspected of bootlegging. Some townsfolk, and Doro was among them, believed the woman carried on after his death, and that the Fultons had helped her. "In May, you admitted to watching them, so I assume you saw something suspicious."

His gaze flickered away and back. "Doro, I can't discuss it here and now," Ev said. "I know you're curious, but please don't poke into this matter. Bootleggers are violent, and they don't think twice about dispatching whoever threatens them. Your snooping might put a target on you. At least wait until I get back." A plea was in his voice.

"I'm not planning to snoop, as you call it."

His gaze widened, as if in disbelief. "Why do I not believe you? You haven't gone three months without sleuthing." He touched one raw wrist. "You were kidnapped by a killer, and not for the first time."

The anxiety darkening his gaze reached past Doro's defenses. "The conductor asked Aggie and me to help." Which was not true, but Ev did not need to know.

His dark brows rose. "Really? How did he know you're an amateur sleuth?"

Since she could answer the question with honesty, Doro smiled. "Two graduate students from Colorado College were on the train, and they heard about some of our adventures from my dad." While that was true, it was not why she and Aggie had finally gotten permission to investigate.

For several moments, Ev gazed steadily at Doro. "Your parents don't object to you cracking cases and being in danger?"

Again, Doro gripped her pocketbook. "They know I love mysteries."

"But they don't know you were tied up in a cellar in December. Or that you confronted a culprit alone in May."

A resigned sigh escaped her. "They don't, and I don't plan to tell them about either episode. Not that I was in peril last May. The confrontation took place in the library's back room. Help was only feet away."

Ev rolled his eyes, while his mouth softened into an almost-smile. "You're incorrigible."

Because she could see he was softening, Doro grinned. "I thought I was intrepid."

Laughter rumbled out of him. "That, too."

Her heart filled with pleasure. "Intrepid and incorrigible aren't such a bad combination."

"Not when they apply to you." His attention returned to her wrists. "Don't dig into the Fultons until I get back. Promise me you won't."

His earnest tone and troubled expression telegraphed genuine worry, not overprotectiveness. "All right, but you'll share some details, won't you?"

A momentary hesitation preceded his response. "I'll tell you what I can. In the meantime, I can't keep Lowery waiting. Tee is with Wade, but she'll be thrilled to see you. We had to walk by Wheaton Hall every day, just in case you were there."

Warmth spread through Doro's heart and soul. "I will be there tonight, and so will Tee."

A wistful smile touched his mouth. "I'll see you two when I get back."

"When will that be?" His earlier reply had been indefinite.

His lips flattened, and his gaze slid away. "I'm not sure. Like I said, a few days, maybe longer."

The indefinite quality of his words bothered Doro, who yearned to ask if he was more than helping the Bureau with his observations. Could he—despite his protestations—be assuming a temporary role as an agent? Knowing he would not admit to such a job, she offered a heartfelt statement. "Please be careful. Very careful."

Ev gently squeezed Doro's hand before stepping away. "I'm only consulting. No danger in that."

Something in his expression belied the words, but Doro did not press him. They were on good terms, and she wanted it to stay that way. "I'll look forward to dinner and a movie. Maybe next weekend."

"Maybe not so soon. For sure, we'll go when I'm home." Ev cleared this throat. "I hope this leg of your trip is uneventful. After all, even a top-notch amateur sleuth deserves a break."

The lilt of laughter underlying his last comment made Doro smile. "After this last crime, I'd like to stick to reading whodunits for a while."

"I'm eager to hear about how you and Aggie cracked another case," he assured her. "Over dinner. Now, I really have to go."

"I do, too," Doro murmured with genuine reluctance. When he moved away, she caught his one hand. "My birthday is coming up, and my grandmother is planning a small party. I hope you can come."

Ev faced her again. "I hope so, too," he replied before brushing a featherlight kiss across her lips.

Heat spread through her. "I better get to the platform," she murmured.

"Have a pleasant journey," he said, before striding away.

As Doro stood staring after him, she felt the warmth give way to a chill. A surge of impending doom washed over her when Ev neared the exit. Not for one moment did she believe he was simply serving as a consultant. But what was he doing for the Bureau? And why wasn't he sure when he'd be home? A few days. Maybe more. And he only hoped he'd be back for her birthday.

With determination, she shook off the troubling thoughts and concentrated on the pleasant feelings left by his fleeting kiss. Although only the second one they had shared, it sent her heart soaring. Soon, she and Ev would share an entire evening. Surely, somewhere in the mix of dinner, a movie, and a drive to-and-from Sylvania, they would have time for a more personal conversation. And there was her birthday dinner. If wishes could bring him back by then, he'd be sitting at her grandmother's table right next to Doro.

Her spirits lifting, Doro headed to the platform. Summer vacation would be over in a few weeks, but the new school year offered an array of possibilities. Exciting ones, ones that did not include working toward becoming the head librarian at Michaw College because, although Doro loved the school, she also...

Abruptly, she halted her train of thought and hurried toward the platform, but not without a backward glance. Ev, almost at the station's doors, turned in her direction. Although the crowd milled between them, Ev lifted one hand. Doro returned the gesture of farewell. No, not farewell. See you soon. Hopefully, quite soon.

Thank you!

Thank you for reading _The Problem Professor!_ I hope you enjoyed it. If you have time, please rate or review it. Comments from readers are helpful and appreciated. I am on Goodreads and BookBub. Most retailers also accept reviews.

https://www.goodreads.com/author/show/21325652.D_S_Lang

https://www.bookbub.com/authors/d-s-lang

For more information, please go to my website or Facebook page.

https://dslangbooks.com

https://www.facebook.com/profile.php?id=100064024056297

You can sign up for my newsletter on my website. I share other authors' work, news about my books, a peek into the writing life, historical tidbits, and more. Your email will never be shared, and you can unsubscribe at any time!

What's next for Doro?

Doro's adventures continue in <u>The Bottled Bootlegger</u>. The fifth book in the series will be out in December 2024.

After seeing Ev Mallow in the Chicago train station on her way home from Colorado, Doro is excited to "step out" with him on their first date. The perfect evening ends on a sour note when a local bootlegger is murdered and his wife disappears. That crime leads to Ev temporarily returning to the Prohibition Bureau, where he goes undercover—much to Doro's dismay. Her worry seems valid when he does not report in, as scheduled.

Doro, not content to wait and see what officials find out, sets her sights on finding him. Soon, armed with information about his possible whereabouts, Doro enlists her best friend and the town constable in searching at a Toledo speakeasy. While the place is less than fifteen miles from Michaw, the bar's raucous atmosphere is worlds apart from any place in the small town. Locating Ev eases her mind, but only temporarily.

The quartet works together to find the killer and unravel a rumrunning ring. When the case is solved, will Ev return to Michaw and Doro? Or will he remain with the Bureau? She is not sure, but she goes ahead with plans to celebrate his birthday. Will the festivity be their last time together? Or will it mark a turning point in their relationship?

About the Author

D.S. Lang, a retired educator, started making up stories to entertain herself as an only child, and she is still making them up. Now, she puts them in writing. She is an avid story-teller and reader, with a To Be Read stack that is overflowing. In her free time, D.S. enjoys swimming, reading (of course), spending time with family and friends, and walking with her dog, Izzy.

A lover of language, D.S. has published over 10 books, with more on tap. Her aim is to write novels that blend history and mystery with dashes of drama, splashes of humor, and touches of romance to create charming stories with authentic details. When you finish one of her books, she hopes you have a smile on your face!

Set during the post-Great War period in small-town Ohio, the books welcome readers into an exciting period of American history, when women were navigating new roles, and the country was dealing with Prohibition and the aftermath of war. Living through those times required spunk, which her amateur sleuths have in spades.

Cantaloupe Pie

While on the train, Doro and her party are served cantaloupe pie, which is described as a cool, refreshing treat on a hot day. The original recipe (which is slightly different) was created by a melon farmer in Texas, who wanted a way to use very ripe cantaloupe. The Texas-Pacific Railroad began serving the dessert on its trains. I've tried the recipe myself. If you like cantaloupe, which I do, it is enjoyable! I used a pecan crust (pre-made) and garnished with pecan pieces. Yummy!

INGREDIENTS

- 1 medium cantaloupe
- 3 ounces cream cheese, softened
- 1/4 cup granulated white sugar
- 2-3 envelopes unflavored gelatin (juicy melons may require 3-4 envelopes)
- 1/2 cup orange juice
- 1 9-inch graham cracker crust
- Whipped cream or whipped topping

Extra melon for garnish

Mint sprigs for garnish

Pecan pieces, if you use a pecan crust

INSTRUCTIONS

Cut melon in half; remove seeds and peel. Cut into chunks; place in blender or food processor; blend until smooth.

Combine 1/2 cup melon puree and cream cheese in blender. Blend until smooth.

Add remaining puree and set aside.

Combine sugar, gelatin, and orange juice in small saucepan. Let stand 2 minutes. Then, cook over low heat, stirring until sugar and gelatin dissolve.

Slowly add above to melon-cream cheese puree.

Pout into chilled pie crust.

Refrigerate until firm.

Spread whipped cream/topping over pie.

Garnish with small melon balls and sprigs of mint. Or use pecans.

Serves 8. Approximately 250 calories per serving.

Doro Banyon Cozy Historical Mystery Series

The Doro Banyon series has a cozier tone than the Arabella Stewart books. History and mystery still mesh as amateur sleuth Doro solves whodunits with a team of colorful characters in small-town America during the 1920s. Various holidays and celebrations (some old-fashioned fun!) are incorporated. Travel back in time to a college campus and crack cases with them!

Prequel-The Lost Exam (free when you sign up for my newsletter)

Book 1-The Catalogued Corpse

Book 2-The Murdered Matron

Book 3-The Jammed Judges

Book 4-<u>The Problem Professor</u>
Book 5-<u>The Bottled Bootlegger</u>   coming December 2, 2024

You can sign up for my newsletter at: https://dslangbooks.com

Arabella Stewart Historical Mystery Series

T he Arabella Stewart Historical Mystery series is set in small-town Ohio after the Great War. Bella returns home from serving as a U.S. Army Signal Corps operator to find her family resort and hometown in dire straits, and the murder of a neighbor adds to the trouble. Much to the dismay of Constable Jax Hastings, an Army veteran, Bella turns amateur sleuth to solve the case. As the series continues, Bella and Jax vanquish the shadows of the war, while solving a series of whodunits with a team of colorful characters. Love and laughter occur along the way. If you love history and mystery mixed with touches of humor, romance, and drama, this series is for you!

D.S. LANG

Book One-A Precarious Homecoming
Book Two-A Lingering Shadow
Book Three-A Lethal Arrogance
Book Four-A Baffling Absence
Book Five-A Fatal Reunion
Book Six-A Surreptitious Undertaking
Book Seven-A Treacherous Accusation
Book Eight-An Uncertain Ceremony

Author's Series Notes

A t one time, there actually was a Mitchaw, Ohio (some-times called Mitchaw Corners). It was the birthplace of many of my relatives, including my dad. At its height, Mitchaw was an unincorporated village surrounded by farms. Like many other small, rural communities, it has disappeared as a separate entity. Now, it is part of Sylvania Township, and subdivisions have replaced most farms.

The town never had a college, nor was it as large and bustling as the Michaw in the Doro books. That is a big reason I dropped the "t" to change the spelling. However, Sylvania is a very real city. It is my hometown and where I still live. Since the 1920s, when this book is set, it has gone from a small village of around 2000 to a small city of 19,000. The township's population is approximately 50,000.